MARK STREUBER

White
Christmas

Homecoming

A Legend is Reborn

This is a work of fiction. Names, characters, places, and incidents either are the product of the author's imagination or are used fictitiously. Any resemblance to actual persons, living or dead, events, or locales is entirely coincidental.

Book design by FormattedBooks.com

ISBN 978-1-7356176-0-2

This book is dedicated to old friends Gino, Diane, Steve, Ken, Barry, Arlene, Mary, Shari, Karen, Eric, and Chris. And to new friends who take delight in old things that become new again.

Letters from War

Christmas Eve 1944

Hey everyone. It's Christmas Eve, and I miss you more than I can say. Did Pa get that new Holstein from the sale barn? It would be nice if he did seein' milk prices are up. How's Squirt doing? Now that he's older, I hope he's doing his share while I'm gone. I know Pa can use the help. I hope the girls are okay.

I don't want to be bossy, but I read from your last letter that big Sis is seeing that Fenton boy. I know of him and seen the way he looks at her. Trust me, he's trouble through and through and she should have nothing to do with him, even though she'll hate me for sayin' so.

Like I told you in my last letter, it gets cold in Italy at night, especially this time of year. But the days aren't so bad... long as the Nazis aren't shooting at us.

The Army threw us a real nice Christmas Eve celebration tonight. Well, it was more of a hodge-podge put together by some of the guys.

Remember that fella I told you about? Bob Wallace? He's that New York entertainer. He and this other fella, Phil Davis, got together and put on a real good show for us. The boys found musical instruments in some of the ruins that seemed to play pretty well, and a few of the guys said they knew how to play 'em. Before we knew it, Bob and Phil had a show put together just in time for Christmas Eve, which is a good thing as they say we're moving up tomorrow morning.

We did find out our General (can't say his name. Can't say the name of the town we're in neither, except that we're in Italy somewhere) well, we found out he's being replaced by another General (can't say his name neither) straight from the Pentagon. I can't say I'll miss much about being here in Italy, other than it's a pretty place when it ain't all shot up. But, I'll miss the General. He was good to us and real smart and never got us into a scrape we couldn't get out of.

I didn't think I'd get the chance to say goodbye, but he and my Company commander, Captain Joe, showed up toward the end of the Christmas Eve show just as Bob was singing White Christmas. It teared the old man up. It teared us all up as we were all wishin' we were home. I'd be glad to shovel a foot of snow with my bare hands if I could be home with you right now.

Well, I gotta go. Dawn comes early around these parts, and I hear this new General is a stickler for order and discipline, which strikes me as odd. I guess it's been a while since he's seen some real action as it gets pretty harried and undisciplined on the battlefield, and any grunt worth his salt should know that.

Anyway, I love you all. Especially you, Ma. I can't wait to get home and gobble down a whole stack of your pancakes, your homemade sausage, and a couple slices of your pumpkin pie to boot!

I'll write soon,

Christmas Day 1944

Hey again. I didn't think I'd get the chance to write so soon, but I'm bored and I miss home, especially on this day. Did you all go to church today? I hope the Reverend gave a real nice message. It's a bit of a silent night around here. We're all sitting on our hands right now, but earlier in the evening that Phil Davis fella I told you about was telling jokes and making us all laugh, which we appreciated as they say it's gonna be a big day for us tomorrow.

They were right about that new General. He's a stickler for discipline. He had us up early for inspection even though we only had a five-mile walk ahead of us. Shoot, we can do that without working up a sweat. It was easier than walking to town with my old buddy George to see the latest Captain Marvel serial playing at the Bijou. Gosh, that was just a few years ago, but now it seems like forever.

I can't tell you what's happening tomorrow, but Captain Joe and Captain Bob were none too happy about the new General's plans. The General called them in for a meeting, and I was assigned to escort them to and from our encampment. As I waited, I heard some sharp disagreements come from inside the tent. Captain Joe was so angry when he came out I thought he was gonna knock over a tree or somethin'.

Even though we've been pushing the Nazis out of Italy, they ain't all out yet. Apparently, a Nazi platoon captured this here town and rounded up all the town folk, and they're holding them hostage in a hotel near the square. Word around camp is that they're using the town folk as bait to try and ambush us (this letter won't go out for a few days, so I can tell you that much). Then we heard they got snipers waiting to pick off any of us Americans who try to free 'em, because they know we'll tr... y

Sorry about that. The Nazis just sent mortar fire our way. They're trying to target our location and take us out tonight if they can. We had a quiet day— there was no fighting at all. But now I guess the Nazis would rather a bloody Christmas over a white one.

Not sure when I'll be able to write again, but I love you always and tell Squirt if he uses my hunting rifle to make sure he cleans it when he's done.

Gotta go...

December 29th, 1944

Ma, Pa. I'm still here. It's been a hard few days, harder than I could've imagined. I'm fine... though I can't say as much about some of the other guys. You'd be proud of the men and women fighting for our country and our freedom. I tell you I ain't never seen such bravery in all my life. I don't know how much I'm allowed to say, but there are some things I have to get off my chest, and writing helps me. I talked with the Chaplain earlier. I guess I just needed to hear a real voice, too.

The battle a few days ago was as difficult as I been in. Captain Joe was right to be angry about the new General's plans. I don't want to talk poorly about our commanding officer, but his plan was flawed (that's my nice word for it.)

We broke through the Nazi lines protecting the town well enough and with very few casualties. Our company, A Company, was ordered to clear the buildings of snipers. Captain Bob was then to take B Company and exter... excritake rescue the Italian villagers held in the hotel. The General was to send in a line of armored vehicles to protect B Company before they entered the hotel, but the General underestimated the size of the Nazi forces and sent them in before we could take out the snipers.

The Nazis lit up the armored vehicles like Christmas trees. They were sitting ducks. We had no choice but to spread out and enter each building as fast as we could and take out the snipers. Luckily the town was not too big.

The firefights were bloody, Ma. I'm just giving it to you straight. I never been so scared in all my life, but we couldn't quit, or more of our buddies would die. Lucky or not, we were able to clear the buildings pretty fast. Just one sniper nest remained on the third floor of a building directly across from the hotel.

Captain Joe, me, Kowalski, and Granger teamed together. As we climbed the steps toward the second floor, a sniper lit up the stairwell with gunfire from the third floor. Me and Captain Joe crashed safely through a door on the second floor. Kowalski and Granger were not so lucky.

We were so angry at seeing our buddies killed that Captain Joe rushed back into the hallway and worked his way up the stairwell like a madman while trading gunfire with the sniper. This time the Captain was hit. He fell to the stairs, bleeding badly.

You won't believe this, Ma. But then I heard a single gunshot ring out... like... a thunderclap from heaven. From the top of the stair, I saw the Nazi sniper who shot Joe fall to his knees. He was dead. He slid down the stair face-first right next to Joe. I tell you, Ma, their noses practically touched!

I rushed up to help, but Joe was delirious with rage and would not stay down. He jumped up and climbed over the dead sniper, drew his pistol, turned into the third-floor room, and fired at the first thing that moved. I saw his face fill with horror, and then I saw him drop to his knees and collapse onto the floor.

With my gun drawn, I entered the room thinking there was another sniper. But what I saw was this young Italian boy plastered against the wall and bleeding badly from Joe's gunshot. I never seen such a horrible sight. I looked around the room. The young boy's family was lying on the floor next to him. The Nazis shot them.

I guess the boy was so traumatized from seeing his family shot he picked up a fallen pistol and shot the remaining sniper. We didn't know the boy was in there, Ma. We didn't know. Joe could not have known.

That is all. I would like to say I feel better getting this off my chest, but I don't. Not yet. Maybe

Mark Streuber

one day. When you see him, please ask the Reverend to pray for us— pray for all of us. We're marching for the front in a few days. Maybe one day this horrible war will end.

I'll be glad to see the girls again and Squirt, too. Tell Pa I love him, and I can't wait to sit next to him on the milking stool.

Love you all,

Chapter 1

November 1954 – New York City

Joe ran his hand through his hair, an exasperated look on his face. "Jarrett, I told you. When you reach half-court, look for someone to pass the ball to. Basketball is a team sport. Remember?"

"Aw, come on, Coach. Every team needs a star," thirteen-year-old Jarrett wise-cracked. He dropped the ball onto his bicep, flexed his muscle, and then popped the ball into the air and back into his hands.

"We got plenty of stars over on Broadway," Joe reprimanded the youngster as he snatched the ball from his hands. "And you sure don't look like you're ready for Broadway. So, let's run that play again. And Jarrett, get it right, or you'll be a *star* at running lines tonight."

Jarrett noted the seriousness in Coach Ross's demeanor and decided he would rather practice basketball than run lines. Joe tossed the ball to Miguel as the boys ran to their positions. Miguel inbounded the ball to Jarrett, who then dribbled past the half-court line. He spied Marcus breaking toward the basket. Jarrett dribbled three more times as instructed. This drew the defender, Cristobal, toward him. Jarrett lobbed the ball over Cristobal's head and watched as Marcus snatched the ball from the air and dribbled to the basket for an easy layup.

"See! That's how you do it, boys. Everyone wins with good teamwork," Joe applauded. "Now run it again until you have that play down perfectly."

"Okay, Coach."

Joe felt tired. After a full day at his regular job and now an hour into his duty as a volunteer basketball coach at the 23rd Street YMCA, he was feeling it. His arm was sore, and his legs were aching. No longer a young man, age was taking a toll on his body, though the lions-share of his current discomfort was courtesy of a half-dozen Nazi sniper bullets that had pierced his legs, arm, and mid-section nearly ten years earlier. "You boys keep playing. I'm gonna grab a cup of coffee and cool down outside. No rough-housing."

"We'll keep an eye on things," Marcus said.

Joe gave a nod to Marcus. He stepped off the court and rifled his hands through Mikey's hair as he waited his turn on the sideline. "Take over for me, Mikey," he said to the youngster.

Only eight years old, Mikey was the youngest and smallest kid at practice. He cast a fearful look toward Joe. "Me?"

Joe smiled. "Hey, just kidding, Mikey. Take over for Jarrett, though. He looks like he can use a rest."

"Okay, Coach!"

Joe made his way to a corner of the gym where a stool held his Thermos, overcoat, and hat. He slid his arms into the coat's sleeves, dropped the hat onto his head, and then clutched the container. The elevator of the nine-story building was just around the corner. He called for it, stepped inside, and pressed a small black button with the faded numeral one. He leaned against the handrail while the elevator lowered him from the seventh-floor gymnasium to the first-floor lobby.

Joe exited the elevator and then made his way around the corner and toward the Information Desk where Lillian worked. She greeted him indolently. "Evening, Joe."

He tipped his hat. "Hey, Lil. I'm just going for some fresh air. Don't let those boys run over you if they come down."

"Oh, there'll be some running, all right. But it won't be me."

He chuckled, tipped his hat once again, and then opened the lobby door to step outside. The crisp November air stung his overheated face. His nostrils drew in the chilled air while his lungs went to work to vacate the stench they had spent the last hour absorbing in the gymnasium— courtesy of fifteen sweaty teenage boys doing their best on the basketball court. He worked his way down a short flight of stairs. The frigid nighttime air constricted the muscles of his battle-worn legs and produced in his stride a noticeable limp. Upon reaching the bottom step, he lowered himself slowly onto the cement and grimaced as the frosty cold penetrated his sweatpants and chilled his rump.

'Just like Army days,' he thought.

After unscrewing the lid from his Thermos, Joe poured the hot black liquid into the lid, took a warming sip, and for the first time that day he relaxed. The brisk nighttime air felt good against his skin, though he was glad to have his coat snugged against his body. Within minutes he felt the need to tug the collar of his coat higher and tighter against his neck and then lower his hat to keep the November chill out— a maneuver he'd practiced more times than he could count sitting in a foxhole in Italy or standing next to an Army Jeep waiting for General Waverly. He dropped his head and sighed as painful memories of the old General came rushing in.

Three blocks away, a cab pulled up to an apartment house. "That'll be $8.50," the cabbie barked out.

"Hold it right there— Huck," Bob said as he glanced at the driver's badge. "We were just gonna run in and get our dates. We'll be right out."

"That'll still be $8.50," Huck repeated.

"All right, buster. Pay the man," a dismayed Bob said to Phil.

Phil bristled. "Pay the man? Why do I always have to pay the man?"

"Because I pay you, and you pay the man. Now pay the man."

Phil removed his wallet from his jacket and handed Huck a sawbuck. "All right, but you stay right here 'til we get back."

"Better hurry," the phlegmatic cabbie barked out. "I'm off-duty in ten minutes, and the Knicks game is about to start."

The two Broadway stars disregarded the starchy cabbie's comments— of course, he would wait for them. They climbed the stairs of the apartment house, opened the vestibule door, and then entered the foyer. Phil scanned the callboxes and found Trudi's apartment number. He pressed the buzzer and then rubbed his hands together. "Oh, boy. We're gonna have some laughs tonight!"

Bob cast a weak smile. Caught in another of Phil's blind date schemes, he was sure the laughs would be on him— again.

There was no response from Trudi. Dismayed by the silence, Phil's expression turned disquisitive. He pressed the buzzer once again.

"Hold your horses. I'll be right down," Trudi's voice finally called out through the intercom.

"That's strange. I don't have any horses," Phil said.

Bob was unamused. "What are you, the Cisco Kid? I thought you told those dames to be ready at 7:30? What's the hold-up?"

Phil shrugged his shoulders. "Don't blame me for the hold-up."

"Well, you're the clown that put this rodeo together."

Trudi appeared through the foyer door. She was wearing her housecoat. "Hi, Phil... Bob."

"What's the hold-up? We have a cab waiting," Phil complained.

"Sorry, fellas. We went to Wu Chow's Mexican Restaurant for lunch. Since then, Doreen's been getting sicker by the hour. I left you a phone call to say we couldn't make it, but I guess you didn't get it."

"We're sure sorry to hear that. We came straight from the radio station. We were doing a plug for the show."

"I hate to stand you boys up, but Doreen is about to toss her guts out, and I'd rather catch it than clean it— if you know what I mean. Can we do this another time?"

"Sure, sure. Some other time," Phil said.

"Got to go. Sorry."

The boys tipped their hats as Trudi disappeared behind the same door she had just appeared. Bob was unhappy. "How do you like that? Our only night off from the show, and we get stood up by a couple of dames."

"Oh, come now, Molly Mundane. The night's still young. What do you say we head on over to the Copa and see what's shaking there?"

"*Everything's* shaking there," Bob retorted. "It's the Copa!"

The two men re-opened the foyer door and descended the stairs. Phil abruptly spun his hat sideways on his head upon seeing that both cab and driver had vanished. "How do you like that? First, we're stood up by the girls, and then we get stood up by a cabbie— for a Knicks game. Doesn't he know who we are?"

"A couple of popsicles, that's who we are," Bob ruefully replied as he tightened his coat against his neck.

"Aw, we can catch a cab over on Broadway," Phil said.

"I think what we'll catch is a cold."

The frigid night air lapped gently at the men's faces while they walked. The streets were quiet. An occasional car passed by, none of which happened to be a cab. Pedestrians were few. A woman walked alone, bundled in a neat and petite package of fluff and fur. Her slender arm extended from her full-length fur coat and held the chain of her miniature schnauzer. Two teenagers with their pompadours and two-tone oxfords walked jauntily on their way to a dance. A burly Norwegian stood outside his door smoking a cigarette. He was oblivious to the cold but attentive to the woman as she and her schnauzer passed by.

Phil gathered his coat close to his body. "Brrr... I should have worn my long underwear tonight."

"And I should have insisted we take that job down in Florida when Maury Susskind begged us to come. It would've been a real treat for the cast and crew, and the thought of a few days in Florida would make me feel a whole lot warmer right now," Bob said as he pulled his coat collar higher against his neckline.

"If I had a drink, I'd drink to that."

Just ahead, Bob spied a figure bundled up and sitting alone on the bottom step of the YMCA. "I'll bet that poor soul could use a drink, too. Look, he's holding his cup out. How about you drop a few coins in there and make a wish."

"I wish you'd pay for once."

Bob dished out a healthy dose of puppy dog eyes to encourage Phil to give up his loot.

"Oh, all right." Phil reached into his pocket, drew out four bits, and plopped them into the man's cup as they walked by. "I hope he doesn't use it for hooch."

Joe lifted his head out of his coat, surprised to see two quarters swimming in his coffee cup. "What the...? Hey, I'm no street bum, you know."

The voice caught Bob by surprise. He turned and stared at the figure. The figure stared back. Bob grabbed Phil by the arm. "Hold on, Phil."

"What's shaking?"

Bob looked intently at the man under the hat. "Captain Ross?"

Joe returned the look and then lurched to his feet. "Captain Wallace? Phil?"

"Well, I'll be. Joe Ross. It is you!" Bob said as he stepped forward and offered the man a hearty handshake.

"In the flesh— what's left of it," Joe solemnly replied as he returned the handshake.

Phil gave a friendly pat to the man's back. "What are you doing sitting here on a night like this? You'll catch your death of cold."

"I *was* enjoying a hot cup of coffee," Joe said as he swished the quarters around inside his cup.

"Oh, heh... Sorry about that. I thought I was doing a good deed, but I guess I goofed."

"It *was* a nice shot."

"Say, we lost track of you after they shipped you out of Italy. After that battle in Montepolina, we weren't sure you were gonna make it home. Looks like you made it back safe and sound, though," Bob said.

"Safe, yes. I'm still working on the sound part," Joe smiled weakly.

"You *were* in pretty bad shape, Captain. I imagine there were plenty of tough days ahead for you."

"More than I could count or want to remember."

"We're sure sorry to hear that," Phil said.

"What keeps you busy now? All done with the Army, I presume?" Bob said.

"Yes, sir. All done. They couldn't use me anymore— not in my condition." Joe then pointed toward the YMCA sign. "This is where I work now— in maintenance. I help keep the place running. It's good work— if you can get it," he quipped.

Cristobal opened the lobby door and stuck his head through the doorway. "Coach, we need you. It's getting a little rough up there."

Joe displayed an easy smile. "Uh-oh, the troops are getting restless."

"As they often do," Bob replied. "You have your own private army in there, Captain?"

"Of sorts. And please, we served three years together. Just call me Joe."

"Yes, Captain," Phil said as he clicked his heels and then playfully stood at attention and saluted before standing at ease. "I mean, Joe."

Joe chuckled at Phil's antics. "I'm a volunteer coach for the boys' basketball team, and I help with other youth events around here— and they sure do need the help."

"I see. Still a leader of men," Bob said.

Joe smiled. "Yes, sir. That's it." He pointed toward the door. "I should get in there before they think I've gone AWOL. It sure was good to see you, Bob... Phil."

"You too, Captain... er, Joe. You keep up the good work now."

"I'm sure those boys are in good hands," Bob said. "I know we were."

"I appreciate that. Well, I better get in there."

Joe stood at attention and saluted the two men, which they respectfully returned. He turned and limped slowly up the stair, clutching the frigid handrail until he arrived at the top stoop. He reached for the lobby door.

Empathy stirred within Bob as he witnessed Joe's tell-tale limp. "Hold on, Joe. Maybe I can come back around and leave you a few tickets for our show *Playing Around.* It's been on Broadway a couple years now. You'd be welcome to bring your wife. It sure would be nice to meet her."

Joe turned toward the two men. "I'm not married, Bob," he said matter-of-factly. "No woman would want me."

It was a startling response. "Maybe a few of the boys you coach, then. And afterward, we can catch up on some old war stories."

"War stories? You mean like trying to make it in showbiz," Phil ribbed, trying to soften the moment.

Joe appreciated the attempt. "That would be nice. Thanks, Captain. Thanks, Phil."

Joe tipped his hat and then followed Cris into the lobby and closed the door.

Chapter 2

It wasn't *Oklahoma*, *Carousel*, or *Kiss Me Kate*, yet *Playing Around* was still a consistent draw, even after two years on Broadway. As the following evening's performance came to a close, Bob and Phil re-entered the stage for a final bow. They presented their finest stage smiles while simultaneously waving to the crowd. It was a show well done, yet the two veteran performers had detected a shadow of change in their audience. The handclaps emanating from the crowd that night were not as vigorous as when the show first opened two years before. Their eyes were devoid of an adoring amazement that they had just witnessed something new and spectacular.

Worse yet, in recent weeks, Bob and Phil had noted in their many audiences a glance here and there at a wristwatch, a check of a purse, or a nod for the door, indicating they had endured the performance more than they had been entertained by it, and that they were on the verge of boredom.

The two men said their final goodbyes. They stepped away from the stage apron and positioned themselves safely behind the descending curtain, closing the show. Ian appeared from the stage wings and threw each man a dry towel. "Good show tonight."

Bob disagreed. "Yeah, good show," he replied sarcastically. He turned his back to the curtain, wiped the sweat from his brow, and then wrapped the towel around his neck.

Phil, too, was uneasy. "You know, Bob. They'll drop us from the penthouse straight into the flophouse if we get a response like that again."

"You got that right, buster."

The two men exited the stage and made for their dressing room, followed closely by the show's dancers. A dull and uninspiring chatter formed between cast and crew: grousing over their sore feet and aching knees; complaints on the late nights and early days the show required; and for the preponderance of dirty dishes, laundry, and bills each person knew was waiting for them when they returned home. The wow factor *Play-*

ing Around had once invoked on audiences, critics and cast members alike had devolved into a monotony of boredom and routine— everything had become routine.

Bob was doleful as he stepped into the dressing room and found an isolated chair to sit in. He let his elbows drop to his knees while he gazed absently at the dirty floor. Restless and agitated, he transferred his stare from the floor to his aging hands and then threw them away from his body as if trying to exorcise the age demons from them.

Phil entered the room and noticed Bob's dismal disposition. "You don't look happy, Bob."

"Aw, your all wet," he glowered. "Can't a man have a few moments to himself? What's your beef, anyway?"

Bob's response put Phil on high alert. He chose a weighty comeback. "I'll tell you what my beef is. It's your demeanor."

Bob responded with a crushing reply of his own. "Yeah? Well, the longer I work with you *de meaner* I seem to get."

"Har-har," Phil said sarcastically. "You keep that attitude and you'll never be happy, and you'll never find a girl. They can see right through that, you know. They see everything."

"Whatever you say, Sigmund."

"No, really. What's eating at you, Bob?"

"I'm worried about the show, Phil. You saw the crowd's response tonight. They're *bored*. I wouldn't be surprised if they're swarming the ticket booth right now asking for their money back. Even our own dancers are bored with our show."

"They're a good crew. They'll come around."

Bob removed his shoes and then kicked them away, which Phil noticed. "Say, now. We've had rough patches with the show before and you've never responded like this. What's got your wickets in a dither tonight?"

Bob eyed Phil carefully. He pursed his lips, took a calming breath, and then exhaled deeply before speaking. "I'll tell you, Phil. I just can't stop thinking about Joe Ross. It was a real gut punch to see him that way."

"In what way?"

"In what way? In what way? Without Joe and the rest of A Company, the Nazis would have flattened us like pancakes that day in Montepolina. And you and me, we'd be in Italy right now pushing daisies. But good ol' Joe, he took the worst of it. And now to see him limping along as a maintenance man, it doesn't seem fair."

"It doesn't seem fair, does it? He's a good man. And he sure seems to enjoy working with those kids. I could see it in his eyes when he mentioned them."

"I saw that, too. I think I'm gonna pay him a visit tomorrow and offer him a few free tickets to the show. You know, let him know how much we appreciate him."

"That's a great idea, Bob."

"Thanks, Phil."

Phil cast an encouraging smile toward his stage partner. "Say, it's not too late. How 'bout we head over to the Palladium Ballroom? It's amateur night, and I still have some new moves to learn."

"Which ones? The Rhumba, Samba, or Mambo?"

"All of them. They're all Greek to me."

Bob's mood lightened. "You're on, buster!"

The dance floor at the Palladium Ballroom was awash with three-hundred eager dancers practicing their hand throws, ducks and combs. Celebrities were sure to be in attendance— Dean Martin, Ella Fitzgerald, Billie Holiday, Sammy Davis Jr., and Peter Lawford were frequent guests.

Bob and Phil climbed the stairs to the second-floor dance hall. As they ascended the stairs, smoke descended into their nostrils as did the ardent odor of three-hundred sweating bodies, while the vibration from six-hundred stomping pulsing feet reverberated throughout the stairwell and shook the stairs beneath their feet. The boys entered the ballroom and glanced toward the stage. The band was in full throat.

"Looky there! Tito Puente and his band are tearing it up," Phil chortled.

"Ho-ho, buster! And that's Marlon Brando pounding the bongos right next to him," Bob remarked.

"Gee, Bob. I think it's gonna be a hot night tonight!"

It was hot— too hot. Bob felt the heat and the sudden press of the crowd against him, both of which he decided not to enjoy. "Too hot for me. I think I'll find a quiet place to rest my dogs and tip a few Bogeys."

"Suit yourself. But you should grab a few steaks while you're at it, cuz I'll be sizzling on that dance floor," Phil said fearlessly. "Grab us a table? Will you, Bob?"

"Sure thing, Cyrano."

Within seconds Phil disappeared into the crowd. He re-emerged, holding the hand of a young female Latino dancer.

Bob pushed his way through the crowd in search of an unoccupied table. As he moved through the room, a gentle hand caught him on the shoulder, and a familiar voice called out to him. "Say, Bobby boy. You gonna cut it up out there, too?"

Bob knew the voice. It belonged to William 'Count' Basie. He turned to greet him. "Ha! Not on your life, Count. If I step foot onto that dance floor, there'll be a two-car pile-up— my left car and my right car," he said while pointing to his pedestrian feet.

"Aw, come now, Bob. You're an old vaudeville hack, same as me. You have some fine dance chops, my friend."

Bob grinned. "Yeah, a couple of pork chops from one big ham."

Count laughed. "Take a table with me?"

"Don't mind if I do."

The two men sat at the first empty table in their path and called for a waiter. "I'll have a Bogey— and make it a double," Bob said.

"A Manhattan for me. Straight up."

"Your show closed for the night?" Bob said.

"We just finished. I'm here to check out the competition."

"Aren't we all. Say, I hear your orchestra is making some big noise right now."

Count flashed a big smile. "Oh, baby! We're as hot as we've been in a long time. Not only that, we just hired this up-and-coming singer named Joe Williams. Wait til you hear him. That man is the cat's meow."

"He's got some pipes on him, huh?"

"Big pipes. Smooth pipes," Count confirmed. "We're cutting a record soon. After its release, I'm taking the whole show on the road. We have gigs scheduled all over Europe. We may even make a road trip to Morocco and Zanzibar. You ever play there?"

"I've wanted to, but as long as *Playing Around* is in production, there's no *Hope* for that."

"Makes sense," Count replied. "Say, you boys still using my songs for your show? I haven't seen a royalty check in a while."

"Oh, we send them by Pony Express," Bob said. "Glad to hear your show is doing well, though. Sounds like it's quite a gas."

"It's hi-octane, my friend! And how's the great Wallace and Davis doing? I haven't been around to see your show lately. You guys still bringing 'em in?"

"Yeah, we're bringing 'em in all right. We're just not sure what to do with 'em once they get there."

Count was confused. "I think you took a left turn on me, Bob."

Bob delayed in answering. He gazed onto the dance floor and caught sight of Phil sweating it out with his audacious dance partner while trying to perfect the 2 and 4 counts of this new dance craze called the Mambo— so different than the 4 count of Swing, which he was more accustomed.

"Count, you ever feel like you're losing a step? You know, like your standing in cement while a steam shovel is coming at you?"

"I'm still not following you, Bob."

Bob withheld his answer. "Where are those drinks?" he said churlishly as he looked for the waiter.

Though he was initially confounded by Bob's bilious disposition, Count made an educated guess as to the cause of his friend's struggle. "You know, Bob. It wasn't all that long ago that me and the band, we fell on hard times. When the war ended, the big band era ended, too. I had no choice but to break up my orchestra. Lucky for me, I never gave up on my music. There was still a fire in my soul— oh man, was there a fire. So, a few years ago, back in '52, we reinvented ourselves into a new 16-member orchestra. But here's the kicker. Rather than playing the *same old clubs*, we went on tour. But not the same old tour— a *European* tour. They loved us there. They rained coin down on us like pennies from heaven!"

"Bring your galoshes then, huh?"

"And your raincoat. If it can happen for us, then it can happen for your show."

"A tour, huh? I see what you're getting at, Count. I know a tour can shake things up and do wonders for the cast as well as the audience. But a tour is hard to do for a Broadway show that relies on a Broadway audience to make it click."

"You ever think of re-envisioning your show? New York is great, but they *got show*. You give the rest of the world *show*, and you just might find yourself *rollin in the dough!*"

"I could use a little of that!"

"Who couldn't," he laughed.

The crowd exploded with applause as Tito Puente finished his set with the song *Mambo Gozon*. Tito Rodriguez and his band prepared to take the stage next.

Exhausted, Phil searched the crowded ballroom for Bob and quickly recognized the famous bandleader who sat next to him. "Whaddya know? It's my old friend Count Basie. I haven't seen you for ages!"

"Hey, ya. Good to see you too, Phil. I hope you don't mind me saying, but you looked a little shaky trying to keep up with that young lady you were dancing with."

Phil dabbed the sweat from his forehead. "That was Caitlin. Dancing with her was like dancing with a whirlwind. Ever dance with a whirlwind?"

"Not since I was seven," Count remarked.

"I think I was nine," Bob reminisced.

"Hey, I should be getting on and leave you two carpetbaggers alone. Next stop for me is *Birdland*. I'll see you boys soon. Bob, you remember what I said now."

"You got it, Count."

Count Basie disappeared into the crowd. "Too bad he couldn't stay any longer," Phil said.

"That's all right. We're not staying any longer, either."

"But we just got here. I've only had a couple of dances," Phil complained

"Don't get frosted. I just need to call Albert."

"Albert? For what?"

"I need him to call Maury Susskind in Florida and see if he can work a deal to get our show down there like he wanted."

"Are you crazy? How are we going to get a whole show down to Florida?"

"Maybe we don't take the whole show. Maybe we take just enough cast and crew to give those Floridians an idea of what *Playing Around* is all about. It'll give us a chance to see how well the show plays with the rest of the country, and it just might be the sauce our show needs to start cooking again."

"It'll take weeks to get that arranged. There's no way to get that done before Thanksgiving, and you already promised the cast and crew ten days off before Christmas. You think they'll want to give that up to do a show in Florida?"

"They might if we make their vacations *paid vacations*. Ten days off *with* pay would make for quite a Christmas present. What do you think, Phil?"

Phil's eye's gleamed as if he were the first person to discover Carol Channing or Ethel Mermen. Bob recognized the look— the look of a man hailing a taxi by stepping directly in front of it. The risk was great, but the reward was greater.

"You're crazy, Bob. But if you think Maury can put a show together in that short of time, then I'll take that ride with you."

"What does that mean?"

"It means, come December, we're going to Florida!"

Chapter 3

The sidewalk was alive with people as the cab pulled to a stop outside the entrance to the 23rd Street YMCA. Bob paid the fare, stepped from the cab, and then pushed his hat tightly onto his head to buttress it from the hiemal breeze. He took a moment to admire the beauty of the nine-story structure in front of him. Built in the Beaux-Arts style, the building was constructed of terra cotta brick and limestone. Two large Corinthian columns made of marble were positioned on either side of the door. A beautiful arch and pediment-style entrance completed the look.

He had long known this was not the first YMCA building in the Chelsea area of New York City. Fire and age had caused the decline of the original 1869

French Renaissance building, which was also located on 23rd Street, nearer to 4th Avenue. The demise of that building led to the construction of this new state-of-the-art building.

Built in 1902, this YMCA contained a marble swimming pool on the lower level. On the upper level was a cork running track cantilevered above a large gymnasium, complete with basketball court. The floors in between hosted a lounge, library, reading room, and leased office space. A separate entrance on 24th Street provided access to the residence rooms— low-budget single rooms and transitional housing for the traveler and those in need.

Bob entered the lobby and approached the Information Desk. "It sure is brisk this morning," he spiritedly said as he rubbed his hands to warm them.

"Can I help you?" Lillian said in an absent tone, unwilling to look up from the registration papers piled high upon her desk.

"Well, I'm a friend of Joe Ross. You know where I might find him?"

"Around the corner. Take the elevator to the sixth floor. Last door on your left."

"Around that corner?" Bob said.

Lillian lifted her arm and pointed without lifting her head. "That corner," she chaffed.

Her lack of attentiveness was dismaying. "Okay. Nice talking with you. I guess."

Lillian noted the irritation in the speaker's voice. She looked up from her papers, smiled weakly, and went back to her work until she suddenly became aware of the person who was standing before her. She sprang from her chair. "Well, I'll be. You're Bob Wallace!"

"I was when I woke up this morning," he quipped and then politely reached to shake her out-stretched hand.

"I'm such a big fan of your show. I've seen it five times."

"I'm glad we were able to grab your attention," he said peevishly.

Lillian did not comprehend the dig but leaned in toward Bob. "I hope you don't mind. Would it be too much to ask for Phil Davis's autograph? He's terribly funny and so charming. And good looking, too!"

"Yeah, he's charming all right," Bob muttered. "I'll see what I can do."

"Wonderful! Tell him my name is Lillian. Spelled with three l's— Lil-li-an."

Mischievously, Bob saw an opportunity to cure Phil of his life-long matchmaking habit. "Say, maybe I'll have him come down here in person, and you two can have a time of it. Maybe you can go to dinner or catch a show. Something like that."

"Oh, that would be marvelous. After all this time, I would finally meet a real Broadway star."

Never mind that Bob was a real Broadway star. He was more than happy to encourage Lillian's attention toward Phil. "I should go. Nice to meet you, Lillian, with three l's."

Bob followed the directions Lillian gave him—around the corner, up the elevator to the sixth floor and down the hall, last door on the left. The door appeared to be ajar. A single knock opened it wide. Inside the room was a bed on a simple wooden frame, a nightstand, and a small dresser. In front of the bed sat an old army trunk. Sitting in his shorts with a wet towel hung over his drooping head sat Joe. The deep wounds and scars covering his legs, arm, and stomach were unavoidable. Hearing the knock, Joe removed the towel from his head and was surprised to see Bob standing in the doorway.

Bob was embarrassed. "I'm terribly sorry, Joe. I had no idea the door would open like that. I thought this would be the maintenance room."

"It's not your fault. Guess I didn't button the door properly."

"You live here, Captain?"

"Yes, sir. I do."

"Looks comfy. So, this is where you hang your hat when you're not working?"

Joe looked around the small room. "Nights, days, weekends, and holidays," he confirmed. "It's not a bad setup. It makes for an easy commute at the end of the workday. Plus, I'm always around if the boys need me."

"I see. Nothing wrong with simple living."

"No, sir."

"What do you say I step outside and give you a chance to get dressed."

"Some fellas are playing a pick-up game in the gym on the floor above us if you'd like to wait there. Just take the stairwell around the corner. I'll be there in a few minutes."

"Sure thing, Joe."

Bob entered the stairwell and climbed the stairs to the seventh-floor gymnasium. Two half-court basketball games of pasty and portly old men were in full swing. He leaned against a wall and watched as the men pushed, grunted, elbowed, grimaced, yelled, breathed hard, cursed, argued, occasionally tackled one another, and in between appeared to play what might be considered a basketball game.

Joe, now fully dressed, joined Bob on the sideline and spent a moment watching the game with him. "I'll bet you wouldn't know this, but when James Naismith invented the game of basketball back in 1891, he did it

at a YMCA Training School in Springfield, Massachu-
setts. He said he did it to provide an athletic distraction
for the men attending school during the harsh New
England winters."

Bob pointed to the men tumbling and fumbling on
the court. "I'm not sure this is what he had in mind."

Joe laughed. "Care to take a turn, Bob?"

"I didn't care to take a turn when I could take a
turn. Basketball was never my thing. I got caught up in
vaudeville at an early age, you see."

"I got caught up in basketball. That was my game,"
Joe said. "I love the teamwork. I love the strategy— high
posts, double posts, spreads, overloads. I was pretty
good, but I wasn't quite tall enough to make a go of it."

"It's a tall man's game," Bob acknowledged.

"It sure helps. Did you know that Harry Gallatin
stands 6'6 and that Connie Simmons is 6'8? I'm a
Knicks fan, you see. At least I was until they traded
Simmons this past year."

"The Knicks? My condolences."

"Oh, they'll come around. They finished in first
place last year."

"It's a great game," Bob said sarcastically as a very
large man crashed to the floor in front of the basket
without shooting the ball.

Joe chuckled.

Bob continued. "You know, Joe. It's a fine thing you're doing— coaching those boys, I mean."

Joe dropped his head and attempted to deflect the praise. "I enjoy coaching. I have a good group of boys too— only a few troublemakers. But I keep 'em in line well enough."

"I'll bet you do. You were always a good leader."

"Thanks, Bob. So, what brings you here this morning? Shouldn't you be getting ready for your show or something?"

"That's why I came. I have tickets for tonight's show. It would be great if you and a few of your boys could join us. It's a clean show. I would think their parents wouldn't mind."

"That would be swell. I'd wager the boys who play basketball for me have never seen a real Broadway show. Their families are working class, you see."

"Whaddya know? We specialize in working class!" Bob said. "The show starts at 7:35 p.m. I'll find a place for you and the boys backstage so you can see first-hand how a real Broadway show operates."

"Swell. I'll talk to the boy's parents, and we'll see you tonight."

Chapter 4

Time.

It was a stage production's nemesis, and it was unrelenting. With every close of the curtain, each performer raced to change from one costume to another and still be on time for the next curtain. Dressers had limited time for *on-the-fly* repairs to the performer's costumes. Make-up artists often had precious seconds to dab and wipe make-up on and off a performer's head and face while stage crews raced throughout their allotted time to properly place the next background scene. It was a symphony of coordinated chaos, a hidden dance obscured from audience view and managed by the internal clock of each cast member who knew the exact time they needed to reappear on stage.

Backstage, Joe and his two young players, Cris and Marcus, were having their own time of it as they witnessed the magic of a Broadway play while seated in an inconspicuous spot in the stage wings. Able to see the entirety of the show, they marveled at the speed the cast and crew moved, all to create the illusion of a seamless production and which they now observed was coming to a close.

"And now, ladies and gentlemen. With Thanksgiving nearly here and with Christmas right around the corner, Phil and I would like to get a jump on the coming holiday and introduce a new Christmas song. We hope you like it."

Mark Streuber

Waiting for Christmas to Call

Was it a dream, was I confused?
Was the brass ring meant for others to choose?
I was a song, without a tune,
A bass clef with its bassoon.
You came along, on Christmas Day,
That's when my heart it started to
Beat with such meaning, I don't know the
reasoning,
Fate placed us on a sleigh ride for two.
Sleigh bells rang, we jingled along,
Singing our Christmas Day song.

It was a dream, you went away,
Said you'd return to me next Christmas Day.
There should've been joy,
There should've been cheer,
On that most wonderful day of the year.
My heart was low, in need of a spark,
It just needed a reason to
Start beating faster, and fill it with laughter,
On a sleigh ride that was built for two.

From April flowers, til Harvest Moon,
I can't wait for next Christmas with you.
From the spring, and to the fall,
I'll be waiting for Christmas to call.

From April flowers til Harvest Moon,
I can't wait for next Christmas with you.
From the spring, and to the fall,
I'll be waiting for Christmas to call.

As the two men completed the final stanza, the audience responded with genuine applause. Bob and Phil bowed deeply and then stood tall and proud. They lifted their arms triumphantly into the air, waved goodnight, and then stepped back from the stage apron while the curtain descended in front of them, closing the show.

Phil was astonished. "Where did that come from? They applauded like we were hep all over again."

"That was seismic," Bob replied, equally thrilled the audience had responded well to their new number.

After receiving their customary towels from Ian, they spent the next few minutes conversing with Albert, who had joined them onstage. Joe and the boys remained in their chairs, unwilling to move until they received instruction from Bob and Phil.

Curiously, a young boy appeared on the far side of the stage and stood silently with his hands at his side. His presence was unexpected. The trio could not help but notice him, and they wondered who he may be. The young lad had also noticed Joe, Cris, and Marcus. Upon seeing their inquiring looks, he unabashedly smiled and waved. They responded with a wave of their own.

Phil finished his conversation and strolled toward the group with a towel draped across his neck. "Well, boys. How'd you like your first Broadway show?"

"It was swell," Marcus replied.

"It was hep. Where'd you learn to dance like that, Mr. Davis?" Cris said.

"Oh, from the back of a Wheaties box."

Bob joined the group. "Quite a show tonight. You boys picked a good night to come."

"It was a great show. And to sit stage side, I mean— wow!" Joe said.

"We're glad you came," Phil said. "It was the least we could do for an old pal."

"And for all your doing for these boys," Bob added.

As they talked, the young boy they had waved to walked inconspicuously to the center of the stage and looked directly into the closed curtain. He crossed his legs and pretend-pulled on an imaginary top hat and then began to twirl— easy and without inhibition— as if he hadn't a care in the world. Bob caught sight of the youngster and nudged Phil. "There he goes again."

It was a moment Phil had waited for. "Oh, boy. I'll be right back."

As the youngster tapped an imaginary dance, Phil tiptoed behind him and emerged by his side. The boy was startled to see him stand so close and was instantly embarrassed. Phil's disposition was one of ease. "It's okay, Bobby. Just do what I do."

Bobby relaxed. "Okay, Mr. Davis."

Phil performed a simple *brush strike shuffle* which Bobby awkwardly tried to emulate. "Not bad. Now let's do a *kick ball change.* You just kick with one foot and then draw it back and get ready to shift your weight to the other foot." Bobby followed awkwardly. Phil chuckled, broke into a simple dance step, and then moved around the stage while encouraging Bobby to mimic him.

Evie had been occupied with a tear in Trudi's costume. With a few quick pulls of thread, she halted the advancing tear and tied it off. "That should do it."

"Thanks, Evie. Say, looks like you have a dancer on your hands."

Evie turned to locate Bobby and was startled to see him dancing with Phil. Embarrassed, she excused herself from Trudi and ran to collect him. "I'm so sorry, Mr. Davis. I've asked Bobby not to do that. I promise it won't happen again."

"It's all right, Evie. I was waiting for him this time."

Joe caught sight of the young woman interacting with Phil at center stage and wondered who she may be. She was not a dancer. Her hair was pulled into a bun, and she wore a simple white blouse above a gray skirt. Her neck and waist held an apron, a pincushion was attached at the shoulder. "Bob, if you don't mind. Who is that?"

"That's Evie. She's a seamstress for the show. I'll call her over."

Joe grabbed his arm. "You don't need to do that."

"Nonsense. Hey, Evie. Come on over. And bring Bobby with you."

"Bobby, come with me," Evie said as she gathered her son and walked toward the men.

"Evie. Bobby. I'd like you to meet an old friend of ours. This is Joe Ross," Bob said.

"It's nice to meet you, Joe," Evie said as she politely offered a handshake. Joe reached for her outstretched hand. It was warm and... rough? "Oh, I'm so sorry," Evie said as she pulled her hand back, remembering the thimble rings still present on her fingers. She removed the thimbles and then extended her hand once more.

Joe smiled brightly. "It's all right. It's nice to meet you too, Evie."

"And these young fellas are Cristobal and Marcus."

"My friends just call me Cris."

"Nice to meet you, Cris. Nice to meet you, Marcus," Evie said. "And this is my son Bobby. I'm sorry he interrupted you, Mr. Davis. The sitter was sick tonight, and I was worried about him being alone."

"Mom, I don't need a sitter anymore," Bobby complained.

Evie looked at him wryly.

"Water under a bridge," Phil remarked. "Bobby's a good kid."

"The best," Bob added.

Joe looked intently at Evie. She was attractive, composed and she seemed altogether kindhearted. She returned his look, which surprised him. He had to speak to her. "I coach boys' basketball at the YMCA on 23rd Street. If you live anywhere near there, you could bring Bobby by. You know, if you have trouble finding a sitter."

"Isn't that interesting. Bobby and I live on 20th Street, just three blocks from there. We have quite a few dancers that live in our building. The rent's cheaper there," she half-whispered.

"That's not far at all. You'd sure be welcome anytime."

"I'm afraid Bobby's not much of a basketball player."

"No experience necessary. Cris and Marcus didn't know much when they started, but now they're good enough to help me coach the other kids. Aren't you, boys?"

"Yes, sir," Marcus confirmed. "Coach teaches us that we're all a team."

His response impressed Evie. "Thank you, Joe. I'll keep that in mind."

Joe was uncharacteristically forward. "You don't have to wait until you need a sitter, though. We have a practice tomorrow. You can bring Bobby by, and we'll be sure to teach him the game and introduce him to all the boys."

Joe's interest in Evie was evident. Phil nudged Bob, who was also aware of his instant interest. Cristobal and Marcus were equally surprised by their coach's unusual forwardness.

"Thanks, Joe. I'll consider it. I will."

Chapter 5

It was an exercise meant to sharpen the boy's hand-eye coordination and to strengthen their chest muscles. The boys stood in two lines directly across from each other— eight boys on one side and seven boys plus Joe on the other. Three basketballs were in play. The side with eight boys was to pass the ball to the boy opposite him, and those boys were to return the ball to the boy on the opposite side and diagonal to him. Each of the three balls was to move as quickly through the line as possible. It was a routine drill, and yet this night it was anything but routine for Ernst.

Connie stood in the line across and diagonal to Ernst. He received the ball from TJ and then smoked the ball toward Ernst, who was still tossing his ball to Jarrett. The ball smashed into Ernst's face, which caused him to reel backward and crash onto the court. He grabbed his face, curled his legs toward his head, and writhed in pain.

The players stood in disbelief as Ernst dropped to the floor and recoiled in agony. Marcus and TJ ran to help Ernst, but Cristobal made a beeline toward Connie. He got up in his face. "Why'd you do that, Connie? Ernst wasn't ready for the ball!"

Joe rushed forward to diffuse the situation. "Step back, Cris. I have this."

Cristobal did not want to, but he did as he was asked and removed himself from the precipice of the altercation. Joe placed his attention squarely upon the instigator. "Gosh darn it, Connie. Why on earth would you do that?"

Connie did not answer. He stood in silence while projecting an indifferent disposition. Cris answered for him. "He did that on purpose. He didn't wait for Ernst to turn his head before throwing him the ball."

"Is that true?" Joe said.

Connie was unapologetic. "He should have turned his head faster."

Joe was livid. "He's only ten years old, Connie. You're eleven, and you're bigger. He's not as quick as you are."

Connie cast a hollow look toward Joe and prepared for retribution. Disheartened and somewhat surprised by Connie's heartless attitude, Joe staid any punishment while he pondered how best to reprimand the young lad. He was also aware he needed to divert attention away from Connie and to check on Ernst. "All right, boys. I want you to run lines. Marcus and Cris, you lead the drill. Connie, you sit on the bench until I'm done with Ernst."

Connie displayed an indifferent look but wisely chose to obey without objection. Marcus and Cris cast a surly eye toward Connie before carrying out Joe's instruction. "All right, two lines. One behind me. One behind Cris," Marcus commanded.

Joe bent down next to Ernst, who sat with his nose and forehead cradled in the palm of his hand. "You okay, son?"

Ernst did not respond but shook his head up and down as tears flowed down his cheeks.

"That's my boy."

Joe held out his hand. Ernst grabbed it and stood to his feet. Joe led him off the court. He retrieved a towel from his gym bag, wet it with cool water from his jug, and pressed it lightly against the young lad's head and nose.

Evie and Bobby stood in the doorway, having witnessed the entire event. Boys could be rough— Evie knew that. Still, she did not want to throw her son to the lions. Having observed how reasonably Joe confronted Connie and how he cared for Ernst, she determined that if there were lions, Joe had shown himself capable of keeping them at bay.

Joe finished with Ernst and then sat on the bench next to Connie, who quickly slid away. Joe closed the gap. "Connie, I don't know why you dislike Ernst. But I won't allow you to treat him this way."

Connie folded his arms and turned his head away from Joe. He did not offer a response.

Joe was agitated. "Here's the deal, Connie. Either apologize to Ernst, or you're off the team. I won't allow a kid that plays for me to bully another kid. Do you understand?"

Tears formed in Connie's eyes, yet he remained defiant. "This is not *your* gym. You're just the maintenance man."

They were stinging words.

"Connie, be careful what you say. Words can kill. And once said you can't take them back. I know that from personal experience."

Connie turned to look at Joe, bewildered by his statement. Joe discerned his expression and knew he did not understand. "What it means, Connie, is that yeah, I'm just a maintenance man. I fix boilers and sinks and help out wherever I'm needed. But I'm more than that. I'm a coach and a teacher, and I care about people, and I care about you. If there's one thing you need right now, it's for someone to care about you. Whatever issue you have with Ernst, you can rise above it. But you can't rise above it by bullying him. I won't allow it. Do you understand?"

Connie was on the verge of tears, and still, he clamped down and would not speak.

"I don't have all night, Connie. Are you gonna apologize to Ernst or not?"

Connie gave in. "All right." He rose from the bench and walked toward Ernst, who sat on the gym floor and against the wall. "I'm sorry, Ernst. I won't do that again."

Ernst looked past the towel he held against his head and glared at Connie. He did not reply.

Joe joined the two boys. "Whatever it is, I hope you two can work this out. You're both good basketball players, and underneath, I know you're good kids. Connie, go get some water and cool down a bit."

Joe watched as Connie made a beeline for the water fountain. It was then that he saw Evie and Bobby waiting in the doorway, which surprised him. "Cris, Marcus. Organize a pickup game, will you?"

"Sure, Coach."

Joe walked toward the door. "Hello, Evie. Hey, Bobby. Glad you could make it tonight."

"Bobby wanted to come and see what this is all about. Looks like you had a rough go of it just now."

"We sure did. Most nights are smooth sailing, but the boys do have their moments. We have some good times, too. Way more good times."

"I see."

Joe pointed to the boys on the court. "The two tall boys over there are Marcus and Cristobal. You met them the other night. They've come to the Y since they were seven-years-old and have played basketball for me since they were eight. They've both become fine young men. And then there's Wylie, Ryan, Jarrett, Karson, Cameran, Edward, Mikey, TJ, Robert, Miguel, and Stephan. Ernst is sitting over there. And that's Connie who just walked past you."

"It's too bad about those two," Evie said privately to Joe. "Looks like the boys on the court are having fun, though."

"Lots of fun. How 'bout you, Bobby? Are you ready to play some basketball?"

Bobby squirmed uneasily. "I've never played basketball before."

Joe cast an easy smile. "That's okay. This is the perfect place to learn. I'll teach you everything you need to know as long as you promise to work hard and listen to your coach."

Bobby turned to Evie. "Can I stay, mom?"

"Joe, would it be all right if we see how Bobby does tonight and then let him decide if this is what he wants to do?"

"Sure. I'm okay with that."

"There's just one problem. I'm due backstage at *Playing Around* by 6 p.m. Can one of the boys walk Bobby home after practice? It's not far— just a few blocks is all. Otherwise, I don't think this will work out."

"I can walk Bobby home," Joe offered.

"Are you sure?"

"Absolutely. I'd be glad to."

Evie pondered the offer. Bobby was her life, yet sitting at home night after night with a sitter was not much of a life for a nine-year-old boy. "All right, Bobby. I'll call you at intermission to see how practice went. Stay by the phone when you get home."

"Yes, mom."

The remaining practice went quickly. Joe spent time on the sideline with Bobby talking basketball— a little of its history and several of the rules. He taught him how to dribble and pass, and he showed him a few basic formations, but he did not let him scrimmage on his first night.

With practice over, Joe walked Bobby home as promised. On this unusually warm November night, heavy sweatshirts were all they needed to keep warm.

"What did you think of your first basketball practice, Bobby?"

"I liked it. My arm is a little sore from all that bouncing, though."

"It's called dribbling. Remember? Your arms will get used to it. If you practice your dribble at home, you'll be amazed at how quickly your arm strength develops. Do you have a basketball?"

"Nope."

"Hmm, okay. If you keep coming to practice, I'll see about getting you one."

"Gee, thanks."

Bobby swung around a light pole and then put his hands in his pockets and kicked an old can lying on the sidewalk. Joe put his hands into his pockets and spied his own dirty can and gave it a kick. "Your mom seems nice. She sure seems to work a lot."

"She works most nights," Bobby confirmed. "I have to stay with Ms. Reade most of the time."

"Ms. Reade?"

"Yeah. She's our next-door neighbor. She's real nice, but she's gone sometimes."

"I see. Where's your dad?"

"Don't have a dad."

"Oh, sorry to hear that."

"It's okay. I never met him, so I guess I don't miss him. Mom doesn't talk about him. She just says the war took him."

"The war took him. What does that mean?"

"I'm not sure."

"Do you know which war he was in?"

"How many were there?"

"There's been quite a few, actually."

"I dunno."

"I see. Do you have any brothers or sisters?"

"It's just me and mom and General Patton."

"General Patton? Who's that?"

"It's my cat!" Bobby snickered. "Mom keeps saying we got to get rid of him because he's a fat cat, and we can't afford to feed him. But she ain't done it yet."

"Lucky cat."

"That's my apartment house up ahead."

Joe looked at the building. "This is your place, huh?"

"Yup. We live on the third floor. Marina and Heather live down the hall, and Trudi and Doreen live on the second floor. Mom says those two are coming over on Thanksgiving so we don't have to spend the holiday alone."

"That sounds like a good neighbor thing to do," Joe said.

"You wanna come up and see where I live?"

"That's all right, Bobby. I should get back to the gym. It sure was nice having you at practice tonight. We have practices twice a week, and we scrimmage against the other YMCAs on Saturday. Tell your mom I'd love to see you at the next practice."

"Okay, Coach."

Chapter 6

Evie sat at her dinette table and cheerlessly looked out her apartment window. The view was atrocious— a fire escape butted against the wall of an adjoining apartment building. Though the view was dismal, it did allow her to look at something, anything, other than the telegram laid out on the table before her. She took another sip of coffee and looked uneasily at the message.

"Why do you need to go in early, mom?"

"I'm not sure, Bobby. There've been some rumors that the show's in trouble."

"What kind of trouble?"

"Like I said, I'm not sure. But if the rumors are true, I'll be at home with you until I find another job—which won't be easy."

"Will we have to move?"

"Maybe. It's hard enough to make rent when it comes due. If we didn't have your dad's pension, then we wouldn't be able to live here at all."

"Couldn't we move in with Doreen and Trudi?"

"They'll be out of a job, too. Now enough of this. There's no sense getting all worked up until we know the whole story."

Bobby leaned into his mom and sighed.

"What's wrong?"

"I like where we live. And we're close to school and the Y, and I like basketball. It's been fun."

Evie gathered her son's face into her hands. "And what about Coach Joe?"

"He's cool."

His use of the term *cool* surprised her. "Cool? Where'd you learn that word?"

"From the gym. All the boys on the team say that Joe is *cool*."

"I see. Well, like I said, tomorrow has enough worries of its own. Let's just worry about today, shall we? Like getting yourself ready to go to Ms. Reade's."

Evie's bus came to a stop in front of the host theatre for *Playing Around— The Durant.* Doreen, Trudi, Marina, Heather, and the rest of the cast and crew arrived at the theatre within minutes of each other and found open seats in the auditorium to sit in. Bob, Phil, and Albert sat on stools in front of the stage. They were pensive.

"Afternoon, everyone. Thanks for coming in early. We have some information about the show that we'd like to share with you," Bob said.

It was an alarming way to start the meeting. Bob's vocal inflection was business-like and impersonal and gave every indication that pink slips were being drawn as he spoke. Evie tightened her grip on the armrest and waited for the dreaded announcement. Trudi noticed Evie's tension and grasped her hand, which steadied them both.

"As you know, *Playing Around* has had two strong years on Broadway. Two years is quite a run for most shows," Bob said proudly.

"And we have all of you to thank for that," Phil said.

"But," Bob continued, "even a successful show like ours starts to run out of gas after a while. You know how it is. Doing the same thing day in and day out can create a sort of humdrum effect for the audience as well as the cast."

"But the show's doing well, Mr. Wallace. We're still playing to full houses, aren't we?" Doug called out from his seat.

"Yeah. We like our jobs. You're not going to close the show, are you? Not before Christmas?" Mara exclaimed.

"No, no. Nothing like that," Phil assured them.

"But that doesn't mean we aren't concerned. You see, it's our belief that our audience is bored with our show. And we know that they know that they're bored. It's undeniable," Bob said.

Phil stood from his stool and handed Bob a piece of paper. "Thanks, Phil." Bob then lifted the paper into the air. "And it doesn't help when our show gets panned by one of our *illustrious* New York writers. Our not-so-favorite critic, Marvin Winchell, was more than happy to send me an advance copy of his latest review, which will be in tomorrow's paper. Let me read it to you."

No More *Playing Around*

How wonderful it is to be back in New York City. I've had the pleasure of spending the past two months visiting several fabled European theatrical performances. The venues were spectacular, the performances sublime— *Les Misérables, Guys and Dolls, The King and I.*

Imagine my disappointment when I came home to New York and attended Bob Wallace's and Phil Davis' revue of *Playing Around*. Sitting through another performance of *Playing Around* was like eating leftovers from a Thanksgiving meal— *the day after* the day after Thanksgiving. The showmanship and originality the show once exuded has sunk into a morass of brown gravy that one uses to cover a dry turkey to make it palatable. There was nothing new and nothing exciting that you haven't seen before.

Clearly, the show has fallen behind other Broadway shows in its creativity and innovation. Unfortunately, *Playing Around* will still draw tourists to its doors that don't know any better. But for the New York theatre-goer that expects more, I say it's time to throw this turkey out.

The review angered the cast. Bob crumpled the paper and tossed it onto the floor. "All of you know how little I think of our friend, Marvin Winchell. Some of you may know that before the war, Marvin and I sang in the same nightclubs. He took it pretty hard when I started playing all the top houses while he played the *outhouses.*"

The joke was a tension reliever. "Not long after, he got out of the singing business. But now he's giving *me* the business. Most New Yorkers won't give his review the time of day, but some will. I hate to say it, but there's some truth in what he says. We *are* losing a step to other shows. So, Phil and I have cooked up an idea that we want to run by you."

"It's like this," Phil said. "Eight shows a week over two years has been wearing us down, which is why we planned to close for a few days in December. You know, to give everyone a break. Right?"

"Right."

"But now an opportunity has come to us that we need your help with. Tell 'em, Albert."

"Thanks, Phil. We've arranged to take the whole show to Florida for three performances at Maury Susskind's *Florida Theatre* in Miami. Maury is a close friend of Bob's, and he's making all the arrangements."

It was a monumental surprise. The cast and crew sprang to attention, suddenly attentive and giddy.

"We know this could put a crimp in your Christmas plans, so Albert has some more news for you."

"That's right, Phil. After we finish our shows in Florida, you'll all receive ten days off *with pay!*"

Doris screeched with delight. "I can't believe this is happening to me!

"I can't believe it either," Phil commented.

Bob was pleased with the response. "The shows are scheduled for Dec. 10th, 11th, and 12th. I know that doesn't give you much time to change any arrangements you've made for the Christmas holiday. But a tour like this just may be what our show needs to make it through another season on Broadway."

Evie was relieved and excited at the same time. The show wasn't going to close, at least if Bob and Phil could help it. And a trip to sunny Florida along with ten days off *with pay* would surely help pay the bills and make for a better than expected Christmas for Bobby. And yet, what about Bobby? She couldn't bring him with her, and she already knew that Ms. Reade would be in Arizona visiting relatives in December. There was no one else that she trusted as much with her son.

Chapter 7

E d Harrison was not a particularly talented fellow. Growing up in Albany, New York, he did not excel as a student, nor did he play sports or participate in band or other organized activities. When the Army drafted him, he could not shoot a gun, navigate difficult terrain, nor did his internal constitution allow him to apply for the more strenuous Signal Corps or Field Artillery.

What he could do was talk the ears off a corn stalk and wheel and deal with the best of them, which made him a prime candidate for Supply Sergeant. Ed knew people, and he knew how to put people together: a buyer and a seller; a consumer and a producer; talent with a talent agent. He was a fixer, a broker, and a middleman all in one. And he was highly likable.

Upon leaving the Army, it was natural that he end up in New York City, where he managed new and up-and-coming talent and matched them to the appropriate commercial, movie, TV show, or Broadway play. Over the years, Ed had developed such a catalog of talent that the network approached him to host his own nightly variety show, on which Bob and Phil had become regulars.

Upon their arrival at the network studios at Rockefeller Center, Bob and Phil exited the elevator on the 13th floor. Long-time receptionist Laura greeted them. "Hey, fellas. You here to see Mr. Harrison?"

"Uninvited, I'm afraid. I hope he doesn't mind," Bob said.

"He's always glad to see you two. I'll let him know you're here."

"Isn't she helpful, Bob? Every time we come, I always say Laura is so helpful."

"Oh, yes. Very helpful."

"Wiseguys," Laura smirked. She phoned Mr. Harrison's private assistant Leah, conversed with her for a moment, and then hung up the phone. "She said they just finished rehearsal for tonight's show and that Mr. Harrison is in his office. He said to send you on back."

"We're on our way. Thanks, Laura."

The boys made their way to the corner office and found Ed reclining in his leather chair while reviewing his notes for the evening's show. "Surprise, surprise," Ed said as he tossed his notes onto the desk. "To what do I owe a visit from the great Wallace and Davis? You two don't show up around here unless you need to do a little promotion for your show."

Bob and Phil eyed one another.

"Oh, I see. Taking advantage of an old army pal, are we?"

"We don't like to say *taking advantage*," Bob said.

"What do you call it then?" Ed asked.

"*Taking advantage*," Phil abruptly confessed.

"At least you're being honest now. What can I do for you boys? This is not about that Marvin Winchell article, is it? I wouldn't give a plug nickel for what that muckraker says."

"We wouldn't either. But there's a little truth in everything, even from a bluenose like him. Which, in a way, is why we've come to see you. We have some news we'd like to share with you."

"Have a seat. Let's hear it."

The boys relaxed into several modern and brightly colored lounge chairs positioned across from Ed's desk.

"It's like this, Ed. The show's doing well, but lately, Phil and I have sensed the audience is not responding like they used to. We've been doing the same routine for a couple years now, and things are getting a little, well... stale."

"Break your dentures stale," Phil confirmed.

"Needless to say, we're concerned about the show's future. So, we hit upon an idea we wanna run by you."

"I'm listening," Ed said.

"We're gonna take the show on the road—"

"— to Miami," Phil interrupted.

"Florida?"

"Yes, Florida. You remember Maury Susskind?"

"Maury? How can I forget? He helped put together my first big showbiz deal. What's that old boy doing now?"

"He flew the coop a few years back and started his own theatre in sunny Miami, right along the beach. He's begged us to come there for years."

"Miami, huh? That's a great place. When are you boys leaving?"

"In December. It's just a three-day engagement."

"Wow, that's quick. Can you get an audience together in such a short time?"

"Don't worry about that," Bob said. "You know Maury. He'll have the place packed out before Thanksgiving weekend."

"Is your crew ready for that? Florida is a big change from your typical New York audience."

"That's what we're hoping for," Phil said.

"Oh? Why's that?"

"If our routines still have some life in them, we need to find that out. If they don't, we need to find that out, too. An audience that hasn't seen our show will help us gauge if it's curtains up or just curtains for us."

Ed tapped a pencil against his desk and pondered their dilemma. "Boys, we've been friends for a long time. I want you to know that what I'm about to say, I don't say lightly."

Bob and Phil leaned forward in their chairs, rested their elbows on their knees, and waited for Ed to lower the boom.

"The way I see it, you boys have had quite a run. From your stage show to your radio show to your Broadway show, everything you've done has been top-notch. Problem is, whether it was Bob and Phil at the *21 Club* or Bob and Phil on KNNY or Bob and Phil at *The Durant*, at the end of the day, it was, is, and always has been Bob and Phil."

"I see what you're saying, Ed. Bob and Phil this and Bob and Phil that and after a while, people get bored with Bob and Phil and they want to see James or Marlon.

"That's it. Have you thought about bringing in any new talent for your show?"

"Not really. It's always been just Bob and Phil," Bob confirmed.

"I don't mean to be harsh, but that's your problem in a nutshell. The audience loves you boys— they do. But fresh faces bring fresh ideas."

"You know this business better than anyone, Ed. You have any *fresh* faces for us?"

Ed pondered the question. "First, let me say that I think it's a great idea to take your show to Florida. If you can make it there, you can make it anywhere," he laughed. "After that, I would definitely add some fresh faces to your show. Let those new guys and gals bust their butts for your show, and in exchange, you can let them tack their shingle next to yours while they make a name for themselves. That will re-energize your audience, and it might give you time to come up with some fresh ideas yourselves."

"Hey, yeah. Then I might have time for a round of golf or to fly fish in the Poconos. Bob's been driving me crazy with work for years."

"Nix, nix. We haven't found any new talent yet. Who do you have for us, Eddie?"

"To start, there's this young dancer named John Brascia. I saw him on Broadway in *Hazel Flagg* last year. He's been in a few movies—*Call Me Madam* and *Torch Song*– if I remember right. And he's appeared on my show a few times in dance roles. That man can dance like the wind."

"A whirlwind?" Phil said.

"I guess. Anyway, I think he's a diamond waiting to be discovered. He dances over at Maybelle's. You should check him out before someone else snatches him up."

"Am I intruding?" a gravelly voice called out as the door creaked open behind them.

"Satchmo! Come on in. You know Bob and Phil."

The two men turned to see the figure peeking through the doorway. "Hey! It's Louis Armstrong!" Phil called out.

"I didn't know you cats were in the house tonight," Louis said.

"We're just visiting," Bob said. "You on tonight's show, Satchmo?"

"Sure, sure. I'm gonna toot my horn and blow that audience right out of their seats."

"No doubt about that!"

Ed had a brainstorm. "Say, why don't you boys join us? Your show is dark tonight, and you can pay me back for all that free advice I just gave you."

"You don't waste any time collecting your debts, do you?" Bob said.

"No, I surely don't," Ed replied.

"What number are you playing tonight, Satchmo?" Phil asked.

"*Sticks and Stones*. You boys remember that one?"

"It's one of our favorites," Bob said.

"Fantastic!" Ed said. "You boys should get to make-up. We're on in a half-hour."

The network broadcast of the Ed Harrison show was at 8 p.m. sharp. As customary, Ed performed his monologue to begin the show. A commercial break followed, after which he introduced the first of his special guests, cowboy ropers extraordinaire, and straight from the Wyoming plains 'The Lasso Lots'. For maximum entertainment, they dressed Ed in various hats, from a Fedora to a ladies Bowler, and lassoed each hat as he held them in his hand without injuring him. A lasso dance was next, once again using the frolicsome Ed Harrison as the object of their hilarity.

"You don't see that every day in New York City," Ed laughed as The Lasso Lots completed their performance.

The audience applauded.

"Next, I would like to welcome one of the most versatile performers working in America today. He plays, he acts, he sings. He's a legend in the Jazz world, and he's an all-around great guy. The incomparable *Louis Armstrong!*"

The crowd enthusiastically applauded as Louis entered the stage and stood next to Ed. "Oh, daddy-o. Thank you... Thank you. I'm so glad to be here with you tonight."

"We're glad to have you, Satchmo. What number are you going to do for us tonight?"

"The band and I worked up a great little number for all you cool cats out there called *Sticks and Stones*. I need a little help to sing it, though."

"Oh? How so?" Ed asked.

"This is an *old* number, you see. And it just wouldn't sound right without a few *old* friends to help me sing it. Boys, come on out here."

Bob and Phil walked on stage, waved to the audience, and then stepped up to their microphones. The surprised audience responded with sincere applause.

"That's what I'm talking about. Ready boys?"

"Let 'er rip, Louis!" the boys confirmed.

Sticks and Stones

I once had a girl, yeah, her name was Rose
Gave me goosebumps from my head down to my toes
But she played around, with every guy in town
Said I'd never be the guy she'd bring around

Oh, sticks and stones, may break my bones
But trombones will never hurt me
When I'm feeling blue, or I've lost my cool
All my troubles slide away when they start groovin'

I had a job, working nine to five
Working hard to keep my own self alive
But my boss come in, said I's no good to him
So he threw me out, like that 'ol Gunga Din

Oh, sticks and stones, may break my bones,
But trumpets and trombones will never hurt me
Though I'm not immune, to a sad sad tune,
I'd rather raise the roof with Duke and Dizzy and Dorsey

I once had a friend, I thought through thick and thin
Closer than Tom Sawyer and that ol' Huck Finn
But he did obstinate, and opinionate
On my merrymakin' revel-atin' ways

Now bring 'em in, all that brass, woodwind
Let the strings and drums join that grand parade
For sticks and stones, may break my bones
But there ain't nothing get me down
When good 'ol Dixie comes around
And lays it down, all those movin' groovin' sounds

Oh, sticks and stone, may break my bones all day
But I'll be revel-atin', and I'll be celebratin'
When that riotous band tears up this here town

Chapter 8

New York City. Exhausting. Non-stop. Noisy. Convenient. Midtown. Gritty. Harlem. Cultural. Expressive. Crowded. Dirty. Broadway. Subway. Statue. Hectic. Wall Street. Exhilarating. Inspiring. Soho. Chinatown. Little Italy. Greenwich Village. Skyscrapers. Watchers. Taxis. Loud. Eclectic. New York City.

Bob and Phil exited the cab and leaned in through the open door to address Huck, who had supplied their ride. "Listen here, Huck. We'll be right back. Are you gonna wait for us, or are you gonna scram?" Phil said.

"It's your dime," Huck replied acerbically. "But dimes turn into quarters pretty fast around here."

"Dimes, quarters, or dollars. We don't have time to flag down another cab. Just wait until we get back," Bob commanded.

"Sure thing, boss."

Phil paid the tab and then turned to enter the building with Bob. Immediately, Huck drove away. Bob and Phil were astonished and then peeved but spoke no more about it.

They pushed their way across the crowded sidewalk to the doorway of Maybelle's Dance Studio in Midtown. A repurposed opera house, Maybelle's provided rehearsal space for aspiring dancers for a $7.95 monthly fee and served as adequate space for an occasional dance performance—as long as the rickety old-time stage held up.

The four-story building that housed Maybelle's was Federalist in style and screamed to all who passed by that the building owner was short on cash. The cement façade was in desperate need of extensive tuckpointing and a vigorous scrubbing. The windows were thoroughly scratched from years of passing hands and overcoats which had rubbed against them. The aged lettering that said *Maybelle's* was steadily delaminating away from the tired glass it had been adhered to.

The two men entered the lobby. Old posters adorned the interior walls of the opera house from when it was the hottest venue in town. Ornate and exquisite architectural elements highlighted every wall and corner of the room, though much of its intricate detail was hidden behind years of dirt and scum, which gave the room a tired and dirty look.

"That's too bad," Phil remarked as he observed the room's sad state of affairs. "Looks like this used to be a grand old lady."

"I'll bet she saw her share of vaudeville stars back in the day," Bob conjectured. "Silent film stars, too."

A half-dozen young girls dressed in leotards and tights were gathered at one end of the lobby. They stretched, talked, and laughed as they waited for their time slot on stage. The opposite end of the lobby held a coat rack and ticket booth.

A deeply wrinkled old woman suddenly appeared and approached the two men from behind. She spoke in a shaky voice. "Can I help you, gentlemen?"

Bob and Phil turned toward the voice and did a double-take as they noted the woman's unusual outfit — a worn black fringed flapper dress, complete with beads and a feathered headband.

"If you're looking for Lon Chaney, I think he's in the cellar," Phil jested.

The old woman's expression became vacant and wistful. "No, I'm looking for Douglas Fairbanks. Have you seen him?"

"Not for twenty years," Bob replied uneasily. "Say, we're looking for a fella. A dancer named John. We heard he might rehearse here on occasion."

"John Barrymore?"

"No, John Brascia," Phil said as he took an uneasy step backward.

"O-oh. *That* John. Yes, he dances here. He's on stage with his dance troupe right now. They're working on a new dance style they call *choreography*. It's not the Charleston, but it'll do."

"Choreography, huh? You mind if we take a look?" Phil said.

"It's four bits for the performance. *Each*."

"Four bits? I thought you said they were practicing?" Bob complained. "You want us to pay four bits for a practice?"

"Somebody has to pay for the lights."

Bob looked disdainfully at the woman and then at Phil and pointed at his wallet. Phil slapped both hands onto his coat pocket and shook his head, pleading silently with Bob to leave his overused wallet alone.

Bob wagged his finger. "Come on, buster. Give it up."

Phil was flabbergasted. He opened the wallet and pulled out the smallest bill he had— a five-spot. "I hope you have change."

"Right through that doorway," the woman directed the men. "I'll bring your change."

As they turned toward the doorway, the woman moved in the opposite direction and vanished.

"How do you like that?" Phil said upon seeing the old woman's ghostly disappearance. "Two hit and runs in one day. First you, and then her."

"Well, we're in, aren't we?"

"Yeah, we're in. But we might not be able to get out," Phil said uneasily. "I'm not sure if that was the *Phantom of the Opera* or the *Ghost of Christmas Past* who just stole my money."

"Whatever it was, you'll be the last to know," Bob said, indicating that in case of a sudden haunting by the old woman, he could make it out the door before Phil.

"Har, har."

They entered the darkened theatre. On stage were a single male, John Brascia, and six female dancers. Tall wooden posts which emulated streetlamps were positioned at various points across the stage. At stage left stood a small table with a record player set upon it. John stood in front of the record player and dropped the needle onto the first song on the record— *Viva Evelyniana* by The Milt Jackson Quartet. Dressed entirely in black, the troupe readied themselves for their unusual number.

"Feel the music, ladies. It's a different time signature— 7/8. So, keep that in mind while you move with the music. Let's try it again from the top."

Seeing the troupe in mid-rehearsal, Bob and Phil picked seats toward the rear of the darkened theatre where they sat unnoticed by the dancers on stage. As the needle moved across the record, the ladies encircled John. The snare drum and trap led the arrangement, followed simultaneously by the electric guitar and double bass. The sax and horn set contrapuntal melodies to the less than usual time signature.

The dancers snapped their fingers and made a clockwise turn around John while he snapped his fingers and walked counterclockwise to them. John then sprang toward Ava and Olivia, which broke the circle and pushed them away from him. He retreated, which pulled them toward him. Back at center circle, he then approached Gabrielle and Halle, who responded in like fashion as Ava and Olivia. He then performed the same routine with Holly and Whitney. Visually, the dancers created an amoeba-like structure with its wave-like motion and form.

The dancers then ran away from John and rounded several of the fake lamp posts. John leaped toward a lamp post, swung around it, and then launched himself toward the second lamp post and swung around that. The dancers ducked and moved in swaying motion as John completed each swing, and then each dancer moved back to stage center and encircled John. He then lit up the stage with a flurry of dance steps while the dancers twisted and twirled and snapped their fingers while moving counter to him.

Phil turned to Bob. "Now that's what I'm talking about. I'll bet *he* can dance with a whirlwind."

"I'll say," Bob remarked. "This is quite the performance. I haven't seen anything quite like it."

"It's what you call *choreography*," Phil asserted.

The dance ended with the song. John wiped the sweat from his brow and then clapped his hands. "All right. Nice job, ladies!" They clapped for themselves and then took a moment to catch their breath. "Okay, kids. Let's take five, and we'll try that again."

As the ladies searched for their towels and water jugs, John sat down on the stage apron and swung his tired legs over the side. Bob and Phil rose from their chairs and walked from the darkened section of the theatre toward the lighted stage.

"That was quite the dance," Bob called out.

John's eyes lit up. "Say, your Bob Wallace. And your Phil Davis," he said as he jumped from the stage and reached out to shake their hands.

"Right on both counts," Bob replied.

"Quite the moves you have. I like your use of the light poles. That was a nice touch," Phil said.

"Thanks. We use props like that to make a dance more interesting. Fred Astaire does that a lot."

"He sure does. There was a lot more going on in that dance, though. We'd like to hear about your techniques," Bob said.

"Choreography, they call it," Phil asserted as if he knew what it was.

"That's right," John confirmed. "Choreography is really just using the body as a tool or an instrument to express motion or form. Some have even said that it is *the voice of the body in dance form.*"

"So, that wavy-looking thing you created is part of it?" Bob asked.

"Well, sure. You see, choreography can be done individually, but it's often collaborative. Using several people or more, we can express an emotion or represent a form, especially when we interpret music that has crescendos and intensity and point and counterpoint. Which is a little of that wave you just saw."

"You mind if I give it a whirl?" Phil asked.

"Do I mind?" John chortled. "I wouldn't mind at all!" The girls of the dance troupe had recognized Bob and Phil and were angling to come over. "Ladies, come meet Bob Wallace and Phil Davis."

The ladies quick-stepped over to the men. "What's shaking boys," Halle said provocatively.

"Look out for that one," John warned. "That's Halle. And this is Ava, Olivia, Gabrielle, Holly, and Whitney."

"It's a real treat to meet you, ladies," Bob said.

"Phil, if you don't mind. Just jump on up there," John said. "Ladies, let's redo the amoeba number. Phil, you stand in the middle while the ladies circle around you."

"Don't mind if I do," Phil said.

John jumped back on stage and then walked to the record player and returned the needle to the start of the vinyl record. "Okay, Phil. Take a minute to feel the music. Feel its emotion and how it's harmonious and then antagonistic and discordant. When you're ready, just move in toward Ava and Olivia, which will force them away from you. They'll stop and move toward you, so express through your emotion and body position how you feel when you are forced away from them. The expression is solely yours. You can crouch, you can backpedal, or you can resist."

"Oh, I won't resist," Phil winked and then looked smugly toward the ladies.

"Oh, brother," Bob said with a shake of his head.

"Okay. This is a good part to start," John said as the needle moved across the record.

Phil took a moment to listen and feel what the music was saying. He then eyed Ava and Olivia. He lifted his hands into the air, crouched, and moved ominously toward them as if creating a scene from Phantom of the Opera. Ava and Olivia responded brilliantly by lifting their hands to their mouths, feigning fright, and moving away from Phil. The ladies then stopped, threw their hands toward the floor in defiance, and leaned in toward Phil, forcing him backward. Phil retreated to the center of the circle. He then moved toward Gabrielle and Halle, who followed the same routine as Ava and Olivia.

Phil embraced the music. Rather than moving toward Holly and Whitney as John had done, he quick-stepped around the circle while spinning and twirling. He slid to his knees and lifted his hands into the air while centering upon the two ladies. They retreated but then pursued Phil, who stood up and back-pedaled. He grabbed Halle around the waist, swung her in a classic spin move, and then drew her near as they reached the center of the circle. The music stopped.

"Yeah! That's it. You felt it, didn't you, Phil?" John said.

Phil was exhilarated. "I did. I became the music. It was a real gas!" He walked to the edge of the stage and then jumped down next to Bob. "Anything to say?"

"Just one word— *choreography!*" Bob mused. "John, can you come down here a minute?"

"Sure."

John jumped from the stage and stood next to the two men. Bob was unusually giddy. "Phil and I have been looking for a way to spice up our show. You know, add a little pizazz to it. We think you might be the pizazz we've been looking for."

John was excited. "Pizazz? As in you want to hire us for your show pizazz?"

"Us?" Phil shook his head sideways. "Just you."

"I see. Not the girls? I mean, I would be happy to join your show, but..."

"But..." Phil repeated.

John hesitated. "I'm flattered, and I really need the work. But the girls, you see, we're a team. We've been working hard to help each other make it. It wouldn't be right for me to leave them like this."

Bob glanced toward the ladies who mulled around the stage and whispered quietly amongst themselves. He then looked to Phil for guidance. Phil shrugged his shoulders and gave an *'I don't know, maybe'* look.

Bob took a gamble. If choreography worked, it would work for everyone, and there would be plenty of jobs to go around. If it didn't, then the show was finished, and they would all be looking for day jobs. "All right, John. We'll roll that dice. Phil and I would like to hire you *and* the girls— a package deal. Can you start rehearsing in a few days?"

John let out a whoop. "Hey, kids! Looks like we're in!"

The ladies cackled with laughter. They hopped down from the stage and surrounded the men. Halle was giddy. "Hey, boys. We should have a party to celebrate. What do you say?"

"Sounds like fun," Phil exclaimed.

Bob sensed danger. "No-o, I'm afraid that's out of the question."

"Out of the question? What's wrong with having a little fun?" Phil complained.

"Have you blown a fuse? We just hired a whole new crew for the show. You and I have some writing to do, buster. Maybe some other time."

"Not even for five minutes?" Phil complained.

Bob was annoyed. "Didn't you hear? Rehearsals start in two days. Savvy? We haven't a minute to spare." He then turned to John. "I'll have our stage manager Albert get in touch with you about the when's and the where's, and we'll see you in a few days!"

Chapter 9

M r. Whitman, Director of the 23rd Street YMCA, sat next to Lillian and discussed new memberships and upcoming events that the Y was organizing.

"Have they started yet, Lillian?" Evie said after she had hurried through the lobby door and then approached the Information Desk.

Lillian glanced at her desk clock. "You're just in time, Evie. You'll need to watch the game from the running track, though. There's not enough room courtside."

"I see. Thanks for the info, Lillian."

"Say, Bobby sure does like being here," Lillian called out, slowing Evie down. "He's been early to every practice the last few weeks."

"He loves it. And he really likes playing for Joe." Suddenly, her countenance fell. "I'm just not sure how to tell him that he can't come anymore."

Lillian was dismayed. "Can't come anymore? Why's that?"

Evie eyed Mr. Whitman. She did not know who he was, but he looked important. She leaned in and whispered quietly to Lillian. "I'm a little embarrassed. It's just that I'm not able to afford the monthly fee right now."

Mr. Whitman overheard the statement. He dropped his pen onto his paper, removed his eyeglasses, and placed them onto the desk. He stood to introduce himself. "Good afternoon, madam. My name is Philippi Whitman. I'm the Director here at the YMCA. And your name is?"

"Evie. Evie Sanders."

"And your boy plays basketball?"

"Yes— for Coach Ross. Bobby really enjoys playing for him."

"I see. Mr. Ross is a good coach then?"

"I think so."

"And he's doing a good job with your boy?"

"Well, we haven't come here very long, but I think he's doing a great job. I think Bobby would say that also."

Mr. Whitman was appreciative of her comments. He leaned in close so others in the lobby would not hear. "Sometimes we're able to offset a portion of the fees for those who are in need. I can't make any promises, but I'll see what I can do."

Evie was unsure. "That would be nice. But I wouldn't want to take help away from those who really need it."

Evie's selflessness was refreshing. "We have a benefactor who helps with these decisions. Let's have him decide. Besides, helping *all* folks has been a mission of the YMCA since its inception."

Evie acquiesced. "Thank you, Mr. Whitman. Thanks, Lillian."

It was a back and forth game. With fifty seconds left on the clock, the 23rd Street team had the ball but were behind by one point to the J Street bunch. Coach Joe called a timeout and huddled with his team. "Okay, boys. We need to be efficient, but we don't have to rush. Cris, you inbound to Wylie. Wylie, you make sure you get the ball over the half-court line in ten seconds, and then I want you boys to work the ball until you get an open shot."

"Okay, Coach."

"Who do you want in?" Cris asked.

Joe ran his eyes past each boy on the team. It was natural for him to pick the best five, but this wasn't a championship game, nor was it a life or death situation. "Cris, Wylie, Jarrett, Connie—" He paused as he looked at Bobby, who had struggled each time he had been in. He could barely dribble a basketball, and he did not understand the rules, but he was working hard and doing what he was told. Still, Joe knew a failure in a pressure situation would leave a mark on Bobby's enthusiasm. "—and Ernst," he said, completing the five-man team.

Connie scowled upon hearing Ernst's name, which did not go unnoticed. "You can sit the bench if you'd like. I can put Mikey in," Joe threatened.

Connie's malevolent disposition retreated. "I want to play, Coach."

The buzzer rang. The ref stepped over. "Get your team out there, Coach."

"All right. Go on, boys," Joe commanded. "Remember, poise under pressure."

The five stepped onto the court. The remaining boys sat on the bench, disappointed they were not in the game but ready to root for their team.

Cris inbounded the ball to Wylie as the clock began to wind. He dribbled toward the first defender, who pressured him. With a quick right step and a dribble, Wylie veered past the boy and toward the half-court line. Another boy moved in to apply pressure. Wylie faked left, and with a beautiful short dribble, he dropped low, preventing the boy from stealing the ball, and then sped past him.

He found Connie open in the high post position and passed him the ball, which drew defenders. Connie dribbled twice and then found Cristobal in the low post with a nice lob pass. Cristobal was immediately surrounded. He passed the ball back to Connie. Ernst was wide open and waving his hands, begging Connie to pass to him. He refused. He tossed the ball over to Wylie, who then found Jarrett in the corner.

Time was running out. Jarrett dribbled toward the basket, hoping to sneak in for a layup, but he was blocked by a gangly red-headed kid. Caught in a pickle, Jarrett lifted the ball over his head and threw it toward the foul line where Connie was open, but he was immediately swarmed by three players. He was trapped and had no opportunity to get off a shot.

The play clock dropped to ten seconds. Connie spotted Ernst wide open in the corner. He despised passing him the ball, but he had no choice. He let the ball fly. Ernst caught it, squared his body, and with two seconds left, he let the ball fly toward the hoop. It clanked against the rim and fell harmlessly toward the floor. The buzzer sounded, ending the game.

The 23rd Street team let out a groan while the J Street boys jumped for joy. Joe threw his hands to his head, disappointed Ernst had missed the shot but equally happy his boys had played like a team. The boys shook hands with the opposing team and then gathered as a group to meet with Joe.

"I'm proud of you, boys. You played like a team today. Ernst, you took a nice shot at the end of the game. Sometimes the ball doesn't drop our way, but that's okay. Everyone had a chance to play, and we gave ourselves a real chance to win."

Connie scowled at Ernst. "If Ernst hadn't missed, we'd have won the game. I should have taken the shot."

Joe glared at Connie. "Connie, you had three kids defending you. I would rather lose a hundred games in a row than let one kid think *he's* the only one that can win a game. *That* would have been the real loss today."

Connie smartly kept quiet and did not respond to the rebuke. "All right, boys. Grab some cookies and a Hi-C and find your parents. Remember, we only have one game left before Thanksgiving."

Evie had watched the game from the elevated running track with the other parents. Intensely interested to see Bobby play, she was equally interested to see Joe. He was a curiosity to her. He seemed capable of being a businessman, a doctor, or a lawyer. Yet, he had settled in at the Y and seemed content to work for peanuts, which she imagined a maintenance man for the Y might make. Why he ended up here, she did not know, but her interest was piqued to find out.

Bobby grabbed a Hi-C and stood next to his mom, who had walked down from the running track. Joe was in maintenance mode with Ernst, determined to not let him despair at missing the last shot. He finished his talk and noticed that Evie and Bobby were waiting for him.

"Joe, I want to thank you for working with Bobby. He really enjoys playing for you."

"He's a good kid. I'm glad you decided to let him play."

Evie smiled warmly. "It was a simple decision, really. It keeps him active, and when he's here at the Y with you, I know that he's safe."

"Thanks, Evie. That means a lot to me," Joe said appreciatively.

Bobby interrupted the moment. "Sorry I didn't play so well, Coach."

"Hey, now. You've only had a few weeks of practice. I thought you played pretty well."

"They stole the ball from me every time I touched it," he lamented.

"Yes, they did. That's because the other team can tell you're new to basketball. Kids pick up on that and then take advantage of you. As you become more practiced and confident, you'll find that won't happen as much."

"I hope so."

"I do want you to practice the sidestep move," Joe said. "When you're on defense, you need to move laterally so that you can stay with your man. And you need to learn how to avoid the *pick*."

Bobby looked down at his feet. "I try. But they keep blocking me."

"It helps if you anticipate when a pick is coming."

"How do I do that? There's just too many kids out there. I get confused."

Joe searched for a way to explain the pick. "Bobby, you remember that night we first met onstage at *Playing Around?*"

"I think so."

"You remember after the show when Mr. Davis showed you some dance steps and said to follow him around?"

"Yeah."

"Well, that's what I want you to do here. You see, basketball is a kind of dance. And your job is to stay with your dance partner. Wherever he goes, you go. Problem is, there's always some fella trying to cut in."

"Which is called a pick," Bobby said.

"That's right. So, what you do, see, is you anticipate where the man you're dancing with will go, and you meet him at that spot. But you need to expect some other guy will want to block you. What you do then is to *sidestep* past him so that you can stay with your man. Does that make sense?"

"I think so."

Joe noted his hesitancy. "How 'bout we practice it before you leave tonight so you can work on it at home?"

"How do we do that?"

"Okay, you be the man with the ball, and maybe we can have your mom throw a pick?"

Evie was alarmed. "Oh, I don't know, Joe."

"Come on, mom. Help me out."

Evie hesitated but acquiesced. "Okay. I'll see what I can do."

Joe cast an easy smile. "Don't worry. I'll go easy on you."

"Okay. But remember you asked me to do this."

"Yes, I did," he said happily. "All right, Bobby. Grab a ball, and when I tell you I want you to dribble to your left. Evie, I want you to stand right here in this spot. When Bobby begins to move left, I want you to come toward me and try to block me."

"Block you?"

"Yes. Just move a few steps toward me and stop is all," Joe said softly.

"Okay."

"All right. Everyone ready?"

"Ready... I guess," Evie said.

Bobby picked up a basketball, and with a dribble, he moved to his left. On cue, Evie moved toward Joe. As advertised, Joe moved to follow Bobby, which put him directly in Evie's path. He did not anticipate that she would come at him so forcefully— they collided. Joe lifted his hands to stop Evie while she held out her hands to stop him. They were too late. The embrace was unavoidable.

"I'm so sorry, Evie. I thought you were gonna take a few steps and stop," Joe said.

Evie was unfazed by the embrace. "Was I? I must have forgotten."

"Mom," Bobby called out. "Get it right!"

"Okay. Let's do this one more time. Evie, go ahead and do the exact same thing you just did, and I'll show Bobby what to do."

"Are you sure?"

"Pretty sure. Ready, Bobby?"

"Ready!"

Bobby dribbled again to his left. Evie moved toward Joe with the exact same steps she had just performed. This time, Joe anticipated Evie's movement and made a 360-degree turn around her while maintaining his position in front of Bobby. Evie turned and put her hands on her hips. "Nice move!"

"Thanks. Every now and then, I can do one of those."

Bobby was also impressed. "That was swell, Coach."

"Like I said, basketball is like a dance. We follow, we anticipate, we twist and turn, and every now and then we do a 360-degree turn to stay with our man."

"Cool."

"So, there you go. Now you can practice basketball while you're at home."

"Or dance with your mom."

Chapter 10

It was Joe's day off. Having just returned from Sunday services, he sat on a wooden chair and polished his military uniform dress shoes. Since his tour of duty had ended in '44, he had little use for those shiny shoes outside a Sunday service. Over the years, they had remained in pristine condition from a profound lack of use. Still, he found it therapeutic to mindlessly rub the black shoe polish against the patent leather material and remember where he had come from and where he had been.

The son of a son of a son of a soldier, he was the latest in a line of Ross' to serve his country and the last man standing. His grandad and grandad's brothers had served in the Civil War. His dad, Alan, had served in the Spanish American War and in The Great War—World War I. He was a Purple Heart recipient and lived long enough to see Joe begin his tour of duty at the start of World War II. Joe's brothers, Marty and Charlie, were Marines. Marty was killed in the early days of WWII at Guadalcanal. Charlie fell during the Korean Conflict.

After enduring the constant flow of blood which had spilled from her husband and children's veins, Joe's mother had faltered. She had lost all hope and was now institutionalized in upstate New York— an unspoken and under-reported casualty of war. Joe would visit her soon, but for the moment, he chose to admire the work that he had just performed on his shoe.

He placed the polished shoe on the floor and then picked up the other, dipped his rag into the polish, and went to work. His mind drifted once more to war and the men he had served with, and he remembered Bob and Phil and how remarkable it was to see them again.

He and Bob were not friends, not in that sense of the word, though they were soldiers in kind. During the war, each man commanded his own Company and was responsible for the welfare of a hundred men. Brothers in arms and members of the same Division, led by General Waverly, they were amicable and friendly, though they often ran in different crowds.

He had only known of Phil Davis. Phil was a Private in Bob's Company— B Company. Phil had developed a favorable reputation within the Division through his ability to lighten the mood of the men through his incessant humor and constant joviality. He was eternally positive, a trait that even a dreadful war did not hold the power to shake. Even on that fateful night, before the attack on Montepolina, Phil was at his best playing cards, telling jokes, and encouraging the men who waited for the next day's battle to stand at ease.

Joe stopped polishing his shoe and then sat up in his chair as he remembered his last encounter with General Waverly. Joe was in the critical care unit at Walter Reed Hospital. After two weeks in and out of consciousness and three surgeries, one designed to save his leg, Joe awoke to find the General standing near his bed. The General heard of Joe's injuries and had faithfully followed his progress. Taking leave from his morning duties at the Pentagon, he visited Joe every day, watching over him as a father would a son.

After regaining consciousness from his heavy sedation, Joe's first remarks to General Waverly were uncharacteristically belligerent, unexpected, and shocking. He lashed out at the General for abandoning the Division and leaving them in the hands of an incompetent General whose only interest was acquiring another star on his lapel. Worse yet, he accused the General of knowing that.

And then, in the presence of military doctors, nurses, and fellow soldiers, Joe called General Waverly a *coward*. It was the unforgivable sin. The insult was akin to an atomic explosion, and it had caught the General in its blast zone. General Waverly's eyes retreated into his skull as he absorbed the dress-down. He could have easily ripped Joe from his sickbed and court-martialed him on the spot, but he did not. He dismissed the thought of retribution, but he could not dismiss the disrespect, even if it was said out of extreme suffering and pain. General Waverly gathered himself into a poised position. He did not salute. He just placed his hat underneath his arm, and with his head bowed, he walked away.

Joe never saw him again. He grieved for days— years— for what he said to the General. He had thought to look him up or send him a note so that he might apologize profusely for his indiscretion, but each time shame would not allow him to pen a simple letter.

A knock at the door interrupted Joe's reflections. "Hold on," Joe called out as he slipped on his shiny shoes and then rose from his chair to answer the door. It was Cris and Marcus.

"Hey, Coach. You look sharp. You going somewhere?"

"Uh-huh. A little bit later. What can I do for you boys?"

"We know it's your day off. But Marcus and I just had to talk with you."

"Uh-oh. Something serious?"

"Not really. But maybe," Marcus answered.

"Okay. Give me a second to grab my jacket and finish up. Let's meet downstairs in the cafeteria. I'll buy you boys a soda pop."

"Told you!" Cris said to Marcus as he cocked his arm and then lowered it in a cha-ching motion. "We'll meet you down there."

Joe chuckled and then closed the door. He eased his way around his bed and made his way to his closet, which held a single jacket, a few ties, a fedora, and his old Army uniform. He removed the jacket from the hanger, slipped it over his arms, and then plopped the fedora onto his head. He closed the closet door and then gazed at himself in a small mirror on the wall. Still young and barely thirty-three, his one good feature was that he still had a full head of hair. '*Not bad for an old grunt,*' he told himself.

He reached for a letter lying on his nightstand with the name *Evie* on it and slipped it into his coat pocket. He looked at his reflection in the mirror one last time. '*You can do this.*'

The cafeteria was small, though it contained the requisite stove, refrigerator, hot plates, and utensils a kitchen required. The fridge held an array of food and an assortment of non-alcoholic drinks. Joe plunked some change into a small money box and pulled out three soda pops. Procuring a bottle opener from a drawer, he unseated the caps from the bottle tops and carried them to the table where Cris and Marcus sat.

"Thanks, Coach," Cris said.

"Yeah. Thanks, Coach. You sure do look good."

"Yeah, we're not used to seeing you in anything but your gray work uniform or your gray sweatpants."

"Well, today is your lucky day. Today you get to see me in my gray suit jacket. Now what's up, boys?"

"We need to talk to you about Connie. We don't want him on the team anymore."

"Why's that, Marcus?"

"He's just not a team player."

"And he hates Ernst."

"Do you know why? When I try to talk to him, he just clams up on me."

"I dunno. We don't see him much. We hear he gets in fights a lot, though."

"Fights? Connie?"

"That's what the other boys say."

"You ever see him fight?"

"We go to different schools," Marcus said. "We didn't know anything about Connie until he moved here and started playing basketball."

"Are Connie and Ernst fighting? Or is Connie fighting with someone else?"

"We can find out."

"Do that, Marcus, and let me know. In the meantime, I agree with you, boys. We cannot tolerate bad behavior from Connie. It'll just end up hurting the whole team." Joe backtracked slightly. "However, I'm not quite ready to kick him off the team until I have all the facts. You find out what you can, and we'll figure it out from there."

"Okay, Coach."

"Now, if you boys will excuse me, I have somewhere I need to be."

"It's a bit muddy outside. Be careful you don't get your shiny shoes dirty!" Cristobal teased him.

"Maybe you'd like to clean them if I do?"

"Whoa! Look at the time. We should go," Cristobal said as he looked at his pretend wristwatch. "See ya, Joe!"

"Yeah, see ya," Marcus added as they sprang from the table and fled through the lobby door with their soda pops in hand.

"See you, boys!" Joe said, followed by a goodbye wave. He downed the last of his soda pop, rose from his chair, and then deposited the empty bottle in the kitchen. His mind was troubled from his conversation with the boys, but he had something far more pressing to think about on this particular morning. He had to keep moving. He adjusted his fedora, smoothed out his jacket, and then made his way out the door of the YMCA.

His walk would take him on the same path that he had traversed many times over the past two weeks while escorting Bobby home from practice. This was the first time that he felt nervous. His leg ached from the cold, or from an extra dose of nerves; he was not sure.

After completing his three-block walk, he approached Bobby's apartment building. He hobbled slowly up the outside stair, entered the foyer, and then pressed the call button. He waited.

"Yes?" A voice called out through the speaker.

"Hey... Evie. This is Joe... Coach Joe from the Y. Do you have a minute?"

"Ah, sure. Hold on a minute. I'll buzz you up."

Evie turned and snapped at Bobby, who was lying on the couch and reading a comic book. "Quick, Bobby. Put that away. And put your glass in the sink."

Bobby scrambled from the couch, grabbed his glass, and placed it in the sink as instructed. Evie moved around the room, stuffing laundry into baskets and picking up a few odds and ends before pressing the buzzer to allow Joe to come up. "Any idea what he wants?" Evie asked as she stopped to look in the mirror and fix her hair.

"Huh-uh."

Joe knocked on the door. Evie moved to answer it. "Hey, Joe. How are you? You look nice."

"Thanks. Sorry to come unannounced. But I wanted to stop by and talk with you and Bobby. Hey Bobby."

"Hey, Coach. I never seen you dress like that."

"Me neither," Evie said as she pointed to his jacket and shiny shoes. "It's a good look on you, Joe."

"Thanks. Once a week, I take this old jacket out of the closet to give the moths a rest."

Evie smiled. "Come on in. We were just about to have lunch."

"Shoot. I'm sorry for interrupting your meal. This will only take a minute. If you don't mind."

"I don't mind," Bobby crooned.

"It's okay with me," Evie said.

Joe removed the envelope from his jacket pocket. "Okay, well... I just wanted to bring you this letter. I think Bobby is doing a fine job learning about basketball and getting along with the other boys. It would be a shame if he had to stop coming to the Y because of the fees. Mr. Whitman told me. I hope that's okay."

"Sure. I know you're both trying to help."

"When he and I talked, I told him what a hard worker Bobby is and how he's becoming a model player. We both thought that he would be a good candidate to receive a six-month scholarship."

Bobby was excited and confused at the same time. "Wow!... What's a scholarship?"

Joe laughed. "It just means that you can keep coming to the Y."

"I can't believe this. You can keep playing basketball, Bobby!"

"Bobby, I hope I can count on you to obey the rules and be a good teammate and to make every practice that you can."

"I sure will. I promise."

"This means a lot to us, Joe. I work so many nights, and I worry about him while I'm gone. But I feel good when he's at the gym with you and not running around on the streets. I was praying we'd find a way for him to keep playing, and I have you to thank for that."

Joe responded with a warm look of his own. "It was nothing, really. Bobby earned it."

"Hey, would you like to stay for lunch? It's not much. It's just a pot of stew. But there's plenty."

"Yeah. Stay, Coach!"

"I'd love to. Ever since I walked through that door, I've been wondering what that wonderful smell was."

Chapter 11

There was no rest to be found for Evie. Once again, Albert sent a telegram and asked that she be at *The Durant* by 3 p.m. for a private conversation with Bob and Phil. He was vague as to the reason for their early arrival. Edna, who was Evie's fellow seamstress and mentor, had also been asked to attend. It was imperative that Evie be there, yet she was disappointed she would miss Bobby's basketball game, scheduled for 4 p.m. If the meeting was short, she could catch the bus and arrive at the Y in time to see part of the game, but she was not hopeful.

Evie arrived at *The Durant* at the same time as Edna. They entered the theatre together and found Bob and Phil sitting with Albert in their private office. Papers were scattered everywhere. "Knock, knock," Edna said as she barged through the doorway without actually knocking. Bob and Phil did not mind. Edna was a celebrated seamstress and a forty-year veteran of Broadway. She was unapologetic in her sentiments and opinions, and with her skills and credentials, she need not be. The show was lucky to have her, and they knew it.

"Afternoon, ladies. Glad you could make it. We have some big news we'd like to share with you," Albert said.

"Big news? Is Orson Welles joining the show?" Edna chortled.

"Welles, huh?" Bob said.

"Marlon Brando will do, too. If he's not busy."

"Edna, my love. We have something far bigger than Orson Welles or Marlon Brando."

"Oh?"

Phil couldn't hold his tongue. "That's right. We have *choreography*."

"That sounds serious. You should see a doctor for that," Edna said wryly.

The comeback caught Evie off-guard and made her laugh. Bob laughed with her. "Well, not to worry. But you have *choreography* as well. And you too, Evie. In fact, the whole show has caught it," Bob said.

"You don't say," Edna said.

"I do say. Matter of fact, if things go the way we plan, I say you two are going to have choreography for a long, long time."

"Is this *choreography* why you called us in today, Mr. Wallace?" Evie asked.

"It sure is. Have a seat, ladies."

"Tell them, buster," Bob said.

"Right. You see, it's like this. This past week we hired a new group of dancers for the show— seven in all. We'll need outfits for each of them as soon as possible," Phil said.

"That's not all. Phil and I have cooked up some new routines for the show, and they're gonna be *big*."

"And when we say big, we mean *Big Apple big*," Phil suggested.

"That's right. We're going all-out— big stage, big scenery, big numbers—"

"—big hairdo," Phil interrupted, lifting his hands from his head in an explosion motion.

"And we're adding color— lots of color! We'll need new costumes for all the dancers, and we'll need them ready for the Florida show in a couple weeks. It's gonna be a lot of work. Do you think you ladies can get that done in time?"

Edna did not mince her words. "If we put Henry Ford himself on the job, we couldn't churn out that many costumes in two weeks."

"I see," Bob said. "Give it to us straight, Edna. What will it take?"

"A job that big would require three or four seamstresses, all as good as Evie. And I'll need a fabric supplier on call twenty-four-seven if need be," Edna said. "This could cost you a pretty penny."

"We got plenty of pennies," Phil chirped. "We just need to turn them into dollar bills."

Edna pondered the challenge. It was a big job, but it was also the type of job that could bring a Tony for Best Costume Design. "Evie, what do you say. You up for this? I can't do this without you."

"Oh, Edna. It's so much work and so little time."

"This is no small-town seamstress shop, Evie. You know that by now. You've risen to the challenge before. Between you and me, I think we can do this."

Evie felt overwhelmed by the sheer amount of work in front of them, but the opportunity was too big to pass up. "I say,... let's do this!"

Edna agreed and then turned her attention toward Bob and Phil. "Not to be crude, but whose butts are we fitting into these new costumes we're making?"

"His name is John Brascia," Phil said. "Along with his troupe of six ladies. We've been working them out over at Maybelle's. Keep in mind that choreography has a lot of movement, so the outfits will need to be breathable."

"Sure. Breathable. But who's he breathing on? Will we need new costumes for her?"

"We're still working on that part," Bob said.

"Mr. Wallace, I hope you don't mind. I was looking forward to Bobby's basketball game today. It's the last one before Thanksgiving. Will there be anything else?"

"Oh, sure. We're done here. Sounds like you ladies have everything under control."

"Thank you, Mr. Wallace."

There was little time for Evie to catch a bus and make the basketball game. She arrived at the YMCA, ran up the steps, and then rushed through the door.

"I'm sorry, Evie. You just missed the game," Lillian called out.

Evie slowed to a stop and then leaned on Lillian's desk. "Shoot. I was hoping to see some of the game. Joe said that Bobby would play more today."

"Well, I don't know about that. But I did hear some comments from our players as they passed by. I don't think the game went as planned."

"That's too bad."

"It sure is. We had beaten the Railroadies four straight games before today. I guess today was not our day."

"I guess not. Well, I should find Bobby. See you later, Lil."

Evie took the elevator to the gym. Several players and their parents filed past her. She found Bobby, Marcus, and Cristobal changing into their sweatpants and sweatshirts while sitting next to Joe. He did not look happy.

"Hey, Bobby. Hey, Joe. Hey, Boys," Evie said.

"Hey, mom."

"Hi, Mrs. Sanders," the boys said.

"Hey, Evie. It's nice to see you."

"You too, Joe."

"How'd it go today?"

Joe pointed at the scoreboard. It said Visitors 34 - Home Team 21.

"Oh, I see. Not so good, huh?"

"Not so good."

"Did Bobby do all right?"

"He did real good," Cristobal said.

"Yeah. He dribbled the ball to half-court without it being stolen, and he got off a couple nice passes," Marcus added.

"That's great, Bobby. I'm so proud of you."

"Marcus played real good, too. He scored most of our points, and Cris had like ten rebounds," Bobby exclaimed.

"They all did good today," Joe confirmed.

Evie detected a subtle hurt within him. "I see. Is everything okay?"

"Boys, can you grab the ball bag and put the balls away?"

"Okay, Coach."

Evie sat next to Joe. He looked at the scoreboard and then back at Evie. "We might've had a chance to win today, but Ernst didn't show up. Some of the boys said he quit the team."

"Quit? That's too bad," Evie replied.

"Ernst was a good player. He wasn't the best shot, but he has some height, and he plays a strong defense."

"Why'd he quit?"

"I know exactly why he quit," Joe soured. "Connie."

"I see. Those two still going at it?"

"Ernst gets along with everybody, and Connie can't get along with anyone. I keep working with him, but he just doesn't seem to respond."

"Sometimes they don't. I've only worked on Broadway for a short time, but I've seen a few dancers like that. They've wanted to do things their way, so Bob and Phil had to let them go. For some people, that's the only way they'll learn."

"Well, I've decided to visit Ernst's house today and talk with him and his father. If they say what I think they'll say, I'll have to let Connie go before Ernst rejoins the team."

"That's too bad. You don't want a bad apple ruining the whole barrel, though."

"No, I don't."

Bobby sat next to Evie, nudged her, and then gave her the *ask him* look. Evie wiggled her knees and knocked them together like a schoolgirl. "Joe, Bobby and I want to thank you for teaching him basketball and walking him home at night. We wondered if you'd like to come over next Thursday for Thanksgiving dinner. I've invited a few girls from the show, too. I hope that'll be okay."

Joe was surprised. "Thanksgiving dinner? I hadn't even thought about that yet."

"Come over, Joe. Mom's a swell cook," Bobby pleaded.

"Of course, I'll come," he exclaimed. "There's no way I'd miss a chance for a home-cooked meal. Is your show closed for the holiday?"

"Yes, we're dark that night. Bob and Phil gave everyone the night off. They said it was the least they could do since they're taking us to Florida in a few weeks."

"Florida? You're going to Florida?"

"The whole show is. Bob and Phil said they want to see how the show '*plays in Poughkeepsie*'," she said in a man's voice and then laughed. "They've also hired some new acts, which is why I was late for Bobby's game today. They want us to make some pretty elaborate costumes for the cast and for the new routines they're creating."

"I'm glad they gave you Thanksgiving off, then. Sounds like you have a lot of work ahead of you."

"I do. At least I have my right-hand man here to help me with Thanksgiving dinner."

"She's making me peel a whole pot of potatoes," Bobby soured. "But since your coming, I won't mind so much."

"That's the spirit. Well, I should go. I want to visit Ernst and his dad before it's too late. I'll see you both next Thursday."

"Sure. We'll see you Thursday."

Chapter 12

Joe washed up, changed his clothes, and then rode the elevator down to the lobby. Lillian was relaxed at her desk. She was leaned back in her chair, with her legs crossed and her feet resting upon a calendar desk pad. She was reading the latest issue of Variety. From the corner of her eye, she spied Joe as he passed by.

"I think that girl is sweet on you," she called out nonchalantly.

Joe stopped to address Lillian's comment. "What girl? What do you mean, Lil?"

"You know what I mean, Joe. Ever since Evie and Bobby have come to the Y, she can't stop looking at you with those marshmallow eyes of hers," Lillian shook her head, crazy-like.

"Aw. You're not jealous, are you?"

"Of you?" she chuckled. "You know my eyes are glued on someone else."

"Really?"

"Phil Davis, of course. Any day now, he's gonna come by and sweep me off my feet."

"It could happen," Joe encouraged her.

"I gotta get him down here first. Bob Wallace promised me an autograph, and I haven't heard boo from him. Say, aren't you two pals?"

"I guess so. Sure."

"Good! Ask him to come down and watch a game or tell him you need help hanging basketball nets or something like that. And then tell him to bring that Phil Davis with him. I got my own scoring to do."

"Lillian Langer. You vixen!" Joe teased.

Lillian would have none of it. "Well, if you guys won't get around to it then us girls got to pick up the slack," she said and then artfully switched the conversation back to Joe. "But not *your* girl. She's cute. And if you don't get your head in the game, it won't be long before some guy sweeps her off her feet and leaves you holding the net."

"I'll keep that in mind. See you, Lil," he harrumphed.

"See you, Joe."

Joe exited the building and was surprised to see it snowing. It was the first substantial snowfall of the season, and it was about time. He was not a particular fan of snow, but the falling crystals did add a certain luster to the city and gave it a peaceful ambiance, even on a busy New York City side street. He kicked his way through the snow dust and quickly noted that the falling precipitation had not hindered shoppers from visiting the local shops to stock up on food and supplies for Thanksgiving. He also noted that with the Christmas season fast approaching, Genoese's Smallware and Supplies store was replete with patrons.

As Joe passed the store, he looked through the window and spied Gino Genoese waiting on customers. Gino caught sight of Joe standing outside the window. He smiled and lifted his hand to wave him in. Joe returned the wave and then gestured that he had somewhere to be and continued on his way.

Ernst's apartment was just ahead. Joe climbed the stairs and entered the foyer. There was no call box, just mailboxes. After verifying the correct apartment number, he entered the elevator for the fifth floor, found the door, and then knocked.

Little sister Ingrid cracked the door, recognized Joe, and then opened the door wide but did not speak.

"Hey, Ingrid. We missed you at the ball game today."

Ingrid glanced toward the floor. "I want to come. But Ernst say he don't want to."

"I figured as much. That's why I'm here."

Hebert approached from the kitchen and stood behind Ingrid. "Hey der, Joe."

"Mr. Fisher," Joe said as he shook Hebert's hand. "I was hoping to talk with Ernst. Is he here?"

"We need da milk. I send him to da store. He vill be back soon."

"You mind if I wait?"

"I verk soon, but okay to vait. You saw de Knicks game last night, Joe?"

"I heard it on the radio. How we can outscore Boston by seven in the first quarter and then lose the game by nineteen points I don't know."

"Bill Sharman. He vas zu gut— too good," Hebert said.

"The Knicks still have a winning record. They'll rebound."

"Better den last night we hope."

"Say, Hebert. Did Ernst tell you that he quit the team?"

"Ya, Joe. It vas no mystery. You know dat good as me. He and Connie don't get along. *Puh.*"

"And I'm sure sorry for that. I hope I'm not repeating rumors, but word around the Y is that Connie is getting in fights with boys at school."

"*Fight* fights?"

"I imagine it to be more pushing and shoving than real fights. I've never seen him with any bruises at practice, though I did see a little cut on his chin last week. You think he's fighting with Ernst?"

"No. Ernst don't have no trouble like dat."

"Okay. It's just that some of the boys have said..."

Hebert perceived Joe's line of questioning. He interrupted him. "Ingrid, komm here."

"Yes, Papa?"

"You school with Ernst. You see him fight da boys"

Ingrid was carefree in her response. "No. He don't fight, Papa. He watches."

Hebert was flabbergasted. "He vatches da udder boys fight? Welche boys?"

"Billy and Ritchie."

"Billie and Ritchie? Dey fight each udder?"

"No."

"No? Who dey fight?"

Ingrid was uncomfortable with the question. She leaned against the couch and partially hid.

"Ingrid!" Hebert called out firmly.

"They fight Connie."

"Connie? Why dey fight him?"

"Papa," Ingrid pleaded.

"Tell me, Ingrid!" Hebert demanded.

"They make fun 'o him cuz 'o his name. They say he got a girl name and pick on him."

The two men were stunned. Connie's bad behavior suddenly made sense. "Why Ernst don't stop dem?" Hebert asked the little girl again.

"Cuz, he afraid Billie and Ritchie beat him up and down, too. So, he don't say nothing. We just watch 'til the teachers come."

Hebert turned to Joe. "Ich wusste nicht— I did not know. Ernst did not speak of it."

"Ernst is a good kid. Sounds like he's getting it from both sides. It's a tough situation for a kid to be in."

"I straighten de boy out. No more vatching de kids beat each udder up. I talk with de Principal, too. He stop dis or I visit de boy's parents," Hebert said sternly.

"Hebert, if you've a mind to, please talk Ernst into coming back to the team. Now that we know the issue, I think we can work with the boys."

"Was ist mit— what about, Connie?"

"I'll have a visit with Connie's parents, soon as I find out where they live, and see if I can put an end to this bullying for good."

"Dey leben in de tenement building behind us. I let not de worse enemy live der. I tought dat to be Connie. But now, maybe no."

Chapter 13

Preheat oven to 350ºF. Grease a 9 x 5-inch loaf pan. Mix together flour, sugar, baking powder, salt, and baking soda in a medium mixing bowl. Stir in orange juice, orange peel, shortening, and egg. Mix until well blended. Stir in cranberries and nuts. Spread evenly in a loaf pan. Bake for 50 minutes or until a toothpick inserted in the center comes out clean. Cool on a rack for 15 minutes. Remove from pan. Cool completely.

The oven was undersized, but Evie had managed to fit an 8lb turkey and a loaf pan of orange cranberry bread inside. Bobby had spent the morning cleaning every inch of the apartment to prepare for their guests. His instructions were clear— do not disturb the bolts of cloth, elastic, sequins, buttons, and feathers that Evie was preparing for the Florida show. General Patton, feline that he was, could not resist such fanciful fare. He pawed, poked, and flitted the shiny and colorful objects, flipping them into the air like mice until Evie finally had enough and locked him in her bedroom.

Trudi and Doreen had arrived hours earlier to help Bobby peel potatoes for mash and to help with other chores. Trudi showed herself to be equal to the task. Doreen, not so much. Though she understood the concept of cooking a Thanksgiving meal, everything Doreen did was accompanied by a plie' or a leg stretch to even out her sore and overworked muscles, which put the pans of food on the counter and stove in jeopardy. Doreen peeled potatoes while extending her leg behind her, which nearly knocked over a pot of boiling water. Then, she set the table while practicing roundhouse twirls, one of which nearly landed on the back of Trudi's head while she sat on the couch folding napkins.

Joe arrived at 3 p.m. bearing a Thanksgiving bouquet of yellow and bronze mums and poms. Bobby answered the door. "Hey, Coach. What are those?"

"Thanksgiving flowers. For your table. I thought your mom might like them."

"I guess. Mom says to come in when you got here. Mom, Joe's here!"

"I'll be right there!"

Joe entered the apartment. A large sofa and two chairs were positioned in front of him. To the right was the kitchen. Across the room was a short hallway that lead to two bedrooms and what he imagined to be a bathroom. Several photographs hung on the wall above the couch, neither of which included Evie or Bobby.

"Did you watch the Macy's Parade on TV this morning, Bobby? They had live elephants walking right down the middle of Broadway!"

"Yeah, I saw. We don't have a TV, but Ms. Reade does, so I watched it with her. I liked the Santa and Rudolph float best."

"I bet you did."

Trudi appeared from the kitchen. "Would you like me to take those?"

"That would be great. I'm Joe."

"I figured. I'm Trudi. Evie's in the kitchen."

Doreen peered around the corner to the kitchen and sized Joe up. "Looks like a fine fella, Evie."

"Doreen!" Evie scolded her in a hushed tone.

"That's Doreen," Trudi said. "Don't turn your back on her or you may get a kick to your head."

"O-kay," Joe said, unsure as to what she meant. "Nice to meet you, Doreen."

"Joe, I'm happy you could make it. I hope you're hungry," Evie said as she appeared from the kitchen while wiping her hands on her apron.

"Hi, Evie. It smells wonderful. I'm getting hungrier by the minute."

"I just pulled the turkey from the oven. As soon as the rolls are done, I think we can eat."

"Is there anything I can do to help?"

"You know how to carve a turkey?"

"I've carved a few in my day."

"It's all yours then!"

Joe waited for the turkey to rest and proceeded to carve the bird, separating the white and dark pieces, wings, and legs. Evie pulled the piping hot rolls from the oven and set them onto the table. The mash potatoes, sweet corn, green bean casserole, and cranberry-orange bread were placed on the table along with the flowers Joe had brought. It was time to eat.

"Evie, you mind if I say a prayer? It is Thanksgiving," Joe said.

"I don't mind."

Joe prayed for the meal, after which the food was passed from one person to another. The conversation began in earnest. "So, Joe. Evie says you're a basketball coach?" Trudi said.

"Yes, ma'am. I coach the boys over at the YMCA. I work there as a maintenance man too, so it's an easy transition from one job to the other."

"That sounds like a lot of work. I'll bet that makes for a long day."

"It can be. But I enjoy what I do. Basketball is a great sport, and it's a great way to keep the boys off the streets and out of trouble."

"I hope you make those boys stretch before they practice," Doreen said. "I've been trying to work this knot out of my calf all day long, and it still won't loosen up," she said between mouthfuls of mash potatoes.

"We do run them through warm-up drills, but they're supposed to stretch on their own," Joe said as he watched Doreen shovel the food into her mouth.

"Unbelievable isn't it," Trudi said as she leaned in toward Joe. "Doreen eats like a horse, yet she's stick thin."

"Because she never stops moving. She's always twirling a leg or an arm or three," Evie said.

"I can't sit still for nothing. I had four brothers— two were older, and two were younger. Being the middle child, I had to stay on my toes," Doreen said soberly.

"That's a big family. Where'd you grow up?" Joe asked.

"Right here in New York City. I was a fidgety little brat, and I drove my mom nuts. She made me take dance lessons to help focus my energy. I guess I just learned to like dancing."

"What about you, Trudi? Did you grow up here as well?"

"In Brooklyn. I've been here all my life. I've never even been out of the city, except one time I did go to Newark. I can't imagine living anywhere else, though."

"I see. And Evie, are you a New York girl, too?"

"No. I'm from a little town in Connecticut called New Milford."

"That's where I was born," Bobby chimed in.

"Bobby, if you were born there, I'll bet it's a swell place," Doreen said matter-of-factly.

"What brought you here?" Joe asked.

"Work. Seamstress work in New Milford is hard to come by. My uncle was a stagehand for *Playing Around*. He introduced me to Edna, and then he talked Bob and Phil into giving me a shot. To be honest, this is his apartment we're in right now."

"It is? He didn't want to eat with us?"

"He's dead," Bobby said dispassionately.

"Bobby!" Evie scolded. "Mind your manners."

"Gosh, mom. He's dead, ain't he?"

"Yes, he's dead," Evie confirmed. "It was tragic. They were working on a hi-rise over on 33rd Street. A scaffold collapsed just as he was walking down the sidewalk. It crushed him to death. We had just moved here and all of a sudden we were alone. But we got to know Trudi and Doreen and some of the other girls from the show. So, we're doing okay now."

"How tragic," Joe said.

"Yes, it was."

"I hope you don't mind me asking. But where's Bobby's dad?" Joe said.

It was a question Evie hoped to avoid. "The war took him," was all that she would offer.

"Joe, can you pass the mash potatoes?" Trudi said.

"Sure." Evie's usage of the phrase '*the war took him*' befuddled Joe, though he decided to move the conversation on. "Here you go, Trudi. So, how did you end up as a dancer?"

"Same as Doreen. Except my mom didn't want me to just become a dancer, she wanted me to become *a star*. That woman made me take every dance and singing class known to women. I was only four-years-old when I started, so what choice did I have? Year after grueling year, I danced and I sang, and I danced and I sang. And where did all that hard work get me? I'm a dancer, all right, but not a star. I wasn't pretty enough for that, you see. Now, I'm just another nameless face in the chorus line."

"That's how it is for us girls," Doreen said. "No matter how much talent we have, most of us girls are just a feature away from famous."

"Doreen!"

"You know it's true, Evie. Men always want the pretty girls to headline; for the rest of us, it's the chorus line." Doreen then looked unabashedly at Joe. "See, if the tip of my nose was just a 1/4 inch to the left and my chin was a 1/2 inch to the right, I would be starring in *Playing Around.*"

"You still have the best legs in the business," Trudi complimented her.

Doreen continued. "Look at Trudi. If her cheekbones were a bit shallower and her lips a little fuller, she would be starring right alongside me. But no, we work our butts off night after night and give the audience everything we have. And when the show is over, and we take off all those pretty costumes, what happens to us? We walk out that stage door, and we dissolve into a crowd of nameless faces."

Trudi picked up the conversation from Doreen. "You see, Joe. When the lights are shining and the music is playing, the men love us. But it doesn't last long— it never lasts long. And all the men who couldn't wait to meet us when we were on stage won't even give us a second look when we walk alone in the crowd. To them, we become a nobody."

Joe poked at his turkey, uncomfortable with the direction of the conversation. He was compelled to respond. "We don't all think that way."

"Pardon?" Doreen said.

"We don't all think about women that way," Joe repeated, staring straight into his mash potatoes.

"Well, looky here, ladies. We have a real gentleman in our midst. All right, Mr. Joe. What way do men think about women?"

Joe was beside himself. This was not the conversation he envisioned he would have at Thanksgiving dinner. He looked to Bobby for help. Bobby was smart enough to play dumb. He shrugged his shoulders. "Thanks a lot, Bobby."

"Go on, Mr. Joe. Tell us what a man really wants."

"Well, there has to be *some* attraction. You know? I mean, you have to like what your girl looks like, even if it's a 1/4 inch to the left or a 1/2 inch to the right," he said, giving a nod to Doreen. "But I think it's more than that."

"How much more?" Trudi asked. "Does she need to have a figure like Marilyn Monroe? A face like Grace Kelly?"

"For some men, maybe. But not for me. For me, the best girl is the one you can be *at ease* with."

"What do you mean by that?" Evie asked.

"You know, can you be at ease with her in the aisle of the supermarket picking out tomatoes or taking in a movie together or showing her off to your friends. Or maybe even watching a Knicks game?" he quipped. "If you can be at ease with her in all those things, and she can be at ease with you in the things she likes, then she's the best girl."

"Where you from, Joe?" Trudi asked.

"Me? I'm a Pennsylvania boy— born and raised."

"Is that what Pennsylvania boys think? Because I can guarantee you the men we *do* meet in this business don't think that way. They're all angling for something else."

Joe paused, unsure how to respond.

"Joe, how did you end up in New York?" Evie said, hoping to derail the precarious conversation.

"Huh? Uh, after the war, I went back to Easton. There wasn't a lot of work there at the time, and I needed to be near a VA hospital to work through a few war injuries. So, I ended up here. I didn't realize how expensive it was to live in the city, so I took a room at the Y and stayed a while, which is how I began coaching basketball."

Joe's announcement stunned Evie. She was completely unaware that he had served in the war. The revelation shook her to her core and brought back painful memories of her failed marriage. She should have known by Joe's age that he had served in the military, but it never came up. She no longer felt *at ease.*

Joe noted the change in her facial expression. "Everything okay, Evie?"

"Oh...yes. I'm sorry. I think all this work this past week is finally catching up with me."

"We've been working overtime for the new show. I think it's taking a toll on all of us," Trudi confided.

"Is that what all the cloth and feathers are for?" Joe asked as he pointed to the varied items stashed in the corner of the room.

"Yes," Evie responded. "We've added seven new dancers to the show, and we need costumes for them by the time we leave for Florida. If I'm not at the show, then I've been here sewing."

"Sounds like a lot of work. I hope Bob and Phil are paying you extra for that."

"They are. Union rules, you know. I don't mind the work. It helps with Christmas coming on, and if the new routines help the show, then we may all keep our jobs a little while longer."

"Makes sense," Joe said.

The meal progressed. Joe noted Evie's lack of participation in their varied conversations. Having an attentive male in attendance allowed Trudi and Doreen to talk willingly and often, making Evie's disappearance in their friendly banter almost unnoticeable. Joe noticed and became increasingly uneasy.

"That was a fabulous meal, Evie. I'd be happy to help wash the dishes."

"You don't have to, Joe. Trudi and Doreen promised they would stick around and help."

Her response was emphatic. She did not want his help. The situation had now become awkward. "I should go. It was great to meet you, Trudi... Doreen."

"You sure are a fine fella," Doreen said.

"It was nice to get to know you, Joe," Trudi said.

"Same here. Bobby, we'll see you at practice next Tuesday. Sound good?"

"Sure, Coach. I'll see you then."

Joe's last goodbye was to Evie. "Thanks again, Evie. It was nice to have a home-cooked meal for a change."

"Yes, it was nice. Goodbye, Joe."

Chapter 14

Ed Harrison occupied the only seat in the theatre apart from Bob, who sat next to him. Together they watched as Phil, John, and his dance troupe rehearsed the newly written dance numbers. The routine was uneven, and the music needed work— even Bob could see that.

"We still have a few things to iron out," Bob confided to Ed.

"You'll need a big iron," Ed joked.

"That bad, huh?"

"Oh, it wasn't *that* bad. It does look like you have some work to do."

"Fair enough. We've only had a week of rehearsals, so I guess that's not too bad a review coming from the great Ed Harrison," Bob needled his friend. "We're writing the routines as we go, you see."

"Did you tell Maury you'd be using his Miami audience as guinea pigs for the new numbers?"

"Not yet. We wanted to surprise him."

"Oh, he'll be surprised. When are you leaving?"

"In ten days. We leave on the 8th, rehearse on the 9th, opening night is the 10th."

"How are ticket sales? Has Maury drummed up an audience for you?"

"What's the latest on ticket sales for the Florida show?" Bob called out to Albert, who watched the rehearsal from the edge of the stage.

"I talked with Maury this morning. He said all three shows have nearly sold out. He asked if we could add another performance on Sunday night. I told him we could only do the Sunday matinee as you and Phil were booked on the night train to New York."

"The night train. You want to leave sunny Florida and come back to freezing New York the same night your show closes? What's your hurry?"

"We plan on doing a big fat plug for the new show that Monday night."

"A big fat plug? On whose show?"

"Yours."

"I guess I'd better invite you, then. Shouldn't I."

"You should."

"Nothing like a little free publicity," Phil commented from the stage.

"Nothing's free, Philly boy. Nothing," Ed corrected him. "I'll make sure to look you two up when someone cancels on my show and I'm in a pinch."

"Sure, sure."

"Speaking of shows, I have my own rehearsal to be at. I'm doing a skit with Dorothy Lamour. We're doing a parody on those traveling movies that Bob Hope and Bing Crosby make. It should be a riot."

"Dorothy Lamour? I would travel with her any day of the week," Bob opined. "Can I join you?"

"Hey, you have your own show to put on tonight," Phil reminded him.

"Oh, the humanity," Bob lamented.

"So, true. Well, I gotta scram. I'll see you boys on the flip side."

"We'll catch you soon, Eddie."

Bob rose from his chair and walked towards the stage apron. He leaned against the sidewall and then rested his arms flat upon the stage. John and his troupe were awaiting further instruction. "Pretty good footwork on that last number, John. Let's keep hammering it out until we have it nailed, though."

"All right, kids. You heard the man. Let's do it again. Ready to go, Mr. Davis?"

"Oh, sure."

Bob then made his way up the stairs and onto the stage. "Phil, come back to the office when you're done with rehearsal. The arrangements are a little inconsistent. I'd like to run through those with you one more time."

"Yes, sir, Mr. Wallace," Phil joked in a squeaky voice.

Bob shook his head at Phil's farcical humor and then made his way across the stage and toward the dressing rooms. Edna was busy mending a frayed hem on Rita's costume. "Edna? How are the new costumes coming along?"

"We're making progress. There's a lot to do."

"Are the new seamstresses keeping up?"

"They're good eggs. They're keeping up all right."

"Sounds like your hitting on all eights, then?"

"We are. And you remember that come bonus time."

"You can count on it." He then caught sight of Evie working on a brigulet for Doris. "Say, Evie. I thought I might ask how basketball is coming along for Bobby?"

"Hello, Mr. Wallace. Very well, I think. He's getting better each week."

"He has a fine teacher. Joe is a natural with the kids."

Evie looked down and away from Bob's searching eyes. "I suppose so."

Bob recognized the aberrant look. "Everything, okay? With you and Joe, I mean? Talk around the water cooler is that he had Thanksgiving dinner with you last week."

Evie was put off. "Who told you that, Mr. Wallace? If you don't mind me asking."

"Oh, you know. It's hard to keep secrets around here, Evie. I didn't mean anything by it. I just thought it was nice that you invited him over."

"Is there anything else, Mr. Wallace? I really should get this brigulet fixed so Doris can get back to work."

"Oh, sure. I won't keep you any longer. I'll see you around, Evie."

Bob walked the hallway to his office and then plopped into his chair, deep in thought. He was sure there had been an attraction between Joe and Evie. Certainly, there was on Joe's part. And he thought Evie had felt the same way.

Phil had finished the last number with John. He wrapped a towel around his shoulders and walked the hallway to Bob's office, where he found his stage partner deep in thought. Phil became uneasy. "You have that look in your eye again, and I don't like it."

Bob did not hide his intentions. "I'm going to the Y tomorrow to see Joe. Wanna come with me?"

"Do we have time for that? The new routines still need work."

"They do. But I think Joe can use some work, too."

"Something going on that I should know about?"

"I was certain that Joe was carrying a torch for Evie, and I thought she had a flame for him, too. But now, I'm not so sure. I thought I'd go down there and see what's dousing their fire."

"Matchmaker, matchmaker," Phil admonished him.

"You're off your nut," Bob said. "Joe and Evie make a nice couple. It would be a shame to see them take a powder on a good relationship."

"Sure, I'll go with you. As long as we can stop and get a massage afterward. My feet are killing me."

"Your feet are killing me, too," Bob joked and then patted Phil on the back. "But I don't know what I'd do without 'em."

Phil was appreciative. "Thanks, Bob."

Chapter 15

Lillian exploded from her chair as Phil and Bob walked through the front door of the Y and approached the Information Desk. "Phil Davis. It's you!" she called out while unconsciously ignoring Bob.

Phil was taken aback. "Who else would I be?"

"Well, of course, it's you," Lillian guffawed. "I thought I'd never see your face around here."

Phil was confused. "I'm sorry. Do we know each other?"

Bob laughed. "You do now! Phil, this is Lillian—with three l's. She's one of your biggest fans."

"Oh, I so am," she said dramatically. She moved around the Information Desk and grabbed Phil by the arm. "You just sit yourself right here next to me. It's high time you and I got to know each other."

Bob took advantage of the opportunity. "Lil, where can I find Joe?" Lillian pointed upward without removing her eyes from Phil. "I see," Bob muttered. Ignored once again, he turned toward the elevator.

"Bob, don't you need me to go with you?" Phil called out with a certain uneasiness.

"Oh, no. Lillian's a huge fan of the show. She's been to see us four times."

"Five times," Lillian corrected him.

"Five times!" Bob repeated. "I think you should stay here and spend a little time with our biggest fan. It'll be good publicity for the show," Bob said as he turned the corner and walked toward the elevator. "Catch up when you can!"

"Bob can take care of himself," Lillian said. "I'd like to hear more about you, Phil. I love when you wear your purple shoes in *Playing Around*. Are you seeing anyone? Do you have any moves you'd like to show me?"

Phil grimaced and slunk deeply into his chair as he wilted underneath Lillian's suddenly overbearing personality.

The elevator opened. The sound of a bouncing ball and the squeal of sneakers against the hardwood floor let Bob know a game was in process. It was a different group of men than he had seen in the weeks prior. These men were agile and athletic and proficient in the game of basketball.

Joe was nowhere to be found. Bob descended the stairs to his friends' room, but he found the room to be empty. Confounded, he worked his way back up the stairs and was happy to see Joe on the running track, having just come out of a service room.

"Hey ya, Bob. I didn't expect to see you here today."

"Hello, Joe. I hope I'm not interrupting your work."

"Not at all. I just finished repairing a few stuck vents. I was about to go down and change into my sweats for practice. School is letting out, and the boys will be here soon."

"No rest for the weary, I suppose."

"No, sir. Not with fifteen boys on the way."

The two men took a moment to lean over the rail of the running track and watch the basketball game on the court below them. "How's your team doing?" Bob asked.

"Oh, we've had our ups and downs. We're not the best at it yet, but the boys are learning. Hey, how's your show coming along? The last time I talked with Evie, she said you hired a new set of dancers and added some new routines?"

"We did. We've added seven new dancers, and they're teaching us the finer points of a new dance form called *choreography*."

"Choreography? What's that?"

"I'm not quite sure. But you'll know it when you see it."

"I don't know too much about showbiz and dancing and all that, but I think I might know what choreography looks like on a basketball court."

"Oh? How so?"

"Well, look at those fellas playing ball below us. See how smartly they move around the court? Each man has a specific job to do. They run cuts and curls, they set screens, they slash and then pop out, and they do it all with one goal in mind— get a man open so he can score a basket."

"Get a man open or get the star player open?"

"Every team needs a few star players. But my philosophy is the team that works together to get a man open— whether that man is the star player or not— has the best opportunity to win. That doesn't happen by chance, you see. It's the coach's job to design that into the play. And when everyone does their part, they make it look as easy as a Sunday stroll. That's what I call choreography."

Bob watched the basketball game on the court below him and contemplated Joe's analogy. "I see what you're saying, Joe. There's a certain movement to basketball I hadn't considered before. It looks like every man gets his crack at the basket. *If* he can get open."

"That's right. If everyone's doing their job, then it's a beautiful thing to watch."

"I can't say it was easy to watch with that other group," Bob said, referring to the pasty and portly group of old men he watched a few weeks prior.

"You have to hand it to those old boys. They've grown a few spare tires around their bellies and sprung a few springs, but they're still out there giving it their best shot."

"Which is how we all should be. I think I've sprung a few springs myself."

"Looks like you're bouncing around just fine to me. Say, it's too bad Phil didn't come with you. Lillian was hoping she might get a signed picture or something."

"Oh, he's here. Lillian pounced on him like a caged tiger the moment he entered the door. I wouldn't be surprised if she's asked him to marry her by now."

"She does have a little tiger in her."

"Maybe I should go downstairs and see if he needs rescuing."

"I'll go with you— in case you need backup."

The two men entered the elevator. Joe pressed the faded number one for the lobby. "So, you never mentioned why you came to see me," he said.

"I just thought I'd come 'round and make sure you're doing okay."

It was a curious thing for Bob to say.

"I appreciate that. I'm fine, I think," Joe said.

"I'm happy to hear that. Say, I was talking with Evie the other day. She says Bobby's doing well. She also mentioned that she thought you were a darn good coach."

"Evie said that?"

"She did. You sound surprised?"

"I am. A little."

The elevator doors opened. The two men stepped from the car and walked slowly toward the lobby. Bob noted Joe's suddenly introspective disposition. "I hope you don't mind me asking, but at one time I thought things were getting along pretty well between you and Evie."

Joe shook his head. "I thought so, too. But now I don't know. Would you mind if I ask you a personal question, Bob?"

"Fire away."

"Have you ever mentioned to Evie that you and I served in the Army together?"

"I don't believe so. Like most guys who served, I don't like to talk about it much. Besides, Evie's only been with the show about four months. I'm confident I've never mentioned it to her. Why do you ask?"

"It was the strangest thing. She invited me to Thanksgiving dinner along with Trudi and Doreen. We had a real good time. You know? And then we got to talking about how each of us came to New York. I told her I came for treatment of my war injuries. I saw her withdraw after that. She hardly spoke to me. I left her apartment not too long afterward, and I've barely talked with her since. She dropped Bobby off at practice this week without stopping in to say hello."

"Did you say something to upset her?"

"I can't imagine how. During dinner, I did ask about Bobby's father. She gave me the strangest response. She said *the war took him.*"

"The war took him. Took him where?"

"That's just it. I don't know, and I certainly didn't want to push the subject."

"Smart maneuver. You say Trudi came over for dinner?"

"Yes. Trudi and Doreen are close friends of Evie's."

"Trudi has a good sense about her, and Phil is good at gabbing with the girls. You mind if I ask him to talk with Trudi and see what she knows?"

Joe thought a moment. "Evie is... Well, she's pretty special. I'm not surprised she doesn't want to be with a guy like me. But if I did offend her, I'd like the chance to apologize. I guess I wouldn't mind knowing that much."

A voice called out from behind the two men. "Is she gone?"

Bob and Joe triangulated the voice and discovered Phil hiding behind a coat rack. "Zoots! Looking for a new suit?"

"Tell me she's not there," Phil whimpered.

Laughter.

"Come on out of there, Phil. We'll create a blockade for you," Joe said playfully.

Phil detached himself from the coat rack, relieved that he now had someone to cover his flank and his rear. The men walked toward the Information Desk, where Lillian had just returned with a hot cup of coffee.

"There you are. Here's your coffee, Phil. Just the way you like it. Steamy hot!"

Phil whimpered.

Bob intervened. "Oh, that's real nice of you, Lillian. But Phil and I are late for rehearsal."

"Yes, we are. It was nice to meet you, Lillian. I'll send that autographed picture right over. Gotta run."

Phil bolted for the door. His abrupt departure surprised Lillian and left her instantly forlorn. Bob did not want to, but he felt badly for her. He did his best to soften Phil's abrupt retreat. "Say, Lillian. It sure was nice to see you again. I'll make sure Phil gets that autographed picture and comes around to see you."

For the first time, Lillian looked squarely at Bob. She knew he was covering for Phil, but she was sensible enough to appreciate the effort. "That would be nice. I would appreciate that, Mr. Wallace."

"It's no trouble at all. Goodbye, Lillian." He then looked at Joe. "We'll see you around too, Joe. I'll let you know if I find anything out."

Chapter 16

General Tom Waverly leaned against his jeep, folded his arms, and then gazed up the slope of his newly created ski run. It was the third such run for the Columbia Inn and Ski Resort at Pine Tree, Vermont. The warm mountain air blew against his cheek and ruffled his thinning gray hair. It was a dubious moment. Development of the new ski run had taken the entire summer to complete. The General had employed a team of arborists and foresters to remove enough trees to accommodate a safe and challenging ski run while leaving the remaining glades untouched. Once tree removal was complete, shaping of the slope was accomplished by small-scale crawlers and by hand.

Grass was planted to prevent erosion and to provide a scenic hiking area for summertime tourists.

This third run, named *Grand Loup*, was longer and higher than the two current runs, though all three terminated in a large bowl behind the Columbia Inn lodge where skiers could enter and exit the lodge at will. The third run was challenging, steep and *green*, and not at all what Tom Waverly wanted to see this far into the winter ski season. He looked up into the blue sky and scoffed. It was not what he wanted to see, either.

The General was no stranger to difficult battles or defying the odds, but it was not in his power to defy the weather. His was to maintain a positive attitude and hope snow would come. But it had not snowed since Thanksgiving and had only snowed once before then. Temperatures were now reaching all-time highs for early December, and he was worried.

He climbed into his jeep and drove a few hundred yards to inspect the ski tows for his first ski run called *Little Lapin* and the second ski run called *Big Renard*. Tow operator Roscoe was waiting for him. "Good morning, boss."

"Morning, Roscoe. Are we ready to test the morning run?"

"Yes, sir. I'll let Clarke know."

Clarke manned the ski terminal on the high end of the mountain. Roscoe flipped the contact switch on the radio. "Clarke, you ready?"

Static. Click. "Yeah, I'm ready."

"Okay. I'll flip 'er on then."

"10-4."

Roscoe pushed the switch to engage the electric motor. The terminal wheel jerked into motion and spun the rope and T-bars around the gigantic wheel and up the hill. The two men watched the motion carefully and inspected for unusual behavior.

"Looks like she's running correctly, boss."

The General smiled dolefully. "No, she would be running correctly with a couple feet of snow under her."

In his steely way, Roscoe sympathized with him. "10-4, boss."

"I'll see you both back at the lodge for the morning meeting," the General said.

"Roger that."

The General reentered the jeep and then drove the short distance to the lodge while commiserating with himself. Ski tows were a big deal back in the '30s and '40s. In 1954 they were old technology. Chair lifts were all the rage, and that is what he had planned for *Grand Loup* as soon as he could afford it. Development of the new run that summer had drained his bank account. He was counting on a busy snow season to allow him to purchase the equipment for the new chair lift the following summer.

The jeep came to a halt outside the lodge. The General exited the vehicle and made his way inside. Granddaughter Susan Waverly greeted him. "How does the ski tow look, Grandpa?"

"It's a little like me— old and outdated, but still able to pull its weight."

Emma approached the General with a basket of laundry. "Good. You can pull your weight by taking these clothes to your room."

"Emma O'Shea," he said, using her maiden name. "That is no way to talk to your employer."

"Yes, but it's how I talk to my brother-in-law. I have more clothes coming. It's your choice whether you want to dress in your room or downstairs where everyone can see you."

Susan laughed. The constant combat between Grandpa Tom and Emma was a regular source of amusement, especially with the lodge devoid of paying customers.

"I'll take them to my room *after* the meeting."

"Suit yourself," Emma crowed as she waved him off with her hand and then walked toward the main lodge to attend the staff meeting.

"I'd better get in there before she commandeers the staff and takes over the whole resort," the General said to Susan, followed by a wink.

The staff assembled and waited patiently for the General to arrive. There were fifteen people on hand: cook and wait staff, house cleaning, ski tow operators, and maintenance personnel. The General stood proud and tall for what would be a difficult announcement. "Thank you all for coming. I won't beat around the bush. All of you know how slow the lodge has been from the lack of snow. You're a fine staff, and I want you to know that I'm doing everything I can to keep this outfit operational. However, I'm faced with circumstances that are out of my control. I'm not ready to sound the retreat, but I do believe it's time to retrench. I'm afraid I'll have to put everyone on half-hours. Just until things get better."

Murmurings and the shuffling of feet ensued, though the announcement did not come as a surprise. Every resort in the area was feeling the pinch and laying off staff.

"I'll work with each of you to define days and hours that I need you," the General continued. "Once the snow flies, you can return to full-time. I know this is a lousy thing to do before Christmas. But sometimes you have to lose a battle to save a war."

"Begging your pardon, General. I have a family to feed. I can't afford to work for half hours. If it's all the same to you, I just assume collect my wages and see if I can find steady work down in Wilmington," Renee said.

"I'm sorry to hear that, Renee. I understand completely. Come by the office after your shift, and I'll settle your account. Anyone else?"

Five more people followed Renee's lead in announcing their intention to quit the lodge, leaving the lodge and the General short-staffed.

"For the rest of you, I'll post hours in the office. Emma can help if you have questions. Thank you, everyone."

The staff dispersed. The General reached for a chair, pulled it from the table, and then sat down to strategize his next steps. Emma stood by the General and observed his dismal countenance. She was aware of the heavy strain the lack of snow had created in him and his stress from the lack of paying customers. She was concerned. "You know I can be a mean ol' bitty at times, Tom. But I know that was a hard thing for you to do."

"I appreciate that, Emma."

"Can I get you a drink, Grandpa?"

"You're a little young to get the drink I need," he smiled. "Just a glass of water will do."

"Yes, Grandpa."

"Better drink it fast. The bankers just arrived," Emma said as she pointed at the door where two men now stood.

The General looked at his pocket watch. "They're always early when it comes time to take my money," he said sarcastically. "Emma, take them to my office and let them know I'll be there shortly."

"Yes, Tom," Emma said.

The General waited for Susan to return with the water. Once he was finished, he walked through the inn and then into his office. Archie stood near the window, looking toward the ski hills. Charles sat in a chair next to the desk.

"Hello, Archie. Hello, Charles," the General greeted the men.

"Hello, Tom. Beautiful day, isn't it?" Charles said.

"Not for a ski lodge."

"Yes. Point taken."

"The place is looking good, Tom. You've made some nice improvements since our last visit," Archie said.

"And your new ski hill looks to be first-rate," Charles congratulated him.

"It would look a whole lot better with a chair lift and snow. I've had to put my staff on half-hours."

"Everyone has. All the resorts around here are hurting. I can tell you that because we've met with every lodge owner this side of Stowe these past few weeks.

They're all trying to cut expenditures or lay off staff to keep their lodges afloat. And every one of them is short on cash right now," Charles said.

"Well, gentlemen. As you can imagine, that's why I've called you here. It's not my way to take on more debt than I can afford, but with the snow deficit we're experiencing, I simply don't have a choice."

"You've done well, Tom. No question about that. Unfortunately, the loan we provided to build the additional ski run has put a strain on our ability to extend you more credit," Archie said.

"I'm not asking for credit. I'm asking for a loan. A loan that I will repay," the General strongly replied.

"Now, don't get upset. We're your bankers, but we're also your friends."

"A friend would have no problem extending another short-term loan. I have an impeccable payment record."

"Yes, you do, Tom. We would never question that."

"Then what, my banker friends, is the problem?"

"Money is tight for us too, Tom. We have to be judicious on who and how much we help."

"I understand money is tight. But that shouldn't make you a tightwad with me."

Archie's expression turned stolid. His words became pointed as he reached deep into his friendship bag. "Tom, you and I grew up together right here in these Green Mountains. We went off to war together, and when we came back, I was there for you when Abigail passed away and when your son Paul and his wife Teresa died in that horrible accident. And you know how I've gone overboard to help you remodel this old grist mill. I know the strain that has put on you and little Susan and how it's consumed you. Heck, you don't even come over for checkers or a game of horseshoe anymore. The point is, you've done a great job with what you've had to work with. But maybe it's time for you to think differently. Maybe it's time for you to think about selling this place and get out from under all these loans."

The General was beside himself. "How can you say that to me, Archie? You know the Columbia Inn was Paul's dream, and it's just about the only home that Susan has ever known. That poor girl has endured the loss of her parents and has lived through a life of upheaval. And you want me to sell?"

"Tom, you've invested everything. Your pension, your life savings— all of it is wrapped up in this place. I know it's hard to hear, but as your banker *and* your friend, it's my obligation to encourage you to sell before you're in so deep you can't get out."

The General was defiant. "So, you're telling me another loan is out of the question?"

Archie's pride was challenged. "Damnit, Tom. If Patton had your stubbornness, we'd have won the war in six months. Yes, I will extend you another loan. But only for ninety days. That's the best I can offer. Even for an old friend."

The General relented. "I'm grateful, Archie." He then moved toward the window and pointed toward the ski runs. "You'll see. The snow will come, and when it does, it'll come in big. Before you know it, the lodge will be filled with skiers, and I'll be down to see you and to repay that loan."

Chapter 17

Evie folded her laundry, laid each piece neatly upon her bed, and then opened the closet door and pulled out her suitcase. Bobby sat next to her on the bed. "Why can't I come with you, mom? I don't want to stay with Beatrice. Her apartment smells funny."

"She's an old woman, Bobby. She still uses mothballs and Coolene. It's just how she grew up."

"Yeah, but it smells. Can't I stay with Ms. Reade?"

"You know she's out of town. And so is Ms. Pleasant. So don't ask."

"What about Trudi?"

Evie was exasperated. "You nut. She'll be in Florida with me. Now pack your suitcase, and I don't want to hear any more about it."

"All right," he grumbled and then left for his room to pack.

Evie watched him leave. She was uneasy about leaving him for such a long time, and yet it had to be done. Five minutes later, Bobby walked back into the room. Clothes dangled from his small suitcase. "Oh, Bobby. You can't throw your clothes in there and expect them to look nice. Here, let me help you."

Unhappily, he dropped the suitcase onto her bed. She went to work to extricate the crumpled clothes from the suitcase and proceeded to refold them. Bobby sat on the bed. "I could stay with Joe," he offered softly.

Evie stopped folding and stared directly into the bed. She was reminded of how abrupt she was with Joe at Thanksgiving and that she had left him hurt and confused. She had not seen him since that day, not even when she dropped Bobby off for practice. "I don't think that would be a good idea, Bobby."

"I like Joe. He's kinda like having a dad."

Evie dropped onto the bed. Bobby was increasingly cognitive that he was one of the few kids in the neighborhood without a dad. She had put it off long enough. It was time to talk. "Listen, Bobby. Joe's a good guy, and I'm glad that you like him. But we've only known him a short while. We don't *really* know him yet."

"Yes, we do. He's nice to me, and he walks me home when you're at work, and he talks to me about basketball and school, and he likes everyone. He even likes Connie, and everyone hates him."

Evie paused long enough to determine how to counsel her son. She chose a path that she had not taken before. "Bobby, have I ever told you about your father?"

"Just that the war took him."

"Do you know what that means?"

"I've never known what that means, mom."

"Maybe it's time I told you then."

"Really?"

"Really! You see, your dad and I met after I graduated high school. He was strong and smart and good-looking. Just like you!"

"Mo-o-m."

"Well, he was. His name was Vince. When I first met him, the war was going poorly. Everyone here in the States was doing their part to help the war effort by collecting cans and metal and other unwanted items to be recycled. The government would then take all that recycled metal and build more ships and airplanes to be used in the war."

"They can do that?"

"They can do that."

"Then what happened?"

"Well, my dad— your grandpa— and I collected every piece of scrap metal we could find. We threw it in the back of his pickup truck and drove down to

Scottsborough, which was the nearest collection point. That's where I met your father. He was collecting cans and metal in his town. Through our conversation, I found out that he was a cousin of my friend Karli. He made plans to visit her, and then he offered to come over and help me with my war garden."

"War garden? What's that?"

"Well, some people call it a Victory Garden, too. You see, during the war, it took a lot of food to feed our soldiers. The government asked everyone who had a yard or little plot of land to grow as much of their own food as possible. That way, we would always have enough food to feed our soldiers."

"I didn't know that."

"What do they teach kids in school, now a day?" Evie said. "Anyway, your father was a sweet man, and he was so nice. It didn't take long for me to realize I wanted to marry him. So we got married. Right after that, he got his draft notice and went away to war. And when he came back, he wasn't the same. You see, Bobby. War changes a person, and it had changed your dad. After he came back from the battlefields, there were nights that he would wake up screaming and other nights when he would sit and stare at the wall for hours without saying a word. You were born by then," she smiled as she ran her fingers through his hair.

"Mom," Bobby complained as he moved his head away. "Then what happened?"

"Well, he had trouble holding a job. He felt bad that he couldn't take care of us, which made him feel even worse. After a while, he began to disappear, sometimes for days. He'd come back and apologize, but then he'd do it again. After about two years of that, he left and never came back. So the reason I say '*the war took him*' is because it didn't give him back. The man who went away to war was not the man who came back from war. Somewhere on those battlefields in Europe, I lost the man I loved, and he never really came back to me. Does that make sense?"

"I guess. But Joe wouldn't do that."

"Your father wouldn't have done that either, but he did. Like I said, war changes a man. Until we get to know Joe really well, we won't truly know how it's affected him. Now, let's get packing. I have to be ready to make the train tomorrow morning, and I want to make sure you and I are both prepared."

Chapter 18

Penn Station was not at all like the train depot in New Milford, where Evie would occasionally board the Housatonic Railway for a shopping trip into the larger towns of Danbury or Bridgeport. While the New Milford train depot was tiny and made of wood, Penn Station was massive and made of stone and steel. It would *not* have made the list of the Seven Wonders of the World, but it quite possibly could have made the list of the Seven Wonders of 20th century America.

The entire eight-acre Beaux-Arts structure was built of pink granite and contained arched decorative steelwork, granite pillars that imagined the Temple of Artemis, and a barrel-vaulted ceiling. The concourse featured a dramatic glass roof which allowed ample sunlight to descend to the boarding platforms below. Train indicators were a massive 16 feet high and were stationed at every boarding gate. The waiting room alone could easily hold a thousand people, and if one looked upward, it was one-hundred-fifty feet just to see the top of the ceiling.

The cast of *Playing Around* assembled on the concourse. Their train, named the *East Coast Champion*, was one in a stable of trains for the Atlantic Coast Line Railway; a passenger train service with four daily runs to Miami. Albert had successfully booked the entire cast on the train, which was no easy task. The route to Miami was a popular destination from New York City, especially in winter.

The *East Coast Champion* was of the newer *Streamliner* class and would provide an easy ride for the cast. With two sleeper cars, eleven coach cars, two dining cars, and a tavern-lounge car, it would be a relaxing twenty-three-hour ride and give the cast time to physically rest and mentally prepare for the rigors they would encounter over the next four days. This would be the first trip for Evie south of Staten Island. Trudi had been to Newark, and Doreen had been to Atlantic City, but Miami would be a new experience for all three, and they were excited.

Bob and Phil arrived at the concourse. After greeting the cast members who waited to board the train, the two men conferred with Albert. "Are we missing anyone?" Phil asked.

"I don't think so. The chorus girls are all here. The band is here, as well as John and his troupe. Edna and Evie, too."

"Will there be enough rail cars?" Bob said.

"Someone may have to ride in the coal car," Phil joked.

"Hey, get with the 20th Century. That's a diesel engine smoking its pipes out there," Bob chided him.

"I know that," Phil chided back. "He always gets this way when he opens that cold and clammy thing he carries in his jacket called a wallet," Phil pretend whispered to Albert.

A voice called out over the public-address system. "Attention! Atlantic Coast Railway with destinations to Washington D.C.; Richmond, Virginia; Daytona Beach; and Miami, Florida; is now boarding at Gate 5 with a departure of 2:25 p.m. Please present your ticket to the conductor upon boarding."

The platform filled with activity. Men, women, and children stood from their seats, handled their suitcases, grabbed their overcoats, and made their way toward the train. Evie handled her suitcase and entered the train along with Trudi and Doreen. A conductor directed Evie to sleeper car A150, where she learned she was assigned a double bedroom with Trudi. Doreen was assigned the double bedroom next to theirs, and she would bunk with Edna. Bob and Phil occupied a drawing-room down the hall.

"Oh, my. I didn't realize the rooms would be so small," Evie commented on seeing the diminutive room for the first time.

"Looks like we're going to be in tight quarters," Trudi said. "You want the top or bottom?"

"I'll take the bottom. If you don't mind."

"It's all right with me. I think your suitcase will go over the door with mine."

"I see. I guess the bathrooms are down the hall?"

"I guess," Trudi said. "When you're situated, do you want to tour the rest of the train with me?"

"I think I'll stay here awhile, at least until dinner. We'll be on the train for a long time, and I want to pace myself."

"I'll stay with you, then. I'll be quiet so you can get some rest. I brought a book *and* a magazine since I don't get to read much anymore."

"Oh? What did you bring?"

"*Look Magazine* and *Murder on the Orient Express*. I thought it might be appropriate since we're on a train."

"I've never read either one. I'm not much of a reader. I've always found it a little boring."

"Well, if you just wanna *Look* at the pretty pictures, the magazine will be right here," Trudi chuckled.

The bustling and scuffing of footsteps and the scratch of bags brushing against the walls of the skinny hallway continued for a short time and then ceased. Lights on the train dimmed, signifying movement. The conductor's voice sailed across the intercom. "Departure for Washington D.C., Richmond, Daytona Beach, and Miami, Florida, will begin in five minutes. Please find your seats."

Already sitting, the two ladies looked out the window toward the East Coast Champion's boarding platform, which was now largely empty. Penn Station was one of the busiest train stations in the world, and there were still hundreds of people stirring about on other boarding platforms waiting to board trains for destinations Evie and Trudi could only guess at.

"You miss Bobby yet?" Trudi asked as she noted Evie's vacant stare out the window.

"I missed him before I stepped foot outside our apartment this morning."

"He'll be okay. Beatrice has raised six kids. She'll take good care of him."

"I know. It's just that this will be the first time I've been away from him for more than a day."

"How did he take it when you told him you were going to Florida?"

"He really wanted to come. But I couldn't see how to manage him and the show at the same time. Never mind the extra expense of it all."

The lights in the train flashed on and off. The conductors closed the outside doors as the train lurched and then slowly rumbled forward. Their route would take them west under the Hudson River and then north through the North River Tunnels before turning southwest at Secaucus and then due south toward Newark and Washington D.C. The powerful E3A 12-cylinder engines, which delivered 2,000 horsepower at 800 RPM, had no problem pulling the fourteen-car train.

With their journey having just commenced, Doreen made an unexpected appearance inside Evie and Trudi's berth. "I'm hungry. You wanna get something to eat?"

"Doreen, we haven't even been on the train a half-hour. How can you be hungry?"

"Well, my stomach, see, it tells my brain it's time to eat, and then my brain tells my mouth it's time to eat. So, I eat."

"What's shaking, ladies?" Phil said as he stuck his head past Doreen's into the berth. "Everyone's headed to the tavern car to get a snack and a drink. You coming?"

"What did I tell you," Doreen said.

"All right. I'll come with you," Trudi acquiesced.

Evie was still unmoved. "I think I'll stay here and catch up on some sleep. I'll see you both for dinner."

Chapter 19

"So many choices," Evie said while perusing the menu.

"I'll have the Salisbury steak with fried potatoes," Trudi said to the waiter.

"Not me. I'll have the lobster cutlet with Parisienne potatoes," Doreen said happily. "I can get all the Salisbury steak I want back home."

"I'm a New England girl. So, I'll have the stuffed crab, Boston style, with sautéed potatoes and a salad," Evie said.

"You two are going to use up all your per diem," Trudi said sensibly.

"We only have one meal to pay for today," Evie replied. "Besides, I can't imagine being able to afford this type of food again. The prices are very reasonable."

Trudi had a change of heart. She lifted her head from her menu and addressed the waiter. "Change mine to the lobster cutlet with sautéed potatoes and the vegetable salad."

The waiter scratched through Trudi's previous order. "Yes, ma'am."

"That sounds good. I'll have that also," Edna said.

Doreen was giddy. "Isn't this fun? Today we're practically in the middle of winter, but tomorrow we'll be in sunny Florida."

"And we'll be living like Hollywood royalty. *I'm sorry, dahling. I can't make the Christmas ball this year. I'll be entertaining Clark Gable and Myrna Loy on my Florida beachfront estate, and I just cannot spare the time,*" Trudi said in a mocking voice.

Laughter.

"I've taken the train to Florida three or four times, myself. When you get to be my age, a little winter warmth does a person good. But you don't have to be rich," Edna advised the ladies. "The package deals the train companies put together make it very affordable."

"Edna Riordan— our world traveler," Evie smiled as she patted Edna's hand.

Edna smiled deviously. "Now, ladies. Let me show you the *right way* to travel. Waiter!"

"Yes, ma'am?"

"With our dinner, I'd like a Tom Collins for each of my friends here, and when dinner is complete, I'd like you to bring us four Champagne Cocktails. You can charge them all to my bill."

The ladies gasped with delight. Doreen poked fun at Edna. "You wicked woman. I'll bet you tell your grandkids you're on your way to Florida for your health when you're really just getting snockered on the train with your friends!"

Edna was surprisingly sneaky and shrewd. "We all have our secrets, don't we?" She then smiled a calculating smile. "You see, on a train you can drink all you want, and you don't have to worry about the drive home."

"Here, here!" Doreen said as she offered a toast with her water glass.

At a table on the other side of the dining car, another foursome had gathered. "Give it to us straight, Albert. What's the final tally?" Bob asked as he picked at his lobster.

"I don't have all the numbers yet," Albert confessed.

"When you do, make sure I'm sitting down first," Phil moaned.

"How about some ballpark numbers, then?" Bob asked.

"Sure. Let's see, the train from New York to Miami for forty cast and crew at $140 per round trip ticket comes to about $5600. Hotel at $30 per night for four nights comes to $4800. Per diem is $12 per day for seven days—"

"—seven days? Why seven days?" Phil interrupted.

"We're in Miami for parts of five days and then two full days of travel."

Bob did the math in his head. "$3300 for the per diem, or something like that."

"$3360, to be exact."

"Now I know why we've never taken the show on the road before," Phil lamented.

"Gee, hearing those numbers makes me think you would've been better off without me and the girls on the trip," John fretted.

"There'll be none of that," Bob said. "You're our hope for the future. If your new routines work, we'll all keep our jobs a while longer."

"No pressure," Phil added as he patted John's back.

John chuckled. "Sure. No pressure."

"You didn't mention salaries, Albert."

"I didn't want to mention salaries," Albert responded. "I'm still tabulating the damage."

"We'll make it work. Don't forget we have paying customers waiting for us in Florida," Bob said.

"That's right. I talked with Maury before we left the train station. With all three shows sold out and with an average ticket price of $8.80, we should rake in over twenty-one thousand bananas. After Maury takes his cut, we should end up about even— I think."

"About even? That hardly makes the trip worthwhile," Phil said.

"If we add the Saturday matinee like I suggested, then we might make a few bucks," Albert said.

"No, we're not doing that. I already told Maury no Sunday night show, and I'm telling you no Saturday matinee. I want this to be an enjoyable trip for the cast and crew. They've worked hard for us these past two years, and a few hours on the beach will do them good. Just listen."

"Listen? To what?" Phil said.

"Shh. Just close that pie hole of yours and listen."

The train was alive with chatter. The doleful conversations Bob and Phil had heard over the past few months were gone. They talked with anticipation of seeing Florida, Florida beaches, and the newly opened hotel to the rich and famous, *The Fontainebleau*, which had been built directly on the white sands of Miami Beach.

"Sounds like a gaggle of geese," John said.

"Happy geese," Albert replied.

"They're as happy now as they were during the first days of *Playing Around*," Bob said. "We may not make any money on this trip, but if John's routines work and the cast is re-energized, then it's worth the effort."

"Boys!" a voice called out as two hands landed on Bob and Phil's shoulders.

"Hot dang! Tito Rodriguez! We didn't know you'd be on this train."

"We arrived late and are just now making our way out of our room. May I introduce my lovely wife, Tobi Kei."

"How do you do," Bob said as he rose to shake her hand. Phil, John, and Albert followed his lead.

"It's very nice to meet you," Tobi replied.

"You folks headed to Miami?" Bob asked.

"Briefly. We're on our way to Puerto Rico," Tito said.

"What a beautiful place to spend the holidays," Phil said.

"It certainly is. But we also have family there. Will you boys be in the lounge later? Perhaps we can chat?"

"Oh, sure. We'll be there," Bob said.

"You going to croon for the crowd tonight, as well?"

"I wouldn't count that out. There's a party atmosphere on the train tonight, and I feel quite the party coming on."

Tito embraced the vibe. "*Wepa!* I have my timbales with me. Maybe I can add a little mambo to your party?"

"O-oh, I don't know. It could get a little loud in there. There's not a lot of real estate in one of those tin cans."

"I'll play very quiet," Tito joked as if that were possible.

Bob laughed. "All right, Tito. We'll give it a shot!"

The lounge was buzzing. The *Playing Around* musicians brought in a guitar, a double bass, and a horn while Tito set up his timbale and cymbals. "You boys pack in the crowds wherever you go," Tito said while pointing at the crowded lounge.

"This time we brought our crowd with us," Phil said, referring to the *Playing Around* cast on board the train.

"I'm glad you brought your band, as well. It's nice to have some accompaniment."

"We can't travel without 'em," Bob acknowledged.

"Estupendo! It would be a shame to waste such a lively crowd."

"We don't want to do that. It's all yours, Tito!"

Tito stepped behind the timbales, revved up the crowd with a short intro, and then introduced his first song, a classic mambo song named *Oh, Maria*. The bass, guitar, and horn joined in.

Oh, Maria,
I just cannot wait to see ya.
I just cannot wait to be with ya.
Do you feel the same way too?

Laughing,
On the portico we're dancing.
On the boardwalk we're romancing.
Under a moonbeam made for two.

Stardust is in your eyes,
that ol' man moon is burning bright,
as I walk along the beach at night with you.

Starfish stop and stare,
at the moonbeams flowing from your hair,
I cannot wait, I must be there with you.
Oh, Maria. Oh, Ma-ri-a!

Tito's song was infectious. Every foot in the room joyously bounced in time with the beat. John was giddy to dance. He looked around the room for a compatible partner and spied Doreen sitting pretty in her bright yellow tropical jumpsuit, which she had purchased especially for the trip. He walked toward her and offered his hand. Doreen gushed with delight. She was not about to pass up the chance to dance. She grabbed his hand, sprang to her feet, and stood beside him.

Floor space was at a premium. The width of the lounge car and the number of people present would make for a challenging dance. John led Doreen with straight-line steps down the center of the lounge car, which pressed the crowd tightly against the walls as they passed by. They twirled and twisted and created a patchwork of steps in between a wayward leg or a stray foot.

Oh, Maria called for a drum solo after the chorus. The band stopped playing while Tito went to work. He banged out the solo on his timbales and cymbal and then went on a search for sound. The bar next to him provided an answer. Drinks with various amounts of alcohol were lined up on the bar waiting to be served. Several coconuts sat in a basket. Tito plinked carefully against the glass rims of the drinks, creating a tinkle and chime effect while alternately pounding on the coconuts. He rapped on the edge of the bar and then onto the window, and then he reached his drumsticks high into the air and pounded against the ceiling of the train.

The crowd went wild. Some played pat-a-cake in time with the infectious sound while John and Doreen moved down the aisle. John lifted Doreen into the air, and while she was upside down, she performed a tap and then an airwalk across the ceiling of the train. He then twisted her around and lowered her gently to the floor as Tito's solo ended.

"Oh! That's what I'm talking about!" Phil said as the crowd exploded with jubilation. The instruments joined in as Tito finished the last verses.

I've got a notion,
To take a sailboat cross the ocean.
And on an island where sands are golden,
Well make a paradise for two.

Oh, Maria,
I just cannot wait to see ya.
I just cannot wait to be with ya.
Do you feel the same way too?

Stardust is in your eyes,
that ol' man moon is burning bright,
I walk along the beach at night with you.

Starfish stop and stare,
at the moonbeams flowing from your hair,
I cannot wait, I must be there with you.

Oh, Maria. Oh, Ma-ri-a!

Chapter 20

The crowd cheered loudly as the New York Knicks appeared from their locker room. Announcer Marty Glickman described to the radio audience the crowd's reaction. He then described to his audience the chorus of boos that arose as the Syracuse Nationals followed the Knicks onto the court. The Nationals were currently in first place with a record of 14-10. The Knicks were treading water with an 11-10 record.

Joe listened to the radio for a few more minutes and then stood up from his bed and clicked the power knob off. He did not want to miss the game, but he had an appointment with Connie's father, and he would not be late. He left the room and rode the elevator to the lobby, where he found Lillian still at work. She had been the first one in that morning and should have left hours ago.

"Lil? Did someone call in sick?"

"Peggy was ill. I told her I'd cover."

"That's too bad— for you and for Peggy."

"No Knicks game for you tonight, Joe?"

"I'm meeting Connie's dad. I don't want to kick Connie off the team until I talk to his dad first."

"It's a lot of effort for you to go to these boy's homes. Can't you just tell the boy he's off the team?"

"Well, Lil. If the Army taught me anything, it's that sometimes we advance and sometimes we retreat, but we all need to hear the same bugle call. If we don't, we'll have chaos."

Lillian was confused. "Not quite sure what you're saying, Joe. I wasn't in the Army."

"Would you let an eleven-year-old boy explain to his dad why he got kicked off the team?"

"Ah, now I see what you're saying. That's probably best. There's no blowback that way."

"Exactly. Say, Lil. I was sure sorry things didn't work out with you and Phil. I know you had your hopes up."

Lillian let her gaze fall upon a stack of papers on her desk. "I knew it wouldn't work. A big star like that has no use for a gal like me."

"Oh, don't talk that way. You're an attractive woman. A lot of guys would like to get to know you better. It's just—"

Lil's attention peaked. "It's just what, Joe? Spit it out. You and I have been friends far too long to keep secrets."

"It's just that you're here all the time. Sometimes I think you're afraid to be alone, so you just come here and work. Aside from a few Wallace and Davis shows, you never go for a walk or take in a movie, which doesn't give the guys a chance to know you outside of work. And sometimes I think you set your sights too high, and you don't give regular guys a chance."

"Regular guys? Like who?"

"Well, Derwood, for one. He's always hanging around the Information Desk. And I even heard him say once that you have a '*classy chassis*'– which is a compliment."

Lillian sidestepped the compliment. "Derwood? You mean *Ol' Firestone* Derwood?"

"*Ol' Firestone*? Why do you say that?"

"Because he's half-bald, and he carries a flat tire around his belly!" She then leaned in toward Joe. "And, he's an accountant," Lillian said with a yawn.

"Sure. He's half-bald, and he needs to lose some weight. But he's a real nice guy, and I think he's genuine. With Derwood, what you see is what you get. And

I'm sure he makes decent money. He works for the firm that handles Gino Genoese's account."

"Sure, he's nice and all. But he's no Phil Davis."

"Just think about what I said, Lil. I'd better get going. See you tomorrow?"

Lil looked fractiously at her friend. "See you tomorrow."

It was cold. It was always cold in New York in December. Joe felt a dampness on his face as the wind blew in from the East River. Snowflakes dropped and then lifted in the air in front of him, courtesy of the unusual wind currents found within a skyscraper city. Joe could have easily reached out his hand to catch them, but he let them fall to the ground, if for no other reason than to brighten the dirty sidewalk on which he walked. The city hadn't experienced a significant snowfall since Thanksgiving, and they would not see one tonight as the weatherman had only predicted a mild dusting.

With four blocks to cover from the Y to Connie's apartment, it gave Joe time to contemplate the trouble that may be waiting for him and to determine how he would handle it, as he was unsure of the character of Connie's dad. The two men had yet to speak in person as neither had a telephone, their arrangements having been made through Western Union telegram.

Joe covered the distance with ease, though his intermittent limp grew more pronounced with the cold and with each city block that he walked. As he arrived at the apartment house, he climbed the steps and entered through the dilapidated door, which creaked and then groaned as he opened it. He walked to the elevator and pressed the button for the third floor— nothing happened. He pushed the button again— nothing happened again. He put his hands on his hips, mildly perturbed, and let out a disgruntled 'harrumph'. It was then that he saw a small sign to the side of the elevator doors that said, 'Out of service.'

'Figures,' he said to himself. He then made for the stairwell, where he ascended three flights of stairs and then walked a long hallway to Connie's door. He took a moment to straighten his coat and gather his composure. He knocked. There was no answer. He knocked again. This time he heard footsteps through the door.

Connie's father, Byron, opened the door with his right hand. His left arm to the elbow was missing in action, clearly a casualty of war. Joe instantly recognized a wooden hand and arm had taken its place. He did not hesitate to offer a handshake. "Mr. Kovacs, I'm Joe Ross. Connie's coach over at the Y."

The man shook Joe's hand vigorously. "Joe, glad you could make it. Just call me Byron. Come on in."

"All right, Byron."

Joe stepped inside the apartment and looked around. He noted that it was smaller than Evie's—much smaller. The kitchen was to his left. It contained a small wood table and two chairs. On the wall, plain hooks were hung to accommodate coats and scarves. In the middle of the room was a worn brown couch that faced an old console radio. An end table was placed to the side of the couch nearest him. Against the wall, on the other side of the couch, was a bookcase. Taped to the wall above the bookcase were three yellowed newspaper articles, their subjects Joe could not make out. Below the newspaper articles, proudly displayed within the bookcase, were a Purple Heart and a Bronze Star.

"Wow! Looks like you earned some medals, Byron. Connie never told me you were military. Where'd you serve?"

"Me? I was career Army until last year. I served in North Africa during *dubb-ya dubb-ya two*. I lost my arm last year in the Korean conflict, so they sent me home."

"I'm sorry to hear that," Joe replied. "I'm Army as well. I was with the 151st Division under General Waverly. I ate six bullets all in one sitting, so they sent me home, too. I guess they thought I was being a little greedy."

"I'm sorry to hear that as well. The important thing is you made it home. Looks like your moving around okay now."

"I'm doing alright. It's a bit harder on cold nights like this. My leg tends to stiffen up a bit."

Byron tapped on his wooden arm. "See, I made out better than you. No problem with the cold," he quipped.

Byron was not at all as Joe had expected. Having observed Connie's behavior over the past few months, he expected his father to be a hardened and unyielding man, not happy and positive. "So, Byron. What do you do for a living?"

"I operate the elevators over at *The Plazas*. I'm on second shift and weekends, which is why I haven't made any of Connie's games. There aren't many jobs for a one-arm man, you see. But that one I can do well enough. It doesn't pay much, but it's steady work, and I pick up all the overtime I can, which is better than sitting here alone."

"Alone? Isn't Connie's mom around?"

"Oh, she's always around for some man, just not for me. When she found out I left my arm in Korea, she left me. She said she couldn't live with a man with one arm, and she sure as heck couldn't live with a man who had a *wooden* arm. So, that was that. And now my son's upset with me, too. So, it's been quite a year for me."

"I hope you don't mind me asking. But why's he upset with you?"

"We always had a good relationship, Connie and me. But since we moved to New York this fall, he's been under some stress. Kids are making fun of his name, and he blames me for that. He had a great name when we were in Philly. But here in New York, the kids don't think so."

"It's not all that unusual a name," Joe commented.

"That's what I tell him. And it's not all that different from Babe."

"Babe? I guess I don't understand."

"In New York, Babe is a great name— because of Babe Ruth. No one thinks twice about calling their son Babe. '*Knock it out of the park, Babe!*' Right? But I grew up in Philly, see. There, Connie Mack was a great name. He coached my hometown Philadelphia A's for nearly fifty years. When I was a kid, I was lucky enough to be a ball boy for the A's during their heyday in the late '20s and early '30s, and I got to know him well enough."

"The A's haven't been too good lately," Joe said.

"Not for twenty-five years," Byron conceded as he pointed to the yellowed newspaper articles on the wall of the A's during their glory years. "Ol' Connie Mack got old, and then the fans got down on him. But he was a winner in my book. He wanted his teams to win, but it was just as important that his players become better men. Even ball boys like me," Byron smiled. "My dad was nothing like him— he was a sourpuss and a drunk. Coach Mack was the man I wanted to be like. So, when it came time to name my own son, I named him after my role model, Connie Mack."

Connie heard the strange voice in the apartment and appeared from his bedroom. He froze upon seeing Joe. "Hey, Connie. You have a minute?"

Connie took a step backward and then stopped. He wanted to run, but there was nowhere he could go. He acquiesced. "I guess."

"I've been talking with your dad. I'd like to talk with you as well."

"About what?"

"Well, basketball. And Ernst."

Connie's face grew pale.

"Byron, would you mind if I had a talk with your son?"

"Ah, sure. I was about to make a pot of coffee. You up for a cup?"

"That'd be great. Connie, would you have a seat, please?" Joe said as he pointed to the couch.

"I guess."

"Connie, some of the boys say you're getting in fights at school. Is that true?"

The lad was ready to defend himself. "It's not my fault. They're always picking a fight with me."

"I see. Do any of the boys on the team pick on you?"

He grimaced. "Just the kids at school. But the boys on the team don't stop them."

"I'm sorry they're not standing up for you, Connie. Why do those boys pick fights with you?"

Connie turned his head away from Joe. "They say I have a girl name."

"Connie can be a boy or girl name," Byron called out from the kitchen.

"He's right, Connie. Besides, your dad says he named you after one of the greatest baseball managers ever. That's a powerful connection. And I'll bet you didn't know this, but one of my favorite players is Connie Simmons. He played for the Knicks for five years before being traded to Baltimore this year. Traitor," Joe winked. "He averaged ten points a game for the Knicks. I'll bet no one makes fun of him. And have you heard about that kid over at Rucker?"

"What kid?"

"Oh, he's fantastic. There's this twelve-year-old kid playing basketball at Rucker Park. He's so good he's already had a write-up in the New York Times. They say he can outplay all the high school boys and that he could dunk when he was just eleven-years-old. You know what his name is? Connie Hawkins. They say he's gonna be a superstar one day. I bet they don't make fun of him, either. Do you see what I'm getting at, Connie?"

"Not really."

"It's not the *name* that makes a man good or bad, small or great. It's the *man* that makes the name great. Every one of those men I just mentioned has or is making their name great. If you work on making your name great, you won't have to worry about anyone making fun of you."

"Yeah. But how do I do that?"

"I'll tell you how," Byron said as he handed Joe a cup of coffee. "Go get the plaque."

"Aw, dad. Do I have to?"

"Go get the plaque," Byron said sternly.

Connie guffawed, but rose from the couch, walked to his bedroom, and removed a plaque from his wall. He returned to the living room and handed it to his father. Byron admired the plaque for a moment and then gave it to Joe. "This is Connie Mack's Code of Conduct. I had a plaque made for it. These are the rules he lived by, and he expected any man that played for him to live by. I keep telling Connie that if he does these things, he can become a fine man just like Connie Mack, and all the other problems will take care of themselves."

Joe read through the rules listed on the plaque.

I will always play the game to the best of my ability.

I will always play to win, but if I lose, I will not look for an excuse to detract from my opponent's victory.

I will never take an unfair advantage in order to win.

I will always abide by the rules of the game—on the diamond as well as in my daily life.

I will always conduct myself as a true sportsman—on and off the playing field.

I will always strive for the good of the entire team rather than for my own glory.

I will never gloat in victory or pity myself in defeat.

I will do my utmost to keep myself clean—physically, mentally, and morally.

I will always judge a teammate or an opponent as an individual and never on the basis of race or religion.

"This is fantastic. I'd like to get a copy of this if you don't mind," Joe said.

"Sure. I can write those down for you."

Joe tried once more to encourage his young player. "Connie, what you're going through isn't easy. I would strongly encourage you to tell your school principal what's going on, and I'll talk to the team about sticking up for you. But you have to do your part. If you do what's listed on this plaque and be the best person that you can be, I just know those boys will stop picking on you, and even better, they'll begin to respect you."

Connie was encouraged. "Okay, Coach."

"Okay," Joe confirmed. "Just one more thing, Connie. Why Ernst? Why are you so angry at him?"

Connie was embarrassed. "Cuz, Ernst is one of the kids that stand there and watch me get beat up. He don't ever do nothing to help."

"Ah. I see how that could make you angry. I'll make sure I have a talk with Ernst about that. Are we good, though?"

Connie was hesitant but hopeful. He looked into Joe's eyes. "Were good, Coach."

Chapter 21

The weather forecast was correct. The snowfall was nothing more than a dusting. Joe kicked the snow into the air while contemplating his visit with Byron and Connie. Life's underbelly was both callous and cruel, harsh and hopeless, and all had left their mark upon Connie and his dad. Joe was happy to have an avenue of resolve for Connie's behavior, yet he was concerned for their welfare. They were barely making it. The coffee Byron served was watered down, made of reused grounds twice over— an old army trick when coffee was scarce. He was also aware of their meager apartment. Minimally furnished, it had an impoverished feel to it. Joe had noticed the newspaper clippings from Byron's days with the A's as the only accouterments to adorn their walls. Connie's clothes were always threadbare. And with Christmas fast approaching, he did not see a tree or decorations of any kind.

As he continued his slow walk down 25th Street, he noticed that Genoese's Smallware shop was still open. He stopped to look at the toys, kitchen items, and other paraphernalia that Gino had on display. A Lionel train set captured his attention. It was a toy that any boy would want. From inside the store, Gino spied Joe standing in front of the large display window and waved him in.

Genoese's was a neighborhood tradition. Passed down from father to son, it had been in business and in the same location for nearly forty years. The Genoese's were purveyors of small household items: hand-held mixers, electric skillets, toaster ovens, lamps, ironing boards, toys, gloves, dry goods, and other saleable items.

Gino was a beloved figure in the neighborhood. He was a businessman, but he was also an *entrepreneur*. He sold Christmas trees in winter, Easter bonnets in spring, patriotic paraphernalia in July, loads of candy for Halloween, and all the items needed for a successful Thanksgiving dinner other than the turkey.

His most beloved attribute was his congenial and approachable nature. When a housewife needed to earn extra money to make ends meet by selling knitted or crocheted potholders or scarves, he never failed to display them for sale. If a young lady wanted to try her hand at entrepreneurship by baking Christmas or Valentine's Day cookies, he always bought tins of cookies to sell in his store and take home.

"You doing some late-night shopping?" Gino called to Joe as he entered the store.

"Hey, Gino. I was just admiring that train set in your window."

"You won't believe how many boys stand outside that window and stare at that train. A lot of them are your boys, I think."

"Is that so? Do you know which boy's?"

"All of them," Gino said matter of factly. "Oh, I don't really know all their names. Jarett maybe, and Miguel and Mikey. I recognized some of them from when I brought cookies and Hi-C to your last ballgame."

"And they sure did appreciate that."

"Well, you do a lot to keep those kids busy and out of trouble. It's the least I can do to help."

"Did your Christmas trees come in yet? It's getting awfully close to Christmas."

"I had three-dozen arrive just yesterday. We're getting ready to close shop, so I hauled them inside already. I set aside a tabletop for you, as usual. You wanna take it now?"

"Thanks, Gino. I'll swing by in a few days to pick it up. Say, how much is it for that train set?"

"She's a beauty, ain't she? She's a six-unit, twin diesel freight train with a Magne-Traction track. It's a complete set— all the pieces you need to get started. I'm selling that for $57.99, plus Uncle Sam's share, of course."

"Ooh, that's a bit pricey," Joe winced.

"It's cost plus fifteen percent. I don't make a lot on those package deals, you know. You thinkin' of going into the train business, Joe?"

"I'm thinking about it."

"I see. You got another boy to help out this year?"

"There's always another boy to help out," Joe said. "I sure do like that train, Gino. But it's almost a half month's salary."

"I tell you what. If you're serious about that train, I can knock off ten percent. It's not much. But if it helps, I'd be glad to do it for you."

Joe thought carefully about the expense. It would put a serious dent in his Christmas plans, but knowing what Byron and Connie were going through it would make the sacrifice worth it. "Deal," Joe said as he shook Gino's hand. "I'll be back in a few days with the cash and to pick up the tree."

Gino grinned. "I don't know what the neighborhood would do without you, Joe."

Chapter 22

A sudden explosion woke General Waverly from his slumber and tossed him out of his easy chair and onto the floor. Bewildered, he looked around to find the source of the explosion. A second blast rang out, which he sourced to the mountain slopes behind the inn. The General sprang to his feet, ran for the back door, flung it open, and then ran outside. The explosions had ripped apart *Grand Loup*, the newly built ski run. The force of the blast created a huge crater and destroyed all the work the General and his team had accomplished that summer. The mountain was on fire.

Out of the fiery flames, the General spied teams of bankers and accountants descending the ski tow toward the inn. Each wore a combat helmet and carried an

M2 Carbine which they promptly unloaded on him. Terror-stricken, he hit the ground and shimmied on his belly into the inn, while bullets sailed over his head and shattered the walls and windows into a thousand shards. Once inside, he sprang to his feet and reached for his rifle secured on hooks above the door. He waited for the approaching assault team to reload. He turned and thrust his gun through the shattered window, pointed, and fired.

The rifle misfired.

He tried again. Each time the rifle failed. Frustrated, he slammed the rifle to the floor and then ran down the hall of the inn and through an open door into the lodge. He instantly recognized that he'd entered the old grist mill before it had been transformed into a ski lodge. It was dark and smelled of oats, flint corn, millet, spelt, and wet barley. The room was heavy with air-borne dust. A steady beam of moonlight streamed through an upper window vent and illuminated the particulates. An owl was ruffled by the intrusion. He hooted, flapped his wings, and then escaped through a hole in the roof.

The unmistakable sound of crying drifted into the General's ears. The weeping came from a wooden door just in front of him. He approached the door, reached for the handle, and cautiously pulled it open. Inside was Susan, at seven-years-old, lying in the hay like a lamb and holding her stuffed animal Polka Dot Pony.

The General was confused. Behind him, he heard another noise and turned quickly. On a large tufted couch sat his wife Abigail and his son and daughter-in-law, Paul and Teresa. The light shown upon their peaceful faces as they enjoyed a cup of coffee together. "Tom, come sit with us. It's been so long since we've been together. We would so like to talk with you," Abigail said.

The General was discontented. "Have you seen Joe? I need him."

"He's not here," Emma scolded him as she walked into the grist mill. "You made it clear you didn't want to see him."

"I was angry. I didn't mean it."

Emma scowled. "It makes no difference now. He's probably lying dead in an alley somewhere."

"I didn't mean it," the General sobbed. "I didn't mean it."

The nightmare faded.

"Grandpa, wake up. You're having a nightmare," Susan said as she knelt next to the General, who had slipped out of his easy chair and onto the floor.

The General's eyes darted back and forth with trepidation as he processed his surroundings. Sweat poured from his forehead. He pushed himself off the floor and back into his chair, embarrassed that Susan had found him on the floor— again.

Susan was concerned. "Can I get you a glass of water, Grandpa?"

"Thank you, Susan."

"I'll be right back."

The General wiped the sweat from his brow and then rested his elbows onto his knees. His dreams were increasing— and increasingly real.

Susan returned with the glass. "Here you go, Grandpa."

"Thank you, Susan."

"Was your dream about that Joe fella?"

"Yes."

"I wonder why. Have you heard from him recently? Maybe you're doing something that reminds you of him."

"Maybe, Susan. I think I need a few minutes alone to work this through."

"Okay. I'll be in the lodge if you need me."

The General drank the water and then set the empty glass on the end table. He rose from his chair, walked to the back door, and looked out the window of the inn. He knew it was just a nightmare, but he was relieved to see the outline of *Grand Loup* in the moonlight and that it was still intact. Seeing his coat on a hook next to the door, he grabbed it, opened the door, and then he walked out into the night. The air had a wetness to it. The weather report called for a chance of snow, but he knew better. He stepped down the stairs and looked up into the expansive sky and noticed a lonely snowflake or two descend and then disappear into the grass, never to be seen again.

He was worried. No snow meant no money coming in for the inn or for his ski business. He had spent weeks analyzing his options, and he was quickly running out of them. The Columbia Inn was on the verge of bankruptcy. If the bank foreclosed, he would need a way to support Susan and Emma, or they would end up homeless. He had to push forward— retreat was not an option.

It did not take him long to conclude that his best plan of attack would be to re-enlist in the Army. It was not a lot of money, but it was sure money, and he could rely on it until he got back on his feet. The General whimpered slightly at the thought of enlisting, but he was determined to own it. Once the thought was set firmly in his mind, he grasped his hands loosely behind his back, walked the stairs into the inn, and went up to his room, where he fell peacefully asleep.

Come morning, Susan found her grandfather at his desk writing vigorously. He was on a mission to finish his letter and then hand-deliver it to the Pine Tree Post Office in time for the day's mail. Emma came in from the kitchen and stood next to Susan. "What's that all about?"

"I'm not sure. Grandpa asked to be left alone until he was finished. And he was *very* serious when he said that."

"We'd better stay out of his way, then. He can be like a Sherman tank when he gets like this."

Susan agreed.

The General finished the letter, sealed it, and then grabbed his coat from the hook. "Susan. Emma. I'm going into Pine Tree. I'll be back in a few hours."

"Can I go with you, Grandpa? I have some medicine I need to pick up at Haney's."

"I'd rather go alone, Susan. I can pick up your medicine for you."

Susan was disappointed. "All right. I'll see you when you get back."

Emma stood next to Susan and watched as the General jumped into his Jeep and drove away. "I wonder what he's doing?" Susan said.

The intrigue beguiled Emma. "I'm not sure. But you can bet your last hairpin I'll find out!"

Chapter 23

Mavis looked through the glass panels of the double entry doors and caught sight of General Waverly as he pulled his Jeep into a parking spot. Always primed for a skirmish with her childhood rival, she prepared to sally with her old foe as he entered the post office. "Good morning, General," Mavis greeted him.

"Good morning to you, Mavis. I have a letter that must be placed in today's post. *First Class.*"

"Sounds important. I'll send it out right away."

The General handed her the letter, which she promptly looked at. "War Department. We're not headed back to war, are we? World War II and then Korea, we can't afford to lose any more boys."

"No, we can't," the General affirmed. "This is a private letter, Mavis. And I mean private."

"Of course," Mavis said, acquitting herself of any wrongdoing. "That'll be six cents."

"You old coot," he said as he removed a nickel and penny from his trousers and tossed them onto the counter.

"Thank you, General," she crassly said as she tossed the change into the cash register and then dropped the letter atop a stack of mail.

"Mavis, if you don't mind. I'd like to see it go straight into the sorter."

Mavis peered over her glasses at the General. Reluctantly, she removed the letter from the top of the stack and dropped it directly into the sorter and into a sealed mailing pouch.

"Thank you. Good day to you, Mavis."

"Good day, General."

The General exited the Post Office while Mavis made quick to ring Emma and ask her about the General's letter, which instantly beguiled both women.

Once outside, the General stood on the sidewalk, placed his hands on his hips, and then glanced aimlessly at the shops surrounding the town square. Twenty-eight shops lined the streets around the square. The town still possessed a butcher and a baker, but the candlestick maker had ceased business thirty years ago. It did, however, have a barbershop, a bank, a post office, a grocer, a hardware store, a diner, a feed store, a fabric shop, a typesetter, and a gas station. This was the General's town, his hometown, and he was proud of it and its people. They were hearty, good-natured, and were generally optimistic, which suited him just fine.

Archie glanced through his office window from inside the bank and caught sight of the General standing on the sidewalk. It was a fortuitous sighting, for he had spent many weeks drawing up plans to help his friend avoid foreclosure of the Columbia Inn and he was ready to present them. Archie grabbed his hat and coat, exited the bank, and then approached the General. "I'm glad to see you, Tom. You saved me a trip up the mountain."

"Ready to foreclose on me already?" the General jabbed at Archie.

"I was ready to foreclose on you last month," Archie jabbed back. "Good thing we're such good friends."

The General softened his tone. "And I'm glad for that, Archie. What is it you need to see me about?"

"I have an idea I wanna run by you." He motioned to a bench on the sidewalk in front of the Post Office. "Have a seat?"

The two men sat down. "Well. Go on, Archie."

"Tom, I've been thinking about the upcoming loan payment, which I know will be a stretch for you to make."

"Archie, you and I have already had this conversation. Remember?"

"Yes, yes. We've talked. But I've done a lot of thinking, Tom. We both know the snow will catch up with us one day, and then you'll have skiers galore filling up that inn of yours. Problem is, there's no way you'll make up for the lost revenue from a snowless Christmas season."

"Archie, tell me something I don't know."

"What you don't know, Tom, is the value of your land. And I'm not talking about the assessed value. I'm talking about the value you can create in the hearts and minds of all those city folk who will pay real money to visit your inn during the winter, the summer, and the fall."

"I'm still not sure what you're driving at Archie. But go on."

"It's like this, Tom. You have land and lots of it. You've added a new ski run this year, and you have room for two or three more. That's all good and well for winter, but what about all that land you own that you *can't* ski on, land that's just sitting there idle the rest of the year? You're paying taxes on that land, but it's not making you a dime. If you come up with a way to put that land to work for you, it can be a stopgap for bad snow seasons like the one we're having this year."

"And what do you propose I do with that land?"

"Apple trees, Tom! I'm talking apple trees! The soil is perfect for it."

"Archie, are you sick? Did you fall off a mountain? Why would I plant apple trees *at a ski lodge?*"

"You old codger. What have I been saying? For year-round income, that's why. You know how unpredictable running a ski lodge can be. Some years the snow is non-existent, and some years the snow is great. But even then, you have steep competition from all the other ski lodges."

"I know all about competition," the General said.

"Don't you see, Tom? You can gain a competitive edge and offset some of that financial uncertainty by planting an apple orchard and maybe even a pumpkin patch. Then you'll have two chances to get those city folk up to your place. Once in the fall to pick apples and experience our beautiful Vermont color season, and if you make a good impression, they'll want to come again to *your* ski lodge in the winter and not someone else's, like those up in Killington of Stowe. It'll be good for you, and it'll provide more business opportunities for the shopkeepers here in Pine Tree."

Archie's idea intrigued the General, and yet the reality of his current situation was undeniable. "Archie, you're my banker and my friend. You, of all people, know my financial situation. I had to lay off part of my staff, and I had put the rest on half-pay. I've already mortgaged all that land you're talking about, and then I gambled the last of my money on that new ski-run. I barely had six cents to mail off that letter I just sent."

"You may not have the money, Tom. But I do."

"What are you telling me, you cagey fox?"

"What I'm telling you is I have an offer for you. You keep the ski lodge; it's all yours. But let's put the rest of that land of yours to good use and plant some apple trees. We'll do it as fifty-fifty partners. I'll take care of all the upfront costs, and you supply the land. And I'll pay my share upfront, which will take care of that loan payment coming due. Afterward, we'll split the profits. What do you say?"

The General looked over his shoulder through the Post Office window and toward the letter he had just mailed. Archie had a good plan, but it too smelled of risks. The letter would be the surest way to real money. "It's a good thought, Archie. But I've risked too much already, and I have to make different choices now. Susan and Emma are counting on me for their support. I'm no longer in a position to put their future in jeopardy."

Archie was discouraged but not deterred. "I understand, Tom. But we have some time. My offer still stands. Let's pray for snow and for you to get that next loan payment made, and maybe you'll see things a little differently once the pressure's off."

The General was not so sure. "Perhaps. I should be going, Archie. I told Susan I'd pick up her medicine at Haney's, and I don't want to forget."

"All right, Tom. We'll talk soon."

Chapter 24

The train rolled to a stop at the Florida East Coast Railway depot in Miami. The cast and crew of *Playing Around* were anxious. Twenty-three hours on a train had been relaxing. Yet, the anticipation of seeing Miami for the first time and of performing in front of a new crowd had created in them a measure of impatience, which was exacerbated by the lengthy trip. Even Phil, the master of mirth, had run out of clever jokes and was forced to revert to his old standbys to keep the cast entertained and their minds from exhausting themselves from the wait.

The depot building *looked* like Florida. It was the length of two standard railroad cars and was situated directly next to the track, with a simple cement sidewalk doubling as the boarding platform. The roof was pitched to 30 degrees and designed to withstand the heavy Florida wind and rain. Corbels were fitted every ten feet under the overhang to help support the weight of the expansive roof. Clapboards were painted a cream white, while windows were fitted with colorful green striped awnings to shed the direct sunlight and rain. The building contained two levels. The first level was for passengers and the second level was for administrative offices and storage.

Bob and Phil were among the first to step off the train and into the warmth of the Miami afternoon. Waiting for them underneath the depot overhang with his arms folded and his legs crossed was their old friend Maury Susskind. "You two look like a couple of dried turnips," Maury called out.

"Same old, Maury," Bob said as he approached the man and offered him a shake of the hand.

Phil was next in line to shake Maury's hand. "You're looking swell. Looks like Florida's been good to you."

"Very good," Maury confirmed. "What a place! We have all the sun and beaches you could ever want. And in the winter, half of New York comes down for a visit. Heck, you can't throw a stick in winter without hitting a matzah ball shop."

"That's a lotsa matzahs."

"Say, I have a cab waiting for you boys. I'll take you to your hotel, and once you're situated, I'll have the cab drive us to the theatre."

"Okay by us," Bob said. "By the way, we hear the show sold out all three days."

"It sure did. When people heard the great Wallace and Davis were coming to town, tickets went faster than fresh bagels in the morning."

"Wow," Phil grinned widely and then joyously tapped Bob on the arm. "Imagine that."

"I wish I could talk you boys into a Sunday evening performance. We could really make some simolean's then."

Phil feigned annoyance. "How do you like that? We've only been in Florida thirty seconds, and he's already trying to rope us into more work."

"Oh, is *that* what you call work?"

"Well, it's not exactly a walk on the beach," Phil replied.

Albert and John disembarked the train together. Bob waved them down. "Hey, fellas. Phil and I are riding with Maury. Once you get the cast settled in, let's meet for dinner at 5 p.m. and then for rehearsal at 6 p.m. That sound okay?"

"Sure thing, Mr. Wallace," Albert replied.

Inside the train, Evie maneuvered her way around Trudi as she placed the last of her items into her suitcase. "There, I think I'm all set."

"Good thing, too. Looks like most of the cast has left the train," Trudi remarked as she peered through the window toward the depot. "I can't wait to see Miami Beach. All that white sand, you know."

"I can't wait to find a telephone and call Bobby."

"He'll be okay. Worry-wort."

Albert re-entered the train and stuck his head inside the doorway. "You two are the last ones. We have a bus waiting, and the driver's a bit impatient."

Trudi was not about to let Evie be hurried. "Albert, have you ever kissed a girl?"

The question was unexpected. He was instantly flummoxed. "Ah, you mean a real girl?"

"Yes, I mean a real girl," Trudi said as she moved slowly toward Albert in a scintillating manner.

"I gotta go," Albert said as he placed his hand on his hat and hurried down the corridor and off the train.

Trudi turned and smiled triumphantly at Evie. "Take all the time you need, sweetie."

Evie laughed. "I'm ready. Thanks for running point for me, though."

It was nearly eighty degrees as the ladies stepped from the train. "Oh, mamma mia! Feel that heat. I think

I'm in heaven!" Trudi said as she stood fully upright and lifted her chin toward the sun.

Evie soaked in the rays with her friend. "I can't believe it. When we left New York yesterday, it was only forty degrees."

Doreen was waiting for them and overheard Evie's comment. "And that's why all those New Yorkers come to Miami. Why should they sit four months of the year in all that cold and snow when they can come to Florida and work on their tan?"

"No doubt," Evie said.

Doreen leaned in close. "And for your information, I'll be wearing one of those newfangled *bikinis* when we go to the beach on Saturday. So don't blame me when all those hunky men are leaning in my direction," she said as she extended her leg and buttocks in a sexy, playful fashion.

"Doreen, you're gonna get yourself in trouble."

"We'll all be wearing them soon enough, so what does it matter? I read in LIFE magazine that Bridgette Bardot and Sophia Loren are already wearing *bikinis* on European beaches. It won't be long before some lady in the U.S wears one and makes it famous. It might as well be me."

"All aboard, ladies," Albert called out, trying to hurry the girls along. The ladies left their conversation on the train platform and approached the bus. Albert turned sheepishly away from Trudi as she boarded so as not to make eye contact. Trudi could only smile.

As the bus made its way to the hotel, Evie noted that it didn't at all look like Christmas. *'Eighty-degree temperature may have something to do with that,'* she thought to herself. Still, as she gazed through the bus window, she noted how different Miami was from New York, and she wondered what it may be like to live here.

Downtown Miami had tall buildings, but none to match Manhattan. And she was sure there would be no outdoor ice rink as there was at Rockefeller Center and no lighted Christmas tree to admire. And yet, Miami had beautiful color; tropical shades of blue and green and brown that imitated sand, sky, and surf. And it had room to grow outward, unlike Manhattan and Long Island, which could only grow *up*. And it had an overabundance of bright, beautiful sun nearly every week of the year.

The bus neared the hotel. When she saw *The Fontainebleau* hotel for the first time, Evie was astonished. The entire cast was astonished. The hotel was semi-circular in shape and seemed to lift from the ocean like a gleaming temple. It was a miracle that Albert had booked the twenty-plus rooms needed for the cast this late into the winter season. When asked about it, he would only say that he had connections, which made him sound like a *mafioso*.

The bus came to a stop at the hotel entrance and was immediately greeted by the bell attendants. After receiving instruction from the head attendant, the cast disembarked and then made their way into the magnificent structure. Their giddy chatter was continuous and uninhibited. As the lobby doors opened, a rush of cold air created by the hotel's conditioned air system greeted them, which provided instant relief from the Florida heat.

Oohs and *ahs* followed as they entered the spacious lobby, which was richly and elaborately decorated and gave all the impression of a grand ballroom. The floor was exquisitely marbled. A black bow-tie pattern had been inlaid every few feet, a nod to the hotel's designer— Morris Lapidus— who was known to wear bowties. Large Corinthian marble columns provided weight to the space, while carpeted circular seating areas provided comfortable places to sit in the nearly football-sized venue. And just inside the entrance was the infamous *stairway to nowhere*.

The ladies had talked endlessly on the train ride from New York about this illustrious staircase. The *stairway to nowhere* was at the same time an ingenious marketing maneuver and a sleight of hand. At the top of the curved stairway was a coat check room— and nothing more. Its sole purpose was to allow every woman who ascended the staircase to check her coat, shawl, or fur and then descend the staircase with all eyes watching and experience what it was to feel marvelously glamourous, like Gina Lollobrigida or Audrey Hepburn on their way to meet Rock Hudson or Gregory Peck. It was pure glamour. Evie hadn't seen anything like it.

The hotel rooms assigned to the cast were not as glamorous as the staircase, but they were lavish. Decorated in French modern, each room provided a view of either the ocean, Biscayne Bay, or downtown Miami. The ladies checked into their rooms, took care of their necessities, and then made a quick tour of the hotel before dinner. The *Boom Boom Room* and the *Pink Poodle Lounge* were high on their list as they had hoped to catch a glimpse of a visiting Hollywood star, of whom it was said were always in attendance.

After dinner, the cast was bussed to Maury's theatre, *The Florida Theatre*, for rehearsal. The *Playing Around* stagehands had taken a different train and were hard at work since arriving earlier that morning. The stage was smaller than that of *The Durant*, though it contained all the necessary stage accouterments to allow the production of a New York Broadway play.

Bob, Phil, John, and Maury had arrived moments before and were in deep discussion with stagehand Fritz on stage requirements and prop positioning. "The mechanicals are in good shape. The fly system and catwalk, too. And the rake is at the right slope," Fritz informed them. "Once the background scenes are hoisted into place, I think we'll be in business."

"What about the angles?" Phil asked. "This stage has angled corners. It's not squared off like it is back home at *The Durant*. We'll want to reposition our props so the dancers can maneuver around them without falling off the stage."

"Which would make for a lousy review," Bob said.

"We'll put tape marks where the cast should stand. That's the best we can do. If they fall off the stage, I guess the audience will get to see a real Broadway play up close and personal," Fritz jested.

"We'll adjust once we rehearse a few times," John said.

"Are your dancers ready?" Maury asked.

"Oh, brother. We can barely keep them from the stage; they're so excited," John said.

"We had to drop the Mandy number, though," Phil said.

"The Mandy number? What's that?"

"It's a new number John and I had cooked up. We have the routines down. It's a take on the minstrel shows of old, but we can't seem to find the right dancer to match with John."

"That's right. The show has pretty good dancers and all. But Bob and Phil want the pace to be fast and furious. Some of the girls we auditioned are having a hard time handling the pace."

"We'll find a girl for that number one day, but for now, we're going with what we know. You'll have nothing to worry about, Maury," Bob said.

"Marvelous. *Playing Around* is going to set Miami on fire and pave the way for more Broadway shows to play here, which will make me a rich man!"

"Don't count your chicks before they've hatched," Bob reminded him. "Those New Yorkers were bored with our show up there. We're hoping these Miamians won't be bored with our show down here."

"You boys will do swell," Maury encouraged him. "Besides, since the day I announced the show, you wouldn't believe the talk around this place. All those snowbirds are spouting off about how *they* were the first to see *Playing Around* and how Wallace and Davis would be nothing without *their* support. You'd think they created the show themselves. The good thing is they've invited all their local friends so they can show you guys off. It's a win-win situation for them and the show."

"We'll take as many wins as we can get," Phil said.

"You got that right, buster," Bob confirmed.

Chapter 25

Showtime— 7:35 p.m.

Maury prepared to watch the opening number of *Playing Around* from the privacy of his booth located just above the theatre's soundboard. He waited until the theatre was near capacity before he ordered the lights to flash and dim, encouraging the audience to find their seats. He looked around for his wife, Mary, who was nowhere to be found. Five minutes later, he ordered the lights to be dimmed again and to flash repeatedly, signifying the show was about to begin. Mary was still absent, and yet with the theatre full, he knew the show must go on. From the phone in his booth, Maury called Albert and confirmed the house was ready and for Bob and Phil to start the show.

The old theatre pro had sat through thousands of these shows in his nearly fifty years in the business.

Yet, he found himself waiting with anticipation and on the edge of his seat as the orchestra struck its first notes and bellowed out a salutatory introduction. After a brief pause, they shifted gears and broke into a jazzy tune. Finally, the curtain lifted.

Female dancers with feathered and jeweled headbands appeared and then moved across the stage with rehearsed precision. Their sequined dresses of red, gold, emerald green, and intense white reflected brilliantly against the luminous stage lights, which created a dazzling show of color. Their smiles were as large as life, and their faces gleamed with delight as they looked out upon the packed audience who leaned on the edge of their seats, being instantly captivated by the imagery.

Bob and Phil remained behind the curtain. They had redesigned the opening number with the dancers in mind giving Trudi, Doreen, Rita, Doris, and the rest of the cast an opportunity to bask in their own spotlight for a few precious minutes. The dancers made the most of it. Their energetic and fast-paced routine enthralled Maury's imagination and instantly transported him into a world of long-forgotten memories from his early days in show business.

It was Florenz Ziegfeld who created the *showgirl*, an ever-present figure in his *Follies* revue. The profession of showgirl was a curious one. Her sole purpose was to adorn the performance with her beauty while increasing the volume of the production, giving the entire show a sense of breadth and largeness.

In Ziegfeld's mind, a showgirl was an exhibit, a work of glamorous art. She was window-dressing meant to allure a titillated public. She was to be seen and admired but not to be touched. She need not sing or dance or possess one talent over another and was often found standing or sitting in perfect stillness, so as to resemble a *mannequin*. A portrait of feminine allurability, she was a picture of innocence while at the same time encouraging trespassing eyes. Often uneducated and from modest vocation, each showgirl possessed the one attribute that Ziegfeld prized the most – beauty.

Maury knew these facts first-hand. Working as a young stagehand for *Ziegfeld's Follies* at the ripe age of twelve, he had seen and heard everything that was to be seen and heard concerning Ziegfeld and his girls, let alone everything the newspapers reported about the iconic man.

Now fifty years later, as he watched the dancers of *Playing Around* move across the stage with precision and expertise, he was reminded that these girls were not *show* girls. They were *chorus* girls, and there *was* a difference.

A chorus girl's greatest asset was her talent— a capable voice, the ability to synchronize in dance with those about her, and a competent understanding of the varied forms of dance— skills that were prized above, but not devoid of, her natural beauty. Chorus girls proficient in these skills were highly sought after.

Maury's wife, Mary, entered the small booth, pecked him on the cheek, and then sat down. "What did I miss?"

"They're still on the opening number. What took you?"

"Little Joey was throwing a tantrum. Marie was having a hard time settling him down."

"Always the mother." He looked lovingly into her eyes. Even at sixty years of age, they were as bright as the day he first met her on the Atchison, Topeka, and Santa Fe Railway. He was reminded of their first meeting— a chance encounter that happened over forty years earlier.

It was heady days for a youngster such as one, Maury Susskind. As Florenz Ziegfeld's penchant for elaborate and daring costumes expanded during the roar of the teens and twenties, he sent then twenty-year-old Maury to California to procure several large crates of Mexican palm fronds and *fresh* California lettuce, avocados, asparagus, cauliflower, and an assortment of fruit to adorn his dancers as a type of *salad bowl* for an upcoming series of shows.

Maury's train encountered some difficulty and was forced into an unscheduled stop in Winslow, Arizona. Mary worked in Winslow as a member of the Harvey House family— she was a Harvey girl. Hungry, Maury entered the nearby Harvey House for a bite to eat and happened upon Mary. It was love at first sight. But Maury had a schedule to keep and a boss to keep happy. Once the train had been repaired, he continued his journey to California. He procured the fronds, fruit, and veggies needed for Ziegfeld's show and then sent them on a freight train ahead of him.

On his return journey, he once again stopped in Winslow to be with his new love, Mary. Feigning illness and other exotic maladies of the day, he exercised every excuse in his playbook to hang out in Winslow long enough to woo his newfound love and eventually convince her to return to New York with him.

After seeing the *Follies* in New York for the first time and then over the next forty years, Mary had numerous debates with Maury as to which profession— chorus girl or Harvey girl— presented the most advantages and opportunities for women and which presented the greater harm. Each profession required discipline, sacrifice, fortitude, and perseverance. Each required its participants to possess a certain skill and to employ it in the most judicious manner. And each gave women an opportunity they longed for— independence, a sense of freedom, and an opportunity to make their own way. And yet, each profession offered its own unique challenge and cost. In the end, they agreed to disagree, but they were also most happy the opportunities were there for the choosing and for each woman to weigh the benefit and the cost.

Male dancers entered the stage next and encircled the ladies, followed by Bob and Phil. They wore grey trousers, "V" vests, and pork pie hats. The crowd applauded enthusiastically. The two men then moved to center stage as the dancers weaved around them like basketball defenders trying to steal the ball. Once they entered Bob and Phil's personal space, they sidestepped around them and then continued to their next designated spot.

"That's new," Maury said to Mary.

The two men then broke into the opening song— *Let Yourself Go*— an Irving Berlin standard. Four more Irving Berlin songs were to be sung during the performance: *Some Sunny Day, Sittin' in the Sun, Homeward Bound,* and *Choreography*. Though not written with *Playing Around* in mind, Bob and Phil, personal friends of Berlin's, had incorporated them into their show.

Bob had known Berlin since his days in vaudeville, as he was always on the lookout for new material. He visited Berlin often at the renowned Tin Pan Alley— a two-block area in New York City— which hosted an unusually large number of music publishers and songwriters. Berlin initially worked in Tin Pan Alley for the

Harry Von Tilzer company and then later went on to work for Oscar Hammerstein's vaudeville house.

With the first number complete, Maury watched as Bob and Phil entertained the audience through a series of physical comedy and one-liners. It was then that he realized what an odd duck *Playing Around* truly was. It was nothing more than a *vaudeville* act in a *revue* format, and its two-year run on Broadway was defying the odds.

Vaudeville and the revue format were long gone. Broadway shows like *Oklahoma*, *Carousel*, *Kiss Me Kate*, and *South Pacific* were the new kids on the block, with each show possessing an engaging plot and strong sub-themes throughout. In today's Broadway, it was a well-written show with a compelling plot that took center stage. Stars abounded, but they were interchangeable and replaceable and subservient to the power of the show itself. The old fashion revue was dependent on its main star, its comedic innovation, or its tawdriness to carry the show.

Maury, a theatre owner for over twenty years in New York and now Miami, examined the show before him with a discerning eye. '*What made Playing Around defy the odds?*' he thought to himself. He did have an answer. It was hard to go wrong with an Irving Berlin song, but its true success must fall upon Bob Wallace and Phil Davis.

Though both men were older and seemed to have lost a step, they had one enormous factor in their favor—their likeability was through the roof. It was the same formula that had extended the career of many vaudeville acts. Those with high likeability went on to star on radio or ever-increasingly on television: Jack Benny, Burns and Allen, Bob Hope, and Groucho Marx. The rest disappeared from public view, many never to be seen or heard from again. Still, given Bob and Phil's likability, unless something drastically changed, it would not be long before *Playing Around* was another footnote in Broadway history.

Maury witnessed a glimmer of hope with the next number— *Choreography*. John and his troupe led an inspiring number filled with emotion and bodily form while retaining the traditional tap and floor dance audiences were accustomed to. Though interesting, Maury noted the routine seemed incomplete without a strong female lead to counterbalance John's strong dance moves.

"That's nice," Mary said.

Maury nodded nonchalantly. "It was okay."

"Just okay? The audience seems to be enjoying it."

"This time. If they come to the show tomorrow night, they may not think so."

Chapter 26

"He did what?" Evie said, amazed to hear the announcement Bobby just made.

"He came over to watch the basketball game on TV. It was really swell."

"Why didn't you ask me first?"

"We tried. Me and Joe called the hotel, but they said you were at the show. Beatrice said it was okay for him to come over. She likes Joe, mom. She says he has nice eyes."

"Nice eyes? I see. Did the Knicks win?"

"Nah, they lost to the Lakers. But Beatrice popped corn on the stove, and Joe told me about the different plays the teams use to make a basket. I never knew there was so much stuff to basketball, mom."

"I imagine there is." Evie's voice trailed off slightly. "So, did Joe ask about me?"

"He sure did. You wanna talk to him? He's right here."

Evie was surprised. His continued presence with Bobby at Beatrice's apartment was unexpected. "Ah, sure. That would be fine."

"Evie?"

"Joe? Hey, how've you been?"

"Cold, mostly. I hope it's okay I spent some time with Bobby. I thought it would be good for him to see a real game. I tell all my players to watch pro basketball so they can visualize what's going on."

"Sure, Joe. I know you're just trying to help."

"So, how's Florida?"

"Oh, I don't even know where to begin. We just finished our last show this afternoon. I think Mr. Wallace and Mr. Davis were happy with it. Either way, I couldn't wait to find a phone and tell Bobby I'd be home in a few days."

"He jumped out of his seat when he heard that."

"I wish I were there to see that. Well, I should probably go. Trudi and I are spending our last night in Florida at a restaurant that we heard about. I should get back to the hotel so I can get ready."

"That sounds swell. I hope you two have a great time."

Evie hesitated before hanging up. She wanted to say more, but she was indecisive. Joe continued to show himself a good man, yet she could not shake her fear that he may turn out like Vince. "Thanks, Joe. We'll see you sometime."

Novello's was a thirty-minute cab ride from Miami Beach to Key Biscayne. Bob and Phil recommended it, having known Novello from their previous visits to Miami. The restaurant was located near a sand dune just off the ocean. It was a unique open-air establishment, and it offered an outstanding view of the Cape Florida Lighthouse.

The cab fare shared equally between Evie, Trudi, Edna, and Rita made the decision to dine out affordable, as did the understanding the clientele at Novello's was slightly more sophisticated than that of other nearby restaurants. The younger cast members elected to dine in Miami's trendy South Beach section, as they heard that is where *the action* was at. Doreen elected the same. Her bikini had accomplished its mission and helped her land a promising young fella, a sailor, who was on extended leave from the Navy.

"Good evening, ladies. My name is Novello. I will be delighted to seat you tonight. Will there be anyone else joining your party?"

"Only if James Dean asks to sit with us," Trudi said.

Giggles.

"Right this way, please," Novello said, unsure as to the object of their amusement. He escorted the ladies through the restaurant to a recently vacated corner table. "May I show you the wine list?"

"I'd like to see it," Trudi said. "We'll be sitting in a train station tomorrow night, so tonight I'm going to celebrate."

"Me too," Edna added.

"And me," Rita said.

"And you, miss?"

"Not for me, thanks."

"Very well, madam. However, our wine list is quite spectacular."

"You're not going to celebrate with us, Evie? We have plenty of our per diem left," Trudi said.

"I know. It's just that I'm trying to save every penny I can to buy Bobby a nice Christmas present."

"I see. That makes sense." Trudi turned to Novello. "Novello, please give my friend a wine list and put it on my tab."

"Yes, madam."

"Trudi, you don't have to do that."

"Consider it an early Christmas present. I wanna make sure you get that present for Bobby, too."

"You're a good friend. You all are."

The wine was ordered. It was then that Edna spotted Bob sitting with an unknown female in the center of the restaurant. "Say, there's Bob Wallace."

"Who's that with him?" Rita said.

"I'm not sure. She doesn't seem very happy," Edna said.

"He doesn't look very happy either," Evie said. "But they're sitting awfully close for two people who seem at odds."

"Maybe they're fighting over the wine," Rita mused.

"Or the wine bill," Edna smarted off. "Let's go over and say hello."

Evie was hesitant. "Edna, we shouldn't interfere in Mr. Wallace's personal time."

"We won't. We'll just visit long enough to find out who he's with," she said deviously.

"Edna, you *are* a devil," Trudi said.

Bob was happily grumpy. The woman he had just met was both intoxicating and suffocating at the same time. Amid his polite argument with her, he turned away to give the conversation time to breathe and spied Evie and the ladies at their corner table. Looking for an easy way to put his disagreement with his table partner to rest, he smiled profusely and waved the ladies over.

"See, we won't have to barge in at all. He's inviting us over," Edna said.

"Top o' the evening to you, ladies. Looks like you took my dinner recommendation."

"We did. It's a lovely place," Edna confirmed and then gave Bob a nod toward his table partner.

"Forgive me. Betty, these four *young* ladies are from my show *Playing Around*. This is Edna, Rita, Trudi, and Evie. Ladies, this is my new acquaintance Betty Haynes."

"It's so nice to meet you, Ms. Haynes."

"It's nice to meet you as well."

"Where's Mr. Davis? I'd be surprised if he wasn't here with you tonight," Trudi said.

"Oh, he's here all right. You can't shake that boy. He's like a Doberman Pinscher. Once he sinks his teeth into you, he doesn't let go."

"I'm not quite sure what you mean, Mr. Wallace."

Bob quieted his humor. "It just means that he's on the veranda dancing with Betty's sister Judy. I'm sure he'll be in before too long. I'll send him your way the first chance I get."

"How nice," Rita said.

Edna was ready to move her group along. "We should get back to our table. It was nice seeing you tonight, Ms. Haynes."

"Likewise," Betty replied.

Bob called out to Evie. "Oh, Evie. Can you stay a minute?"

"Yes, Mr. Wallace?"

"I was wondering how Bobby was doing? You know, with the basketball team and all."

"How nice of you to ask. He loves it. The boys on the team are good to him, and he takes every opportunity to be at the gym to practice."

"How old is your son?" Betty asked.

"He's nine-years-old. An adventurous nine-years-old, I might add."

"Those were the days," Bob remarked. "Say, Betty. It sure is a small world. Bobby's basketball coach was your brother Benny's unit commander during the war."

"You don't say."

"I do say. His name is Captain Joe Ross."

"Captain Ross? Oh yes! Benny talked about him quite often in his letters home. He said Captain Ross was the bravest man he'd ever met."

"I'll say. He practically saved our whole Company single-handedly. If he hadn't taken out this crow's nest of Nazi snipers during the Battle of Montepolina, I might not be here tonight."

"A hero then?" Evie said.

"He sure was. He paid dearly for that privilege, though. He took six bullets to the body. One bullet practically shattered his right leg. We thought he was a goner, but somehow he pulled through. A testament to his resolve, I think."

Evie was astonished and then disgusted with herself. "That's why he walks with a limp? How could I not see that?"

Betty observed Evie's countenance. She detected in her expression a hint of concern for Joe beyond that as Bobby's basketball coach.

Novello approached the table. "I'm terribly sorry to disturb you, Mr. Wallace. There's a gentleman at a private table that would like to take a photograph with you."

"A photograph? No, just tell him I'm busy and offer my apologies."

"Certainly, Mr. Wallace. But... forgive me. Perhaps you may reconsider his request? I think him to be a very important man."

"Important, huh? What's his name?"

Novello spoke the gentleman's name deftly. "Howard Hughes."

Bob's eyes lit up. "Howard Hughes? That is an important name. Ladies, if you'll excuse me. I think I should take a photograph with Mr. Hughes. I shouldn't be long."

"Be my guest. You wouldn't want to keep Mr. Hughes waiting," Betty said.

Evie became uncomfortable. "I really should get back to my table, Betty. It was nice to meet you."

"Stay a moment, Evie. At least until Bob or Judy come back. I'd look silly sitting here all alone."

"Yes, of course," Evie acquiesced and then took a seat.

"It's a remarkable coincidence that you and I should meet. My brother Benny had the highest regard for Captain Ross. Have you known him long?"

"About a month. Bob and Phil invited him to the show one evening, and we met there."

"And he coaches basketball?"

"Yes. He's a volunteer coach at the YMCA. He works there also— in maintenance."

"A career man," Betty chuckled.

"I suppose..." Evie's voice trailed off.

"Everything okay, Evie?"

"I think so. I'm just processing what Bob said. I didn't realize that Joe was a war hero. I don't think he would ever tell me so himself."

"The good ones don't."

Evie looked closely at Betty. She appeared honest and forthright. It was possible she could provide an impartial voice for the uncertainties that she had regarding Joe. "Betty, would you mind if I ask you a question?"

"Go right ahead, please," Betty said as she pulled her chair closer to Evie's.

"Joe seems like a really great guy. He's so good to my son Bobby and all the other boys he coaches, but...."

"But?"

"But, do you think it strange that a guy like Joe, a war hero no-less, works as a maintenance man at a YMCA?"

"I see. Do you disapprove of him being a maintenance man?"

"Not at all. It's just that I find it strange he settled into *that* position after the war."

Betty identified with Evie's question. "I think each man handles their involvement in the war differently. My brother Benny has struggled since the war ended. He was to take over the family farm when he returned, but he's had trouble adjusting. He's in Alaska now. I think he's still trying to make sense of everything he endured in the war, and so far, he hasn't been able to do that— even after ten years."

Evie became teary-eyed. "My husband was like that."

"Was?" Betty asked.

Evie looked around the restaurant hoping their conversation went unnoticed and discovered that Trudi, Edna, and Rita were involved in their own conversation. She returned her gaze to Betty. "He died... After the war. He came home to me, but after two years of drifting in and out, he finally left. The war had changed him. I could see it in his eyes. It was as if he wasn't there. I knew our marriage would never be the same, and I think he knew it also."

"How tragic. I'm very sorry for your loss," Betty said as she held Evie's hand.

"I'm so sorry, Betty. We're practically strangers. I didn't mean to lay my burdens on you like this."

"War affects us all, not just the ones who were there. We all have trouble making sense of it from time to time. I hope you don't think I'm intruding, but is that your concern with Joe? That he'll leave you like your husband did?"

"Yes. I'm afraid of entangling myself with a man who hasn't made sense of it yet. My fear is that he's hiding out at the Y until he does. I can't risk going through that again, and I never want to put Bobby through that."

"I see. How long has Joe worked at the Y?"

"Since the war ended, I think."

"Hmm, that's a long time. I guess it's possible he may be hiding. But it's also possible that he *has* made sense of the war, and he found the YMCA to be the best place for him. It could be just that simple, Evie."

Evie's spirit lifted. "What wise words, Betty. I never thought of it that way."

Betty appreciated the warm response. "I know you need to get back to your table. I should go find my sister Judy. She's easily swept off her feet when she starts dancing, and she loses all track of time. It was so nice talking with you. I hope we meet again."

"I would love that!"

Chapter 27

It was just a scrimmage, a five-on-five game between players on his team, but it was good practice for a real game. "Nice. Nice! Good ball movement. Keep it going," Joe barked out from the sidelines. Cristobal was wide open. He received a bounce pass from Stephan and took it to the hoop for a layup. "That's it," Joe called out. "Do it again."

Jarret inbounded the ball to Miguel, who dribbled past the half-court line. He found Bobby open and tossed him the ball. Bobby dribbled sideways around a defender and then passed the ball to Connie. Connie tested the key. He drove for the basket, which drew two defenders. This left Marcus wide open. He made a bounce pass to Marcus, who then fed Jarret, who took it to the rim and scored.

"Great teamwork," Joe called out as he clapped his hands. He blew his whistle to stop play and then turned to the remaining players on the sidelines. "Mikey, you go in for Miguel. Ernst, you're in for Connie. TJ, you're in for Karson."

Mikey, TJ, and Ernst stepped onto the court. Connie was having fun, and he did not want to come out, but he knew he should step aside. He held out his hand for Ernst to slap tag, the traditional basketball gesture when players trade places on the court. Ernst was surprised; Connie had never acknowledged him in that way before. He slapped his hand and continued onto the court. Joe watched the exchange, contented. Connie was showing signs of improvement.

The scrimmage continued with each player getting his turn to develop his skills and grow as a ballplayer. Joe, ever the captain, was fastidious in his observance of each player and where they needed development and where they excelled.

At the top of the hour, Joe blew his whistle to end the practice. "All right, boys. Gather 'round." Their shirts dripped with sweat as they surrounded Joe. "Fine practice, boys—really fine. You've come a long way since we started practice this fall. We didn't have a winning record this year, but we've made a lot of progress. We've added some new players. We learned how to handle adversity, and we learned what it's like to be a man and compete. The world is a hard place, but if you keep working hard and you do what you know to be right, I believe you boys can accomplish anything you set your minds to."

The boys applauded Joe's words.

"As you know, this was our last practice before Christmas. For you boys who'll still be around, we'll start practice again in January. I hope to see you then. Now, hit the locker room if you need to, and Merry Christmas, everyone!"

The boys huddled together and then reached their arms into the circle as Marcus led the call. "One, two, three, go Y go!" the boys chanted in unison and then broke for the locker room.

"Marcus and Cristobal. Can you stay a minute?" Joe called out.

"Sure, Coach. What's up?"

"You two have played for me for a long time. I want you to know how much I've appreciated your leadership and your help with the other boys over the years. But next season, I'd like to see you play for your high school team.

"We like playing for you, Joe," Marcus stated strongly.

"Yeah. You're the only coach we've ever had."

"I'm happy to hear that, boys. I am. But you'll both be freshmen next year, and your team will need you—your school will need you. And besides, you won't find any college scouts hanging around a YMCA. If you two keep working hard and you do well in school, I think there's a real chance for you to qualify for a college scholarship, and who knows, maybe you could play for the Knicks one day," Joe grinned. "Merry Christmas, boys."

"Merry Christmas, Coach."

Lillian entered the gym and approached Joe. "Hang on to your hat, Joe. Mr. Whitman wants to see you in his office right away."

"Right now? I promised to walk Bobby home."

Bobby approached from the locker room with Connie trailing behind him. "Coach, if it's okay with you, me and Connie are gonna walk home together. His apartment is not far from ours."

"Problem solved," Lil commented.

"It's okay with me, Bobby. And thanks for doing that, Connie."

Connie smiled ever so slightly and nodded.

Joe took the elevator to the second floor and knocked on Mr. Whitman's door. "You asked to see me, Mr. Whitman?"

"I did. Have a seat, Joe."

"All right."

"Joe, if I have my math right, you've worked at the Y for the better part of ten years."

"Sounds about right, sir. Is there something wrong with my work?"

Mr. Whitman scoffed. "No. There's nothing wrong with your work. We have the best facility this side of the Hudson, thanks to you. I called you in here to talk about an opportunity. I got word this morning that Mr. Ries, the Program Director at the YMCA in Queens, is retiring at the end of this month. They're looking for a new Program Director, and I want you to apply."

"Me? I'm just a maintenance man."

Mr. Whitman leaned across the desk. His burly arms wrinkled a stack of papers. "Joe, do you know how many times over the last ten years I've had a parent of one of those kids you coach thank me for hiring you? Dozens!" he said matter of factly. "You're *not* just a maintenance man. You're a decorated soldier and a war hero, and you've been a hero to a whole division of boys who have left your program better young men than when they came. No sir. You're not just a maintenance man."

The conversation caught Joe off guard. "Queens? That's so far away."

"Oh, it's not that far. It's just across the river a bit. You'd be responsible for the whole program, though—not just basketball. And you'd need to organize classes for adults and kids. Your pay would double, and you wouldn't have to fix latrines any longer," Mr. Whit-man grinned.

"I'd love that. When do they need an answer?"

"Friday. I told them you're the man for the job. But they already knew. Word gets around, you see."

Chapter 28

From a Railway Carriage
by *Robert Louis Stevenson*

Faster than fairies, faster than witches
Bridges and houses, hedges and ditches;
And charging along like troops in a battle,
All through the meadows the horses and cattle:
All of the sights of the hill and the plain
Fly as thick as driving rain;
And ever again, in the wink of an eye,
Painted stations whistle by.

Here is a child who clambers and scrambles,
All by himself and gathering brambles;
Here is a tramp who stands and gazes;
And there is the green for stringing the daisies!
Here is a cart run away in the road
Lumping along with man and load;
And here is a mill and there is a river;
Each a glimpse and gone forever!

Evie tossed the complimentary train guide complete with poem by Robert Louis Stevenson onto the floor and looked out the window of the train into the darkened sky. It was late, even for a seamstress who works far into the night at a Broadway show, but she could not help but contemplate the long train ride still ahead for her. With the heavy holiday traffic nine days before Christmas, Albert was unable to book a return trip to New York City for cast and crew until Monday night, and that not until 10 p.m. It would be Wednesday morning at 7:30 a.m. before the train arrived at Penn Station. The unusually long trip home was due to scheduling logistics which required the *Havana Special* to stop at every station along the route from Miami to New York.

Bob and Phil were lucky. With only two tickets to procure, Albert had booked them on the *East Coast Champion* the same night the show closed so they could make the Ed Harrison show by Monday evening. They will have arrived in New York nearly two days before Evie and the rest of the crew pulled into Penn Station.

Evie could not wait to see Bobby and tell him all about Florida and to give him an early Christmas present— several seashells that she had collected with Trudi and Doreen as they walked along Miami beach.

A sleepy Doreen appeared in the doorway of their roomette, downcast and glum. The sailor she had met on the beach a few days earlier, she found out, was married to the sea— or so he said. He made it clear to Doreen that is where his first love lay.

"Don't fret, sweetie," Trudi encouraged her. "There are always more fish in the sea."

"Sure. But did you see those hunky arms of his? He held me so tight before we left I thought I might burst."

"Don't do that. I don't want to clean up after you again," Trudi said petulantly.

"You excited to see Bobby?" Doreen asked glumly.

"More than excited!"

"And what about Joe?" Trudi said quietly from her bunk.

"Joe?"

Yes. Joe."

"I think so. I've thought of him a lot on this trip, and I realize how unfair it was to compare him to Vince. That wasn't right of me."

"Well, honey. You'd better make your move before some pushy gal decides she's ready to go to the hoop for him."

"Doreen, a basketball analogy? I thought you didn't care for that sport," Evie said.

"I don't care for that sport. But I care for men. And if you want to win a man, sometimes you need to give him the full-court press before some other gal does."

"Good night, Doreen," Evie scoffed.

"I'm just saying."

"Good night, Doreen," Trudi added and then blew her a kiss before burying her tired head into her pillow.

Evie could not sleep. The irregular clackity clack emanating from the driving wheels as they pressed against the steel track became more pronounced as the train grew quieter and its passengers fell off to sleep. There was no room for her to sit up, her chair having been turned into her bed. She could only lean against the wall of the train, curl her feet under her and stare out the window. She pulled her blanket close and reminisced about her time in Florida. She thought of Bobby and whatever she was to do with this man named Joe.

Thirteen hundred miles away, Joe sat on the stairs of the YMCA. He sipped his coffee and looked beyond the tall buildings that overshadowed him and gazed into the darkened sky. Though it was now mid-December, it had remained unusually warm and did not feel any colder than it did back in November when he sat on those same steps and encountered Bob and Phil for the first time. He lowered his head, drew his coat around his neck, and then dropped his chin above his coffee and allowed the steam from the hot liquid to warm it.

His life, once so simple and phlegmatic, had become noisy and uneven. The new job opportunity was at the top of the disruption list. He liked the idea of becoming a Program Director— leading was never an issue. But he hated the idea of leaving 23rd Street. It had taken him years to make the impact he was now making in the lives of the boys he coached. That feat would not easily be replicated at a new YMCA, let alone with a new set of boys and their parents. He did like the idea of making more money which meant he wouldn't have to room at the Y any longer. That fact was especially enticing as he thought of Evie and Bobby. He still could not understand what he'd done to turn Evie away in such an abrupt manner, but he was certain a small room with a single bed at the local YMCA was not enticing for any woman.

Another two-hundred mile north, Susan Waverly threw her lined surcoat over her shoulders and stepped out the kitchen's back door and into the yard. The few dinner guests they had that night had left, which gave her a few moments to ponder the strange day. She folded her arms tight against her body and stared into the sky. A million stars stared back, reminding her of how small and insignificant she was. She knew the Columbia Inn was in trouble— the whole town knew— yet she was powerless to do anything about it.

And yet, the unexpected arrival of Bob and Phil, Betty and Judy at the inn that day was nothing short of a miracle and had resurrected within her a glimmer of hope. To see her grandfather light up like a kitten under a milk cow was a wonder to behold. And then the phone call Bob made that afternoon to Albert with the request that he summons the cast and crew of *Playing Around* to Vermont in three days for a Christmas Eve show had filled her with a bouquet of hope that somehow their fortune would change and that snow would fall, and the inn would fill up with paying customers and that all would be well with the world again.

Emma stood in the doorway of the kitchen and interrupted Susan's soliloquy. "Susan, there's still some tables to clear."

"Okay, Emma. I'll be right there."

Emma observed the sixteen-year-old's unsettled countenance and felt a tinge of grief. Susan was as sweet as a Cox's Orange Pippin apple in September, and yet she could ski the boots off any man, woman, or child this side of Telluride. She had lived her entire life in Vermont with most of that right here at the Columbia Inn, even when it was a grist mill and barn full of mice, barn owls, and fermenting hay. It would be a hard day to see Susan pack up all her belongings on that dreadful day the bank came for the note on the inn. It broke Emma's heart.

"Emma, do you think Bob and Phil's idea to bring their show up here will help us?"

"As long as they pay for their food and lodging upfront, it'll help for a little while," she said, withholding her pessimism. "We may get some free advertising from it. But without any snow, I'm afraid it will just delay the inevitable."

"Well, we should pray for snow then," Susan said.

"Sure, we'll pray for snow. But what I'd really like to pray for is an answer to what was in that letter the General sent to the Pentagon last week. I'm still beside myself that Mavis wasn't able to steam that letter open."

"Emma, that would be an invasion of Grandpa's privacy."

"Let's just call it a covert operation for the good of the community."

Chapter 29

Evie felt the bed rattle and sway. Or maybe it was the twitch her body had developed from two days and thirteen-hundred miles on a train that awakened her from her afternoon sleep. She massaged her tired eyes and then focused on the alarm clock next to her bed— 4 p.m. It was still Wednesday, or at least she thought it was. She sat up and leaned against the headboard. The waning rays of sunlight shone through her apartment window and rested upon the train guide that she had brought home with her. She remembered a portion of the poem contained within— *'here is a child who clambers and scrambles, all by himself and gathering brambles'*. Bobby would be home from school soon, and she could not wait to see him.

She gathered her thoughts. Bobby would expect dinner. What would she make? She had also thought to make a tin of oatmeal cookies to thank Beatrice for watching Bobby, but she was too tired. That would have to wait for another night. With no time to make a proper dinner, TV Dinners were pulled from the freezer and placed into the oven. Soon the aroma of turkey, cornbread, peas, and sweet potatoes filled the kitchen. As they cooked, Evie readied herself for Bobby's arrival.

He walked calmly through the door, tossed his books onto the couch, and found Evie in the kitchen. He cast a disinterested look her way and made pretend that he hadn't missed her at all. "Hey, mom. What's for dinner?"

"That's it? No hug for your mother? Just a *what's for dinner?*"

Bobby couldn't pretend any longer. He leaned into his mom and hugged her tight. "Aw, mom. I'm glad your back." He pulled away from her and looked into her eyes. "Did you get me anything?"

"I did. Come and see!"

Bobby trailed her into the bedroom and watched as she removed two seashells from her still packed suitcase. "What do you think of these? I found them on the beach. Amazing, huh?"

"I'll say," Bobby said as he put both seashells to his ears to test the myth that you can hear the ocean when placing a seashell next to your ear.

"Do you hear it?"

"I think so."

"That's not the only surprise I have."

Bobby dropped the shells onto the bed and began to rummage through the suitcase. "What else did you get me?"

"Stop that now. There's nothing more in there. It's not what I brought you, but what you and I are going to do tonight."

"Tonight? What?"

"With the extra money I made from our show in Florida, I figure it's time you and I get our very own Christmas Tree. I called Mr. Genoese when I got home this morning, and he said he had one tree left and that he would save it for me."

"Can we look for presents, too?"

"You can look, but don't get your hopes up. Santa didn't make that much money in Florida," she winked. She hesitated before asking the next question. "Bobby, would you be okay if Joe came over and helped us put up the tree tonight? It would be nice to have another man around to do the heavy lifting."

"Gosh, mom. I wouldn't mind at all."

"I was hoping you'd say that. We'll go see Joe right after dinner, and if he's up for it, we'll get the tree together."

As they had planned, they finished their dinner, and with no dishes to clean other than a toss in the trash of a few tin trays, Evie and Bobby set out to visit Joe. Another cool December night allowed them to wear their light coats as they walked and talked on the way to the Y.

"She had a TV, mom. So we watched every night. Beatrice fell asleep a lot, so I got to pick what I wanted. I saw the Wonderful World of Disney and Roy Rogers and Dragnet and Father Knows Best. And on Saturday I got to watch Howdy Doody. Can we get a TV, mom?"

"One day," Evie said.

They reached the door of the Y, walked up the steps, and entered the lobby. The ever-present Lillian was laboring away at the Information Desk. "Hey, Lillian."

Lillian recognized the voice and looked up from her papers. "Well, don't you look tan. Did you just get back from Bora Bora?"

Evie laughed. "No. I was in Florida. Do I really look that tan?"

"You're as brown as a coconut. I guess that's why I haven't seen you around here in a while. I've seen Bobby, though. Hey, Bobby."

"Hey, Lillian."

"Lillian, is Joe around? We have something we'd like to ask him."

"I'm sorry, Evie. Joe's not here."

"Oh, that's too bad. Do you know when he'll be back?"

"That's just it, Evie. He's not coming back."

"What do you mean he's not coming back?"

"He's taken a job at the YMCA in Queens. He's been there the past few days getting to know the place. He's going to be the Program Director. It's a big deal."

The revelation stunned Evie and knocked her back a step. She tried to speak but could only fidget with her hands.

"He can't leave!" Bobby called out. "Joe can't leave!"

Lillian felt chagrined and put her hand to her mouth. "Ooh, I wasn't supposed to tell anyone about that. Joe wanted to tell the boys himself. Bobby, you need to keep that a secret. Okay?"

Bobby's eyes teared slightly. He didn't respond. Evie gathered her composure. "I'll make sure he doesn't say anything, Lil. I promise."

"Thank you, Evie. And Bobby, don't let that news make you a stranger around here. Joe tells me you've been a good addition to the team. I'm sure they'll get a good coach to help with basketball."

Bobby remained silent.

"We should go. Thanks for everything, Lillian."

"Take care, sweetie. We'll see you soon."

It was a miserable walk to Genoese's. Neither Evie nor Bobby spoke more than ten words the entire way. They hardly had a chance to experience what life would be like with Joe, and now it appeared that chance was gone. They opened the door to Genoese's and walked inside. Gino was busy with another customer. "Be with you in a minute, Evie."

Bobby looked cheerlessly at the toys that Gino had stocked for Christmas: a Gilbert Tool Chest with saws and hammers; a Tom Corbett Space Academy with rocket ships and flying saucer; a Howdy Doody TV game and a myriad of cars and trucks in various shapes and sizes; and a Joe Palooka Bop Bag.

"I see you sold that train set in the window," Evie said as Gino finished with his customer.

"I sure did. The man who bought it just picked it up. There'll be at least one happy kid for Christmas this year!"

"That's nice for them. We're just here to pick up the tree, Gino."

"It's a good thing you called this morning. I had a lot of people ask about it. I even had one person offer double the price for it. But I told him the tree was spoken for, and a deal is a deal."

"I appreciate that. It hasn't been a good night for us, and if we didn't have a tree to bring home, it would have gone over like sour milk."

Gino detected the despair in Evie's voice. "Sorry, you've had a rough night."

"Me too. What do I owe you?"

"It's $7.99 for the tree. The stand is $1.99, and I'll throw in a candy cane for each of you. I hope that'll brighten your night."

"Thanks, Gino. You've always been so nice to us."

Carrying the tree and the stand three blocks from Genoese's was not easy, but it was manageable. Carrying it up the stairs to their apartment was the hard part. Following the twist and turns of the stairs, they reached the second floor and rested. Trudi and Doreen burst out of their apartment, giddy as schoolgirls. "We saw you come up the stairs. Did you hear the news?" Trudi said in a happy panic.

Their sudden appearance jolted Evie from her malaise. "What news?"

"They just delivered a priority telegram from Albert," Doreen gushed out loudly.

"From Albert?"

"Yes. Bob and Phil want the entire cast to come to Pine Tree, Vermont—"

"—wherever that is," Doreen interrupted Trudi.

"Shh," Trudi scolded her. "They want the whole cast in Vermont in three days. They want to put on a show for their old commander and get this— Albert says we'll all get a Christmas bonus!"

"Yippee!" Doreen shouted. "We'll be rolling in the dough. This'll be the happiest Christmas ever."

"Did we get a telegram, mom?"

"I don't know," Evie answered.

"Let's find out," Trudi said. "We'll help you with the tree."

Doreen carried the stand while Bobby climbed under the tree to lift with his shoulder. Evie and Trudi each grabbed an end. They lifted it effortlessly up the stairs and then stopped at the door, which Evie quickly unlocked and opened. Slipped underneath the door was the same telegram Trudi and Doreen had received. "Well, I'll be," Evie exclaimed upon opening it. "It looks like we'll be spending Christmas in Pine Tree, Vermont. And Bobby, this time you're coming with me!"

Bobby's eyes lit up. "Really?"

"You know it. You'll be out of school for the holiday break, and there's no way I would spend Christmas without you."

Bobby's spirit jumped. Depressed from the news about Joe, his spirit lifted exponentially, as did Evie's. They could not have foreseen that their *Blue Christmas* would turn into *a-rockin' Christmas tree* decorating party, but it did. The ladies carried the tree inside and helped to stand and decorate the tree using the small number of ornaments Evie had pulled from her trunk: garland, some glass bulbs, an angel, and tinsel.

Bobby turned on the console radio and tuned in to Perry Como, Frank Sinatra, Jo Stafford, and Patti Page sing their latest Christmas songs. Trudi and Doreen danced with the music and frolicked with each other and then Evie, and then with Bobby and General Patton. Evie baked gingerbread cookies while Trudi popped corn, which they ate, tossed at one another and General Patton, and then threaded with string and wrapped around the tree. The foursome stepped back from the tree and admired their work. Evie was contented with its look.

"What a beautiful tree. Now, all we need are presents!"

Several blocks away, Joe had arrived at Connie's apartment and knocked on the door. Byron was surprised to see him. "Joe? I didn't expect to see you tonight."

"Sorry about that, Byron. I thought I'd take a chance and see if you were home tonight."

"It's my night off. I was just listening to the radio. It's getting close to Christmas, and every now and then, they'll play a Christmas song or two."

"Tis the season. Say, Byron. Is Connie around?"

"Jarrett invited him over to his apartment to watch a show. Can you believe that?"

"That's great news, Byron. In more ways than one. You mind if I come in?"

"I don't mind."

"Swell. Stay right here," Joe said. He stepped back into the hall and hurried to the stairwell, where he retrieved a large package wrapped in brown paper. He stepped back inside the apartment and handed the package to Byron. "I didn't want Connie to see this. I just picked this up from Genoese's. It's a Christmas present for you and Connie. Well, more so for Connie. But you may find some interest in it also."

"A present? What is it?"

"I can't tell you that. It's a Christmas gift. You have to wait until Christmas to open it!"

"Joe, you didn't need to do that."

"Actually, I did. I know things have been tough for you and Connie. I happened to be at Genoese's a few days ago to pick up a Christmas tree and figured this might mean something to Connie. So, I decided to get it."

Byron was flabbergasted. "I can't take this from you, Joe. It wouldn't be right."

"I thought you might say something like that, Byron. But listen here. You can give me a thousand reasons about the how's and the why's of why you can't accept this. But I have one reason why you should."

"What is that?"

"You and me, Byron. We were soldiers. We didn't fight in the same battles, but we fought in the same war. We laid our lives on the line every day for our country, even though it cost us dearly. We're brothers in arms, you see. And when one brother is down we pick him up, because we know that when we're down he'll pick us up. That's what brothers do. So, I'm asking you— one soldier to another— that you accept this gift. If you can't do it for yourself, at least do it for Connie."

Byron's eyes welled up as he wrestled with the thought of accepting the gift. Joe's words hit home. He put down the package and then lifted his right hand to his forehead, stood at attention, and saluted. Joe returned the salute.

Byron then bent down and picked up the package. "It's been a while since Connie has had something like this. I better hide it from him until Christmas, or he might tear into it and spoil the surprise."

"Sounds like a good plan. Merry Christmas, Byron!"

"Merry Christmas, Joe!"

Chapter 30

General Waverly stood at the pinnacle of *Grand Loup*. Bob and Phil, Betty and Judy stood beside him and marveled at the view. "It's so beautiful here," Judy exclaimed.

"I'll say," Betty agreed. "It feels like we're on top of the world."

"Not quite," General Waverly corrected her. "We're only at elevation 3930 feet. If you look due north on a clear day, you'll see Mount Mansfield. It's the tallest mountain in Vermont at 4393 feet."

"It would take a whole lot of shoes to cover those feet," Phil joked.

"But only one to cover your pie hole," Bob snickered.

"Can't you ever play along?"

Bob disregarded Phil's starchy comment and then looked down the hill of the future ski run. "It sure will be nice when it's finished, General. I can already see myself making a few christiana and stemming turns down that hill."

"Is that what you see?" Phil said. "Because I see you platzing and klutzing all the way."

"Wiseguy," Bob said.

"General Waverly, I hope you don't mind. How did a man who spent his entire life in the military end up owning a ski resort near a small town in Vermont?" Betty asked.

General Waverly looked off into the distance. It was a private memory, but he chose to recount it for her sake. "This was my son's dream. And then it became my dream."

"Oh, I didn't know you had a son," Betty said.

"I didn't either," Bob remarked.

"You didn't think Susan came from a tree, did you?"

Bob was embarrassed. "I had thought to ask about her parents. I never heard you talk of them when we served together, sir."

The General became introspective. "He was a good man, my son. And he loved these mountains. You see, I was born in Pine Tree, over there. And so was my son," he said as he pointed south. "And all the land you see from Pliny Creek to Haystack Mountain to Old Pond Road and then to Pine Tree Road is Waverly land, which has been in our family for nearly one-hundred-fifty years. And Vermont, as you know, is snow country, or at least it used to be," he scoffed due to the lack of snow that year.

"It will be again, sir," Phil encouraged.

The General was not as hopeful. "I chose to leave these mountains and join the Army so that I might see the world and find out what I was missing. Can you believe that?" he said as he pointed to the mountains all around them.

"It's a beautiful place, sir."

"I fought in the Banana Wars down in Panama and Haiti, and then I fought in the Great War, and then for a while, there were no wars. Marianne, my wife, stayed here all that time and waited for me. She was raised in Stratton, just over there," he said as he pointed north. "By then, I had seen enough of the world and I realized the place I had always wanted to be was right here in Pine Tree. I came home, and Marianne and I had a son. We named him Paul."

The wind picked up and blew cold against Judy's neck. "Ooh, I think I'm getting a chill."

Phil moved in close and put his arm around her shoulder. "Don't mind me."

"What a guy," Judy remarked with an approving tone.

The General continued. "As soon as Paul could walk, we would take him climbing and skiing in these mountains. When he was older, he was the one who had the dream of turning the old grist mill into a ski lodge. Ski resorts were starting to become a thing then— Stowe and Pico and Big Bromley— oh, back in the late '30s, I suppose."

"How old was Paul then?" Judy asked.

"He must have been nineteen. He and Teresa married right out of high school. She was quite the skier herself. They had Susan the following year. Like so many other men, Paul enlisted after the bombing of Pearl Harbor. He said he couldn't stand by and watch while his father and all his friends went off to war. I believe you boys enlisted about the same time?"

"Yes, sir. I was a member of the ROTC program in college. It helped pay my tuition. When Uncle Sam called, it was my duty to serve," Bob said.

"I wasn't that smart," Phil said. "For college or ROTC. But that didn't stop me from doing my duty, sir!"

"What happened then, General?" Betty asked.

"Paul was a gifted skier. The National Ski Patrol had targeted him for recruitment by that time. The Ski Patrol was a civilian unit, as you know. Even so, the Army placed them in charge of recruiting for a brand-new military unit— the 87th Mountain Infantry Battalion. After he enlisted, Paul was sent to Washington State where he received specialized training in mountain and arctic warfare— on skis no less," the General chuckled.

"They fought in Northern Italy, didn't they, General?" Phil asked.

"They did. By that time, they were assigned to a military unit— the 10th Mountain Division. It was a bittersweet time for me. When we began the allied invasion in Salerno, Paul and the 10th were pushing north toward Nauders in Austria. It seemed like he was always two steps ahead of me with Nazi and fascist troops separating us every step of the way."

"How did he pass away, General?"

The wind blew hard against General Waverly's neck. He bowed his head to deflect the wind. Remorse overwhelmed him. "After the war, Paul came back to Pine Tree while I finished my career at the Pentagon. He started work to transform the mill and barn. To make ends meet, both he and Teresa worked for the National Ski Patrol, which provided outdoor emergency care, mountain rescue, and avalanche assistance. Who would have thought the thing my son loved the most would end up taking his life and the life of his wife?"

"What a tragedy. I'm so sorry for your loss, General," Bob said regretfully.

"Very sorry to hear that, General," Betty added.

"Worst day of my life," General Waverly admitted. "It happened about seven years ago. Word came of an avalanche just north of here. There was a driving snow that day. Eight skiers were swept away by the slide. They called in every available ski patrol member. They searched for hours. A second slide occurred. Paul and Teresa were both in its path. When they found Paul, he had passed away from a broken neck. Teresa was found alive, but she died from injury and exposure a few days later. With little Susan to take care of, I retired immediately from the Army and vowed to finish the work my son had started and to fulfill his dream."

"Poor, Susan. To be so young and to be without her mother," Judy said

"Susan is a strong girl. It took a long time, but she's come to terms with their death. It helped to have her Aunt Emma around."

Betty was surprised. "Emma is your sister?"

"Sister-in-law. My brother passed away in the Great War."

"You don't say," Phil said.

"My brother was a good man, too. Emma has had a hard life without him. It was good for both Emma and Susan that we stay together. That's why this place is so special. Keeping this place alive is keeping Paul's spirit alive, and it helps us remain together as a family."

It was hard information for the group to digest. "I'm getting a little chilly myself," the General said somberly. "I think it's time we get back to the inn."

"I, for one, will be ready for a cup of hot cocoa when we get back," Judy said while wrapping her arms close to her body.

"Or maybe a spiked eggnog," Betty added.

"No-o. A hot buttered rum for me," Bob said.

"I'll take one of each," Phil quipped.

The group piled into the Willy's Jeep Wagon. The General drove them carefully down the twisting and turning access road located on the far side of Columbia mountain. They drove past the access roads that tied into *Little Lapin* and *Big Renard* ski runs and then continued down the mountain toward the inn. As they came to a stop in front of the inn, General Waverly called out to Bob. "Bob, can you spare a minute?"

"Why sure, General. Phil, I'll see you inside."

"Aye, aye, Captain," Phil said with a quick salute. "We'll get the place warmed up for you."

As the group entered the building, Bob turned and addressed the General. "What can I do you for, sir?"

"Bob, are you a religious man?"

"Oh, I don't know. I believe in the Almighty, I guess. Sure. Why do you ask?"

"I've had these dreams. Emma and Susan know about them. But I keep them to myself mostly. I don't want to worry them, you see."

"What are your dreams about, General?"

"I keep seeing my wife and son. They seem to be waiting for me. And then I see Susan when she was a little girl. I've never had dreams like that before, but I guess I'm not too surprised by them. What surprises me is that I keep seeing Joe Ross in them, and that is confounding me, son."

Hearing the General speak Joe's name was a surprise. "How long have you had these dreams, General?"

"Since Thanksgiving."

'Weird', Bob thought to himself. That was the approximate time he and Phil came across Joe at the YMCA. He chose to withhold that information for the time being.

The General was introspective. "In war, you see a lot of death. You know that, Bob. Most of it was honorable. Some of it wasn't. I miss my wife and son and daughter-in-law more than I can say, but they lived their lives to the fullest, and they died with honor. I have no regrets about that. My one great regret is that I left the men of the 151st Division in the hands of an incompetent General, and I knew it. It cost this country a lot of good men, and it cost me one of the closest relationships I ever had outside my family."

It was the first time Bob witnessed the General tear up. "Captain Ross?" Bob said.

"Captain Ross," he confirmed. "I visited him every day when he was at Walter Reed. He was unconscious most of that time from the trauma of all his surgeries. When he awoke and saw me there, he cursed me out, like I've never been cursed before. And then he called me a coward in front of all those injured soldiers and their doctors. He wounded me, son."

"I'm sorry to hear that, sir."

"He wounded me. But I was the one who wounded him and all those men who died. Joe was right. I was a coward. I didn't stand up to Command when they ordered me back to the Pentagon. It was my fault Joe was lying in that bed. He knew it, and I knew it."

"That's a heavy burden to bear, General. Were you able to talk with him about that?"

"I tried. It took me a few months to realize that Joe was hurting when he said those things and for me to put my pride back in its place. When I finally went to see him, I found out that he'd been discharged. I looked for him, but he never seemed to show up anywhere. Not in the phone book and not by a street address. My resources at the Pentagon couldn't even find him. I never did find a way to tell him how sorry I was."

Bob was speechless. It was possible his chance encounter with Joe was not such a chance encounter after all. If Christmas had any magic at all, he was sure he would find out soon enough.

"It sure is a fine day to take a walk. I hope you don't mind, but I can use some time alone to think."

"I understand. I'll see you inside, sir," Bob said somberly.

Bob left the General and then entered the inn. The smell of cocoa and buttered rum filled the entryway with an enticing aroma. He followed the sweet scent into the lodge, where he found Betty, Judy, and Phil sitting next to the piano and sipping their drinks. Bob ordered a buttered rum, which Mr. Becker, the bartender, prepared. He then joined the trio at the piano.

"Everything okay?" Betty asked after seeing Bob's somber disposition. "You look a little wet under the lids."

"The General didn't assign you to KP duty, did he?" Phil said.

Bob deflected the comment. "No. Nothing like that. I just had a bit of dust blow in my eye. I've put the wipers into overtime trying to work it out," he said while mimicking a windshield wiper with his hand.

"We were just going over the new routines for the show. It's awfully nice of you and Phil to invite us to be a part of it," Betty said.

"Believe me. When we saw you kids sing and dance down in Florida, Phil and I knew you were the bee's knees. Didn't we, Phil?"

"We sure did. We saw you sing and dance, and we said *you're the bee's knee's and we need to add you to the show.*"

"How exciting! The Haynes Sisters working with Wallace and Davis. I don't know about you, but I'm thrilled," Judy exclaimed.

"We're awfully glad to hear that. Phil and I stayed up half the night writing your parts. And Judy, after seeing you dance, we have a number called *Mandy* we want you to try out. Our lead dancer John should arrive with the cast tomorrow, and he'll show you the steps."

"I'm up for it if he is!"

"Say, why don't we practice a little now?" Phil suggested.

Judy was game. "Fine by me."

"Bob, can you pound a few keys for us? Something smooth and easy so we can get our feet under us. How about *The Way You Look Tonight*? You know, the one by Kern and Fields."

"Oh, good one! Betty, would you join me at the piano?"

"I'd love to."

"Okay, Judy. We'll just tap around a bit. Just follow my lead, and we'll see where it goes."

Bob plinked the keys of the piano, setting the tempo and rhythm of the song. Phil tapped a simple brush step. Judy followed with her own brush step. Phil followed with a scuffle, which Judy mimicked. Phil continued with a riff walk which Judy copied but added her own flare. Bob began to sing. Betty alternated each verse with him.

As the song progressed, Phil and Judy added to each other's repertoire. When Judy introduced a new move, Phil would follow, and if Phil reached deep within his closet of dance tricks, Judy didn't miss a beat. She was more than able to add her own flourish to each move. As the song neared the end, Bob picked up the tempo slightly and replayed it one more time, as much to admire Phil and Judy's artful dance as to admire Betty, who sat wonderfully close to him on the piano bench.

Music from the lodge wafted into the lobby of the inn. Susan and Emma, curious of its source, entered through the lodge doors. As they listened to the music and watched the dance, the song's melody was too catchy to resist. They moved their feet slightly and swayed in time as Bob and Betty sang.

General Waverly entered the lodge, having completed his short walk. The General was not a man of show business nor of music, but he remembered *The Way You Look Tonight*, a song that he had danced with his lovely wife Marianne when he was a younger man. It gave him pause.

Emma caught sight of the General presently lost in a sentimental moment. It had been a long time since she had a dance, a long time since she had held her own man in her arms and been in love. She was sure it had been a long time since the General had experienced the same. She was not about to let this opportunity pass by. She approached him. "Have a dance, Tom?"

He was immediately put off and embarrassed. She was his sister-in-law, after all. "Emma, I don't care to have a dance."

Emma was not be denied. She brought out the Howitzers. "I'm not asking. *I'm telling*," she challenged as she put her hands to her hips and waited for his response.

The General was disconcerted. "Why, why I ought to...."

Emma didn't wait for an answer. She grabbed the General's hands and lifted them into hers. "It's music, Tom. You're supposed to move your feet to it."

General Waverly was stuck between a rock and a hard place. Emma had outmaneuvered him, and the songbirds on stage had taken notice. His first inclination was to retreat, but he decided the honorable option was to wave the white flag and surrender. "Oh, all right. You old bird," he groaned as he moved his feet in time with the song.

Susan wondered at the sight. Grandpa begrudged Emma's advance, she could tell. But deep within his facial expression, a smile protruded. It had been so long since she had seen him enjoy something as simple as a dance, so long since the pressure of the inn's debt and the memory of all his personal losses had allowed him a few moments of unencumbered joy.

The General caught sight of Susan. She looked just like her mother Teresa when Paul had asked her to their first prom all those years ago. She was beautiful. Emma noticed the General's loving look toward Susan and released him. He walked toward his granddaughter. "Have a dance, Susan?"

"I would be delighted, Grandpa."

Phil and Judy lost interest in their dance. They gathered around the piano and enjoyed the most precious of moments with the General and Susan. Bob played the song's melody long enough to give the General a few precious moments with his granddaughter. Of all the dances they had seen, they would not have missed this one for all the world.

Chapter 31

Time stood still. Marcus and Cristobal sat at their classroom desks and stared at the second hand of the clock. Every tick of the hand seemed to take a minute. Every minute seemed to take an eternity—3:56; 3:57.

"Marcus, there's only a few minutes left, and you haven't turned in your assignment," Mrs. Stulken said.

"Oh? Ah, sure. Here you go," he said as he handed her the paper.

"Doodling? Was that your assignment, Marcus?"

"Oh, sorry. It's Christmas time, Mrs. Stulken. Can I do the assignment when we come back from break?"

"I'm not happy about this, Marcus. But seeing that it's Christmas, I'll let it slide this time."

"Thanks, Mrs. Stulken."

3:59 p.m.

Cristobal looked at Marcus. Marcus closed his books. They waited.

4:00 p.m.

The bell rang. The two boys grabbed their books, exploded from their chairs, and sped toward the door. "Slow down, boys! You're going to hurt someone," Mrs. Stulken yelled out.

The classroom doors flung open as the hallways filled with gleeful students. Happy chatter and hoorays filled the air. School was finished for the year. Christmas time was here!

For the moment, Christmas mattered little to Marcus and Cristobal. They weaved and dodged their way through a meandering mass of students, past their lockers where they tossed their books, and then past an unsuspecting teacher who was caught off-guard by their race for the door. They burst through the school doors and onto the sidewalk. Miguel, Robert, Stephan, and Jarret followed closely behind after bursting forth from their classrooms. They were desperate to keep up.

At the middle school, Connie, Ernst, TJ, and Miguel were the first to break out of their classroom and then out of their school. They sprinted across the playground and jumped the chain link fence to join up with the lead pack of boys racing down the street ahead of them. From the elementary school, Mikey joined the chase along with Wylie, Ryan, Karson, Cameron, and Edward.

Like water that sifts through a crack, word had leaked that Joe was leaving the 23rd Street YMCA. He had called an after-school meeting to address the rumor. Huffing and puffing, the boys reached the Y, crashed through the front doors, and ran past Lil, who was so unnerved from the sudden onslaught of boys that she ruffled her papers and dropped them onto the floor.

Lil was peeved. "Slow down boys, or you'll hurt someone!"

The boys did not listen, nor could they wait for the elevator. They raced up the stairs and onto the basketball court, where they found Joe, who was awaiting their arrival.

"Say it ain't so, Joe. Say it ain't, so," Marcus said in between coughs and wheezes.

"Settle down, everyone. You've rushed in here like your pants are on fire. Take a minute to catch your breath, and then we'll talk. Grab a drink of water if you need."

The boys breathed in and breathed out, calming their anxiety. Joe counted the boys. "Looks like everyone's here. Wait, I don't see Bobby. You boys know if he's coming?"

"He wasn't in school today," Robert said. "Teacher said he left town."

"Left town? On the last day of school? Do you know where he was going?"

"Huh-uh," Robert shook his head no.

The announcement discouraged Joe. If Bobby was gone, then Evie was gone, too. He had hoped to talk with her before Christmas. "Okay. Well, I'm glad you boys got my message. I want to address a rumor. I'm not quite sure how it started," he said as he looked beyond the boys to Lil, who had taken the elevator and now leaned against a wall and listened in. "But how it got started really doesn't matter. It's the decision that matters."

"What did you decide, Coach?" Cristobal asked.

"I'm getting to that. As you boys heard, I was offered the job as Program Director over at the YMCA in Queens. I had a chance to visit that location the past few days. I met with the staff and toured the facility and got to know some of the boys over there. They seem to be real fine boys."

Mikey started to tear up. "He's leaving us. You're leaving us. Aren't you, Coach?"

Joe dropped his hand onto Mikey's head, and slowly lifted it back up and smiled at him. The boys waited anxiously for his answer. "It's a big promotion, becoming a Program Director. And I'd be able to afford my own place."

Joe paused. "But I've decided that I'm *not* taking the job in Queens."

The boys nearly jumped out of their sneakers. "Hooray! Joe is staying!"

"Why'd you change your mind, Joe?" Connie asked.

"Well, it's because I've decided to take the job as Program Director here at 23rd Street."

It was unexpected news. "What? What does that mean? You're going to be Program Director here?" Cristobal said.

"I am. When I told Mr. Whitman that I decided not to take the job in Queens, he said he just found out that Mr. Krob would be retiring next summer. He said if I can wait until summer, then the job would be mine."

"That's boffo!" Jarret exclaimed.

"It'll still be a change. I'll be responsible for the entire program, so I won't be able to spend as much time with you boys. But my goal is to coach the boys' basketball team every year. So that much won't change."

"That's great, Coach!" TJ said. "I really didn't want to play for anyone else."

"I appreciate that TJ," Joe smiled and ruffled the young boy's hair. "I know your folks are expecting you at home, so I won't keep you any longer. I just wanted you to hear the news straight from the horse's mouth."

The boys gathered 'round and gave Joe high fives and pats on the back. The younger boys gave him a hug. Within minutes they dispersed and had left for their homes. As the last boy left, Lillian approached her old friend. "That's wonderful news, Joe. I'm so happy for you— and for us. I thought I'd have to break in a new basketball coach."

"It was a hard decision, but it's the right decision. Besides, who would I watch the Ed Harrison show with if you're not around?"

Chapter 32

Susan snapped the sheets in the air to work out the wrinkles and then went to work to fit them to the bed. She was in a rush. The cast of *Playing Around* was arriving and room preparations were behind schedule. Emma had called the maids and kitchen help back to full schedule, but on such short notice, the inn was understaffed. Susan filled in wherever she could.

With the sheets fitted and the pillows placed, Susan's job was complete. All the rooms in the inn were now ready for guests. A car horn sounded. Susan looked out the window and saw John standing outside the inn providing direction to the cast as they arrived. They were coming in waves now.

A bus had arrived earlier in the day carrying the stage crew. They were the first to receive their room assignments. After checking in, they immediately went to work to unload the stage props, as their work would be the most laborious and time-consuming.

Susan hurried downstairs to help Emma, who was working alone at the front desk. She entered the lobby and slipped behind the reception counter.

"Finally," Emma said in exasperation as a dozen people stood before her at the check-in desk. "My position was about to be overrun."

"I'm sorry, Emma. I just finished the last of the rooms. I came as fast as I could."

"That's all right, dear. Can you take these two up to room 222?"

"Sure." Susan looked at the woman and her son. "Can I take your bags for you?"

"How nice. We can manage, though."

"Right this way. My name is Susan, by the way."

"I'm Evie. This is my son Bobby."

"Nice to meet you," Susan replied as she led them across the lobby and then up the stairs. "Are you both dancers?"

Bobby giggled. Evie let out her own funny laugh. "No. I'm a seamstress for the show. I take care of the costumes for the dancers."

"I was just *playing around*," Susan joked. "We're so happy that you came. We don't have many Broadway stars visit us in Pine Tree. None at all, really. Well, this is it— room 222. Let me know if there's anything that I can do for you."

"We will. It was nice to meet you, Susan. I'm sure we'll see you around."

As Evie unlocked the door, Susan turned and called out to Bobby. "Hey, Bobby. My grandpa says he isn't expecting many kids for the show. Maybe I can show you around the ski lodge later on. And if we're lucky enough to get some snow, I can show you how to ski."

Bobby was delighted, yet he felt a tinge of awkwardness at the thought of hanging around *a girl*. "Thanks."

Susan made her way downstairs to help the next set of guests, Trudi and Doreen, who were placed across from Evie and Bobby in room 223. By the afternoon, all the cast and crew had checked in. Dinner was next on the list. Emma and Susan transitioned to the lodge, which was still half-staffed. They sat the guests, took their orders, served entrée's and main courses, and helped with every request the kitchen staff asked of them. By night's end, they were exhausted, and yet there was still cleanup to be done. The lodge had to be ready to serve breakfast in the morning.

General Waverly was equally exhausted. During the day, he had performed his own duties carrying bags, greeting guests, and running errands for Emma and Susan. For those who drove their automobiles, he directed traffic and parking. Gathering with the ladies at the end of the evening, he was complimentary of their exceptional service. "Ladies, you did a top-notch job today. The guests told me more than once that they were very happy with your service."

"We'll be out of business if we don't take care of the guests," Emma replied. "Now, I have some business of my own. I'm going to my room and drop my head onto my pillow and sleep for a week."

"You worked hard too, Grandpa."

"Thank you, Susan. It sure is nice for Bob and Phil to bring their show up here. I just hope it's not all in vain."

"It won't be, Grandpa. You'll see," Susan encouraged him.

As morning came, Bob, Phil, and John worked with Fritz on the design layout for the stage and finalized their plan for modifications. They were happy the General was wise enough to plan for entertainment when he designed the lodge, though in its current condition, the stage was below Broadway standards.

With the opening of the show in just five days, there was much to do. Rehearsals began in earnest. Judy's prolific dancing had encouraged Bob and Phil to add the *Mandy* number to the Christmas Eve show.

By late afternoon John and Judy had also created a new number— the *Abraham* number— and were hard at work perfecting it. Bob had left the Columbia Inn to visit *Iron Leaf* typesetters in Pine Tree as handbills were needed to promote and advertise the show. General Waverly had also commissioned him to pick up the daily mail from Mavis at the Post Office as he still hadn't received his return letter from the Pentagon.

With the arrival of the cast and an energetic and promising first day, the following morning couldn't have been more different, and it created a great deal of anxiety for Susan and Emma. As quickly as she came, Betty had left the show for a job in New York. Susan knew that because she delivered the letter from Betty to Judy herself and then watched from the shadows as Betty privately contracted with the General for a ride to the train station. Bob and Phil were in deep disagreement with one another. Judy was in constant tears, and time was running out for the show to be ready by Christmas Eve. Trudi, the most capable dancer and singer, was asked to fill in for Betty, if she was unwilling to return from New York and rejoin the show.

Bob himself then left Pine Tree for New York. Upon learning that the Pentagon had turned the General down for reenlistment and having been informed by Emma of his desperate financial condition, he had arranged a spot on the Ed Harrison show to make a televised plea to the officers and soldiers of the 151st Division to come to Pine Tree, Vermont on Christmas Eve and honor General Waverly. He also intended to visit Betty.

After arriving in New York and making his television announcement, Ed Harrison congratulated Bob on his performance. "You did a bang-up job, Bob. Do you think the men will respond?"

"I think so. At least, I hope so."

"And Betty? Do you think she'll come back to Pine Tree with you?"

"It's hard to say. I've wronged her somehow, and I don't quite know how. Let's just say I won't be holding my breath."

"I'm sorry to hear that. When are you heading back to Vermont?"

"Tomorrow morning. I have one more stop to make tonight."

"Oh?"

"Joe Ross. Phil and I crossed paths with him last month. The General has asked about him, so I thought I might pay him a visit and offer him a personal invite."

"Joes Ross? I haven't heard that name in years. He made it back then, did he?"

"He did— barely. Since we've been reacquainted, Phil and I have been on the lookout for him. I think he's needed that."

"We never leave a man behind," Ed confirmed.

"No, we don't, Eddie. No, we don't."

Chapter 33

Joe sat with Lillian in the lounge of the YMCA, having just watched the Ed Harrison show on television. The request for the men of the 151st Division to join Bob at the Columbia Inn in Vermont had left him stunned and speechless. He felt cold. His leg began to ache. Lillian turned off the TV and sat quietly next to him. Finally, she broke the silence. "You gonna go, Joe?"

Joe shook his head no. "The last time I saw the General, I embarrassed myself badly. I think it's safe to say he would never want to see me again."

"Is that a fact? Or is that fiction?"

"What do you mean?"

"I mean, did *he* say he didn't want to see you again, or did you just make that up?"

Joe looked intently at Lillian. "*He* didn't say it. But I know for a fact that I cursed him out and that I did it in front of the whole world. So, why on earth would he want to see me."

"You were injured, Joe, and under heavy sedation. You told me that yourself. The General *had* to have known that."

Joe was conflicted and mildly perturbed. "Whether I was sedated or not doesn't change what I did." He shook his head in disbelief. "This is all so sudden. I need some time to think. I'm going upstairs."

Lillian was unwilling to let Joe indulge himself in a morass of self-pity. "Sure, run upstairs and wallow in your misery if you want. But remember this. I've heard you say more than once that you've wanted to make amends with the General if only you had the chance. Well, this is your chance, Joe."

"I know you mean well, Lil. But he won't want to see me."

"Don't you think that's for him to decide?"

"I suppose."

"You suppose? Well, suppose this. While you're here brooding about, the rest of your Division will be in Vermont celebrating with the General. If you don't go, you'll not only be letting him down, you'll be letting the men of your Division down. Let that fact sink into that thick head of yours, why don't you. I'm going to make some popcorn."

Joe was defenseless against Lillian's astute argument, yet he was not in the mood for popcorn. While she headed for the kitchen, he took the elevator to the gym and found a dark corner to hide. His mind was in turmoil and his spirit was screaming within him. Duty called and yet— the General? Had the mark he inflicted ten years earlier healed? Or had it become infected and rancid as an open wound that never heals. There was no way for him to know. He wished to God the word *coward* had never left his mouth.

Thirty minutes later, Bob entered the front door of the YMCA. Lillian had just grabbed her coat to leave for the night. "Hey, Lillian. I hope I'm not too late. Is Joe around?"

"Mr. Wallace," she greeted him. "I was just about to lock up."

"I'll just be a few minutes. I promise."

"He's upstairs."

"Thanks, Lil. I'll make sure to get those tickets for you and your friends."

"Backstage passes?"

"Sure. Backstage passes."

Bob took the elevator to the sixth floor and then to Joe's room. He was not there. As he stood in the hallway, he heard the echo of a ball bouncing in the gym above him. He entered the stairwell and made his way to the gym. The lights were turned down. Only a single lamp illuminated the court from the backboard to the foul line. Joe was shooting free throws.

"Hey ya, Joe," Bob said, interrupting his shot.

Joe was cheerless. "Bob? What are you doing here?"

"I made an appearance on the Ed Harrison show. I thought I'd come by and see you while I was in town."

"I had no idea the General was living in Vermont. It's a nice thing you and Phil are doing for him."

"You saw the show."

"I did."

"It's the least we could do. During the war, that man got us into and out of more scrapes than I care to remember. Phil and I saw an opportunity to help him out of his own scrape, so we took it."

"I see. So... what brings you here?"

"Actually, you're what brings me here. I had hoped to talk you into coming to Pine Tree with me."

Joe transferred the basketball he held in his hands to one arm, and then lowered his head. He did not speak. Bob broke the silence. "General Waverly has asked about you."

"Me? Why would he ask about me?"

"Well, it was more telling than asking. It was no different than what you told me a while back. He said that last meeting in the hospital was one of the greatest regrets of his life. That and abandoning the 151st when he knew he should have stayed."

"He said that?"

"Word for word— pretty much. I was hoping it might be time for you and the General to make amends. You know, shake hands and let bygones be bygones."

Joe shook his head. "I'm sorry, Bob. I don't think I can make it."

"You can't make it? I don't understand. Surely someone can cover your shift for a few days."

"It's not that. There's just too many bad memories for me."

"I don't mean to be heartless, Joe. But we all have bad memories— every one of us. We all saw things we can't get out of our minds. And when they rise to the surface, we have to push and shove those memories back into those dark corners whence they came. It's a tough business for us all."

Joe became emotional and slightly hacked. "Bob, you don't know what I did. You don't know what horrors I have to deal with night after night, year after year."

Bob went on the offensive. "Good Lord. What is it that's torturing you like this, Joe?"

Joe's eyes teared. He felt as if knives were scraping against his sinews. "I killed him, Bob. I killed him."

"Killed who, Joe? Who did you kill?"

"That Italian boy— in Montepolina. I didn't mean to," he said as he began to weep. "I had to take out those Nazi snipers. You remember, don't you, Bob? I couldn't let any more of our boys get shot up."

Bob became emotional. "I remember. You saved our bacon that day. You were a hero."

"I wasn't a hero. I was a murderer. When that sniper shot me, I lost control. I stormed into that room and I shot that boy, that sweet little Italian boy. You should have seen his eyes. He looked at me with absolute terror as he hit the wall and then slid to the floor and died. I can never forgive myself for shooting him, and I can never be around those men again. It would just bring back those horrible memories of what I did."

"No, you got that all wrong. That boy didn't die."

Joe's face collapsed into confusion. His voice cracked. "What did you say?"

"I said that boy didn't die. *He lived.* As did his mother. Not so for his father and sister."

Joe was in pain. "I saw him die, Bob."

"You saw him hit the floor from your gunshot. But then you passed out. More of our boys came up the stairs right after you and dragged you out of there. They found the boy and his mom still alive. We got them down to the medic straight away, and then we evac'd them to a field hospital. We found out later they were both going to make it about the same time we found out you were going to make it."

The news was excruciating and aberrant. Joe could not fully speak for ten seconds. Bob watched him restively, and then it dawned on him. Joe's presence at the YMCA all these years suddenly made sense. "Oh, I see. That's it, isn't it? Your work here with these boys. All these years working with them was to make up for the life of that little Italian boy you thought you took."

Joe wiped the tears from his eyes. "Bob, if you don't mind, this is too much— it's too much for me to process right now. I need time to think this through. I hope you understand."

Bob wanted badly to help, but he knew Joe would need time and space to work through this new information. "Sure, Joe. I understand you need time. I'll make sure to come and see you when I get back to town."

"I appreciate that," Joe said with his head slumped toward the floor.

Reluctantly, Bob turned and walked toward the same stairs that he had come up. As the stairwell door closed behind him, he heard the basketball release from Joe's hands and then bounce aimlessly across the gym floor. He then heard the sound of two knees as they dropped to the floor. Joe bowed his head, placed both hands over his face, and wept. His weeping progressed from a sob into a cry and then into a wail. His mind travailed from the juxtaposition of killing the young boy to the knowledge that the boy was still alive, and he was unable to adequately process the change.

In the stairwell, Bob thought to return to him and help, but he knew that what Joe needed now, only Joe and his Maker could provide.

Chapter 34

Lillian had climbed the stairs in secret, listened in on the conversation, and then made herself invisible when Bob descended the stair and made for the elevator. She cried all night. When morning came, she hoped a hot breakfast at Gwen's Diner would bring a little comfort and peace into Joe's morning— and hers.

"Two eggs over easy, a stack of hotcakes, and a couple slices of bacon," Joe ordered with the waitress, Erin.

"Anything to drink?"

"Coffee— black. Thanks."

"And you ma'am?"

"I'll have two eggs, hash browns, and a side of sausage. And a cup of coffee."

"All right. That'll be out shortly."

"You really didn't need to do this," Joe said.

"Just call it an early Christmas present," Lil replied.

Joe smiled bucolically. Lillian detected a calmness in his demeanor and a peace in his spirit, as if he had spent the night wrestling his demons and won. She did not know what time of night he finally pulled himself from the basketball court and then back to his room, but she was sure it was late.

"Two days until Christmas," Joe exclaimed as he looked out the window of the diner.

"That's right," Lillian confirmed as she looked out the window with him.

The neighborhood shops were decked out in their finest Christmas regalia. Blue, red, and green lights flickered on and off in the store windows. Shoppers bustled past the diner's window in search of last-minute gifts before the shops closed for the holiday. Conversation between the two old friends was solemn but peaceful. Finally, four plates of eggs, bacon, hotcakes, and sausage were placed on the table in front of them.

Hebert, Ernst, and Connie entered the diner and were surprised to see Joe and Lillian enjoying a late breakfast. "Hey der, Joe. Hey Lil. I did not expect you here dis morning."

"Morning, Hebert. Hey boys," he waved to the two youngsters.

"How you doing, boys?" Lillian said.

"Hey, Ms. Langer."

"Connie, your dad not with you?" Joe said.

"Someone called in sick. He had to work."

"That's too bad," Joe said. "But I'm glad to see you out this morning."

"I verk Christmas Day, but not today. So, I tought to take de boys for breakfast and gift shop. Not many days left, you know," Hebert said.

"No, there's not."

"Take a seat, ya?" Hebert said to the boys.

"Right this way," Erin said as she directed the boys to a table two seats over.

Hebert leaned in toward Joe. "I want to say tanks for de work you done with de boys. Ernst, you see, he and Connie have it patched up. More a misunderstanding between boy's den anyting, but dey finally work it out. I have you to tank for dat."

Joe was happy to see Ernst and Connie sitting together. "Boys just need help seeing all sides of it sometimes. It's nice of you to bring Connie shopping with you."

"It was de right ting to do to help de boys get along. Say, I saw de Ed Harrison show last night. You served with de 151st, ya? You go to de Veer-mont with de unit to celebrate Christmas with de General?"

"I thought about it. But I have to be truthful with you Hebert. This time of year, I just don't have extra money for a train ticket to Vermont, let alone for food and lodging. I thought I might send the General a note. You know, wish him well and for a Merry Christmas."

"Dat's hard luck, Joe. Christmas is pricey for de working man."

It was an easy out for Joe. "That's it exactly, Hebert."

Hebert nodded. "I go now. Glad to see you bo't."

Though the menu hid Connie's face, he had strained to listen in on Hebert's conversation with Joe. He processed the words '*I don't have money for a train ticket*'. His thoughts ran to the train set stuffed under his father's bed. He had gazed at it every day for weeks when it was in Genoese's big picture window, and he knew the price of it to the penny— $57.99.

It was a secret as to how it found its way under his father's bed. But as a duck is to water, it was no surprise that Connie had found his way to it. He also knew his father could never have afforded such a luxury. In his mind, it could only have come from Joe.

After its discovery, Connie had ample time to un-loose the packaging and then ogle, poke and prod the train set and then re-tape it sufficiently to not raise suspicion it had ever been opened. It now dawned on his young mind that Joe had inadvertently traded his train ticket to Vermont for the train set under his bed. He felt bad for Joe.

"And you?" the waitress asked Connie.

"Huh?"

"It's your turn to order, Connie," Ernst said.

"Oh, ah. I'll have pancakes."

"Just de pancake? No egg or sausage?" Hebert said.

"I can have more?"

"I say, dis my treat, Connie. Now eat!"

"Yes, sir. I'll have what he just said."

"Two of each?" Erin asked.

"Uh-huh."

"Coming right up."

Joe and Lillian finished their breakfast and then bid goodbye to Hebert and the boys. When their breakfast was complete, the boys left the diner and walked the neighborhood shops looking for presents. Connie returned to his apartment with a Christmas gift for his father— an electric can opener. This new technology would allow his dad to open cans of corn, peas, carrots, and his favorite New York chowder, without Connie there to open it for him.

Connie had no money of his own, but through his concern for the boy, Hebert had contracted with Connie to wash his car once a week throughout the summer months in exchange for the money to buy the can opener now. Connie was ecstatic to have a gift for his father, yet as the day wore on his conscience gnawed at him — *Joe could not go to Vermont because of the train set under his bed.* He felt increasingly troubled.

Later that day, with his father still at work, Connie pulled the train set from under the bed, unwrapped it, and then looked at it long and hard. Decaled for the Erie Railroad, the train engine had a die-cast metal frame and trucks. It sported a super-powerful worm drive, had authentic detailing and possessed a working headlamp that could pierce the night. It was beautiful... and... it should not have been his. He knew that. He had done nothing to deserve it except to win the attention of a coach who did his best to keep the team bully at bay. Connie made an impulsive decision. He rewrapped the train in the brown paper in which it came and then ran out of the building toward Genoese's.

The shop was busy with customers. Connie waited patiently with package in hand while Mr. Genoese served his paying customers. When he had finished, he approached Connie. "What do we have here?"

"I need to return this train."

"Is that what's inside the package?"

"Yes."

"And you want to return it *before* Christmas? Is something wrong with it?"

"I don't know. I've never opened it. I just need the money."

Gino was confused and concerned that his paying customers may be watching the transaction. "Follow me to the storeroom, and I'll see what I can do."

Connie followed Gino as directed. "Have a seat, son. Can I examine the package?"

"Sure."

Gino unwrapped it and looked it over carefully. "Your right. It hasn't been opened. There's just one problem."

Connie's heart sank. "What?"

"I'm curious. How did the train set that I sold to one man end up in the hands of a boy who wants to pawn it for money?"

"It's not like that, Mr. Genoese."

Gino leaned forward and set his hands to his hips. "Tell me the truth, son. Did you steal this train set?"

Connie was awash in fear. "I didn't steal it. I got it as a Christmas present. Honest."

"Is that a fact. I sold this same train set to a man I know very well, and now you come in here *before Christmas* and say to me that it's yours and you want to sell it for money? I think you stole this train, young man, and I'm going to call the police."

"I didn't steal it. Joe gave it to me, and now he can't go to Vermont because he spent all his money on this stupid train so I could have a present for Christmas. It's my fault he can't go."

"Hold on now. Take it easy. I'm sorry for getting angry at you, son. You say it was Joe that gave you this?"

"He gave it to my dad to give to me for Christmas."

"And you want to sell it back to me?"

Connie's eyes were wet with tears. "Joe needs the money so he can go to Vermont and be with his Division."

Gino was aware of Bob's announcement on the Ed Harrison show. "Did Joe ask you to do this?"

"He don't know. I was hoping to get the money and surprise him."

"What's your name, son?"

"Connie."

"Connie? That's right! I saw you at the basketball game a few weeks back." Gino put his hands across Connie's shoulders. "I'm sorry for accusing you like that. I should have known better. Forgive me, please?"

"It's okay, Mr. Genoese."

"Thank you, Connie. Believe it or not, you've done a wonderful thing today."

"I did?"

Gino turned and picked up the train set and handed it back to Connie. "Yes, you did. Keep the train set. That's what Joe wanted."

"I can't. Joe needs the money to go to Vermont!"

"Don't you worry about the money. I'll take care of that. Joe has done a lot of good for this neighborhood.

I know there'll be people willing to help him out. Now, I need to make some phone calls. You just get this train set back home and make sure it's wrapped nice and neat so your dad doesn't find out you've been into it. Merry Christmas, Connie!"

Chapter 35

Emma, Judy, and Susan had also watched Bob's appearance on the Ed Harrison show the previous night. Phil had not. Neither had the General. Bob had left strict instructions with Phil that he should not let the General see Bob's announcement to the men of the 151st Division on television or the surprise would be ruined.

To carry out his mission, Phil successfully feigned a leg injury which drew the General away from the TV set for the entirety of Ed's show. His performance was a success, as the General truly believed that Phil was injured.

The ladies, however, eagerly watched the show and approved of the manner of Bob's plea to the men of the 151st Division. They were remarkably happy until Judy asked a simple question, "Emma, how many men are in a Division?"

Emma sprang from her chair while her mouth simultaneously hit the floor. Shock contorted her face, constricting the blood vessels in her head, which then paled her face.

"Good Lord. What have we done?"

Judy and Susan sprang to their feet to steady the old girl in case she fell. "What is it, Emma?"

"Fifteen thousand."

"Fifteen thousand?" Judy said.

"Fifteen thousand men in a Division. All coming here on Christmas Eve. What are we going to do?"

It was an enormous number, the magnitude of which bowled Judy and Susan over. All three women dropped back into their chairs at the same time. They repeated Emma's line, *'what have we done?'*

Emma collected herself. Though she had never served in the military, she had served in General Waverly's private army and was a seasoned soldier when it came to battle tactics for and against him. She went to work to save the day. An energetic phone call to Mayor Allison was the first order of business. She explained their dilemma and demanded an emergency meeting with the people of Pine Tree the following morning. She argued that an invasion of men, women, and children was on their way to Pine Tree, and the battle to feed and house an army that big was too much for one little inn. It would take an effort by the entire town to rescue their plan to honor General Waverly on Christmas Eve and to provide hospitable living quarters for their guests.

The Mayor concurred with Emma's assessment and agreed to call a town meeting. Communicating the emergency meeting to the town folk in a matter of hours was of little concern. A quick call from Emma to Mavis and with the help of the New England Chapter of Busy Bodies of America grapevine, the announcement was successfully relayed.

The following morning the fleet had assembled. An armada of cars, trucks, scooters, bicycles, and two horse and buggies converged on the town square as if gathering for battle. Pine Tree Town Hall was overrun with curious and eager townsfolk. There was not an empty chair or an open space to lean against a wall.

Mayor Allison took to the podium. Emma stood by his side. "Thank you for coming, everyone. I am quite sure no one here could have expected to have a meeting the day before Christmas Eve, but here we are. Emma has asked to speak to you on behalf of the Columbia Inn and our friend General Tom Waverly. Emma."

"Thank you, Mayor. Every one of you knows the General and what he's meant to this town, not to mention our country. He's lived in Pine Tree his entire life, outside of his military service. And he put a lot of you to work when he started renovating that old grist mill into a ski lodge. He's never failed to come to your aide when you needed help to dig out after a snowstorm or to help build the hall that you're standing in right now."

"We know all that, Emma. What's your point?" Walt said.

Emma signaled battle stations. "My point is this. We have an unknown number of soldiers and their families coming to Pine Tree tomorrow night for the Christmas Eve show. If even one-tenth of the 151st Division shows up, we'll be overrun, and we won't have enough food or beds to accommodate them. That will ruin the evening for the General and hurt his pride. And it will put a black eye on the entire town."

"Shouldn't you have thought of that before Bob Wallace went on the Ed Harrison show and made that announcement?" Clancy demanded.

"That's right," Shelly scolded. "We should have been asked!"

"Hold on, now," Archie called out from the crowd. "Let's keep calm, people. We can worry about how this should have been handled another time. Our problem is here and now. Think of the opportunity we have in front of us. Hundreds, maybe thousands of people may come to our town tomorrow night. That will give us an opportunity to put Pine Tree and the Columbia

Inn on the map. If we make a good impression, those folks will want to come back again and again. Think of how that will help your businesses and the value of your homes and land."

"There you go again, Archie. Sounding like a banker," Stanley chastised him.

"I am a banker, Stanley," Archie chastised him back.

Mayor Allison jumped into the fray. "Archie's right. No matter how we got to this point, this is no longer a Columbia Inn problem. This is a Pine Tree problem."

"What should we do, Mayor?" Curtis asked.

"I'm working on that."

"Why don't we focus on the obvious," Archie said. "Mr. Cisco, you're the train conductor. The train typically arrives around 4:30 p.m. each day. Is that correct?"

"That's correct."

"How many cars?"

"Five. There are sixty seats per car, which is the standard run for Pine Tree."

"And we all know that one bus per day comes to Pine Tree. A bus only holds 50 people. Between the train and the bus, that's 350 people," Archie said.

"We can do the math, Archie," Walt said. "Why you doing the math is the question."

"I see what Archie's getting at. There's only three ways to get to Pine Tree— by train, by bus, or by car.

That limits how many people can come here at any given time," Mayor Allison said.

"But how many by car?" restaurant owner Tyler asked. "How can we possibly figure that out?"

"I'm not sure how to compute that," Archie responded. "That's the great unknown."

The room went quiet. Thurl, a mechanic, broke the silence. "Hard for a California man to get here in just two days whether he's driving, flying, or by rail. Texas or South Carolina men, too."

"I see what you're saying, Thurl," Archie said. "Everyone, we have to keep in mind that this is a difficult decision for people to make on such short notice—even for those in the New England area. Most people will have their Christmas plans set in stone and have families and relatives to care for. That should keep the numbers down even if they do come by car."

"Emma, how many people does the Columbia Inn hold?" Mayor Allison asked.

"We have the inn and four bungalows. Altogether, about 250 people."

The crowd gasped.

"Good Lord. That's not much," Shelly said.

"And what if more come than you can handle?" Millie chimed in.

"That's why we need your help. The Columbia Inn doesn't have enough beds, and we don't have enough food. But you do!"

"What do you mean, Emma?" Shelly asked.

"What do I mean? I mean, every one of you has pots and pans, don't you? You all have beds and sheets and a table to eat at. And you have the most important thing of all— hospitality. The people of Pine Tree have always been known for their hospitality. So, I'm asking you, no, I'm begging you to share a little of that hospitality right now."

Archie was the first to sign up for duty. "Emma. I'm in." He then walked to the podium, stood beside her, and addressed the crowd. "Listen, everyone. Tomorrow night is Christmas Eve. I know this will put you and your family out on that most blessed and sacred of nights. But isn't this what Christmas is all about? If ever there was a night meant for giving, it has to be Christmas. I want you all to know, me and my family, we'll open our home and our table and our beds to anyone who needs it."

Emma and Archie's declarations touched the people of Pine Tree. Mayor Allison was the next to sign up for duty. "Emma, you can count on Alice and me, as well."

"And me too," Thurl offered.

"Sign me up," Walt said as he gave in to the will of the town.

"How do we get started, Emma?" Millie said as it became clear the entire town was ready to sign on to the plan.

"Ladies, you're with me. We can work out the logistics of food and rooms. Archie, you were an Army Captain. Can you develop a battle plan for the men?"

"I'd be honored."

"And above all, you cannot let the General know. This must remain top secret!"

Chapter 36

Battle plans were drawn up. The people of Pine Tree went to work to prepare for the arrival of the Division. At times the town resembled a madhouse. Men, women, children, and beasts were put to work to ready the town for the certain onslaught of visitors. Rooms were cleaned, sheets were washed to a sparkling white, pillows were fluffed, windows were washed, dishes were cleaned and shined to a spot-free finish, yards were decluttered and freed of debris.

A food list was created. The kitchen staff at the Columbia Inn could handle up to 250 dinner guests. The women of Pine Tree would supplement the meal by preparing selected food dishes in their homes. Then, at the right time, they would deliver their items to the back door of the inn to be served to the dinner guests. Whatever food items a woman did not have in her fridge or cupboard, she would send her husband, child, or herself to the neighbor's house to borrow, beg or steal— a bag of flour or sugar, sticks of butter, a sack of potatoes, fresh cream and milk. If her neighbor did not have the item, she would run to market, which was quickly running out of supplies.

The men were then sent to the neighboring towns of Wilmington and Brattleboro to collect the needed supplies and replenish the local market. It was an automobile square dance as driveways were emptied and then filled through their constant search for goods, dry and wet, to keep the women making and baking.

The reservation desk at the Columbia Inn, manned by Emma and Susan, became ground zero. Calls rolled in throughout the day. When all the rooms were let, they worked with the Sunshine Motel in Pine Tree to reserve rooms. When those rooms were let, they worked with each soldier to assign them to a local household. Though it was not ideal, the soldiers were more than happy to stay with a local family for the privilege of honoring General Waverly.

Phil was assigned to keep the General occupied and away from the reservation book. If the General recognized any of the names, it could blow the whole operation. Emma and Susan coded every man's name thought to be an officer or whom the General may have known personally. Phil then dragged the exasperated General to town for a doctor's visit for his injured leg. To keep the General away from the inn as long as possible, he insisted on a scenic drive through the Green Mountains and asked to stop near the woods for a bathroom break, during which he craftily snuck back to the jeep to let the air out of a tire or two.

The cast and crew of *Playing Around* were put to work at the inn and in town. Judy and John, Trudi and Doreen, arranged for local dance students and the youth choir to fill out the show's closing number— *White Christmas*. Young Bobby possessed a serviceable tenor voice and was given a role in the choir. Evie, an excellent cook, was assigned to help in the short-staffed kitchen baking pies and helping with side dishes.

Archie assigned the men their own set of tasks. Christmas lights had long been hung in the town square. Additional lights were purchased and hung across the streets from one lamp post to another. American flags were flown near the war memorial to add a patriotic touch to the festivities.

It was critical to quantify the actual number of soldiers approaching Pine Tree. A signal corps was put in place on the main road to flag down approaching drivers and direct them to the appropriate lodging— all without alerting the General. Archie worked closely with Mr. Cisco to tabulate the actual number of passengers who had purchased tickets on the Christmas Eve train. Along with the number of rooms that were booked at the inn, Sunshine Motel, and in homes, Archie then tallied the numbers and worked with the men to arrange logistics for transportation, the next circus trick that would need to be performed.

When the soldiers arrived for the Christmas Eve show they would be assessed as to their barracks location. Those staying at the Columbia Inn would be transported directly there. Those who were quartered at the Sunshine Hotel or a local residence would be transported to their respective quarters and then transported one more time to the Columbia Inn— and in time for the show. When the show was finished, they had to be transported back to their lodging in town. It was a logistical challenge, and it would require every available car and driver the town could spare.

Above all, secrecy was paramount. This was a covert operation. If the General sniffed a conspiracy, their cover would be blown and the surprise ruined. It would take a team effort on each person's part to maintain the ruse.

The planning, cooking, baking, and cleaning went on well into the night. By midnight, the town folk had settled down, tired but happy. Tomorrow was Christmas Eve, and it was shaping up to be the most unusual, albeit exciting Christmas Eve they had ever witnessed.

Chapter 37

Christmas Eve Day, 1954

The YMCA would remain busy with patrons until closing time. It would be work as usual for Joe. The boiler would need to be checked for leaks and drips, the pool would need skimming, the faucet in the third-floor bathroom would need repair— just another day at the office.

Joe showered, dressed in his skivvies and t-shirt, and then sat on his bed. It was early, but he thought to turn on the twinkle lights of his table-top Christmas tree to add a bit of cheer to his otherwise doleful day. He stood from the bed, flipped on the switch, and took a moment to admire the colorful lights.

'Merry Christmas, Joe', he said to himself.

A small package lay underneath the tree— from Lil. It was the size and shape of a wallet. He had hoped it may be a pocket-size transistor radio that he could carry with him and listen to the Knicks game while he worked. But it was a wallet.

Joe put on his work uniform and took the elevator down to the kitchen to make a pot of coffee. Leaning against the counter, he stared absently past the pot as it gurgled and bubbled coffee into the clear knob, and he wondered where Evie may be. He suspected she was in Vermont with the show, but he could not be sure. He became somber. The day had barely begun, and already his *White Christmas* was turning steadily *blue*. With the perc done, Joe tipped the pot and poured a long pour into his Thermos. He took a calming sip.

"Morning, Joe," Lillian said as she rounded the corner to the kitchen.

"Oh, hey, Lil. Merry Christmas Eve."

"You too, Joe. Do you have a minute? I need you to look at something."

"Right now? I was gonna check the boilers and make sure they're running full-on."

"Yeah. Right now. If you don't mind."

"All right," Joe said, slightly exasperated.

"Follow me, soldier."

Joe followed her out of the kitchen and into the lobby, where he was instantly startled to see it full of people— all awaiting him. "What's this about?"

Gino spoke for the group. "We got you something, Joe."

"Me?"

"You."

Gino handed him an envelope. "We want you to go to Vermont to be with your Division. We took up a collection— me, Hebert, Byron, Marcus's dad Larry, Cris' dad Mateo, the folks from Gwen's Diner, Alger's pizzeria, Blooming Acres flower shop, Bauman's clothiers, Sutliff's General Store, Solon's Sporting goods... The whole neighborhood pitched in a little. Lillian and Mr. Whitman, too. Lot of those folks couldn't be here this morning as they had to work. But they were all happy to chip in."

Joe looked inside the envelope. It was two hundred dollars, at least. "I can't take this from you. It's not right."

Byron stepped forward. "Oh, yes, you can. It's your turn to let your friends help you for a change— soldier."

It was payback.

Joe could not have imagined when he awoke that morning it was his turn to be on the receiving end of a helping hand, but he chose to accept it. Joe shook

Byron's hand. "Thanks, Byron. Thanks, everyone. I don't know what to say."

Hebert piped up. "You say *I must get to de station before da last train to Veer-mont goes.*"

"But I haven't started my shift yet," Joe exclaimed.

"You don't have to," Mr. Whitman said. "I asked Charlie to cover for you today. Now go get yourself packed and get on that train."

"This is unbelievable. I'm indebted to you all."

"No, Joe. We're indebted to you. You've made a huge impact on the boys you've coached over the years, and the neighborhood is all the better for it," Mr. Whitman said.

While Joe's friends and shopkeepers made their presentation, Lillian had made herself busy on the phone and was in an increasingly tense conversation with the caller on the other end. She removed the handset from her ear and dropped it onto the hook. "Well, if that don't beat all."

"What is it, Lillian?" Gino said.

"I called the train station for you, Joe. All the seats are booked. There's no more room on the train to Pine Tree."

It was painful news. "Son of a gun. What do we do now?" Byron said.

"The bus!" Larry said. "What about taking a bus to Vermont?"

"Great idea!" Mr. Whitman said.

Lillian picked up the phone and made a frantic call to the bus depot as the group gathered around to listen. "I'd like a ticket to Pine Tree, Vermont, please." She listened for a moment and was suddenly perturbed. "Yes, that Vermont!" she stated strongly to the ticket agent. She listened closely again. "Uh-huh.... Uh-huh... You don't say..." The group tightened around Lillian, nearly sitting on her lap in the process. "You don't say," she said again. The group inched ever closer until she became exasperated and waved them off. "Okay... If that's the way it has to be." Lillian hung up the phone. The group took a step back. "They have a seat. But the bus leaves at 9 a.m. You have to hurry, Joe!"

Joe's day had been turned upside down. He was suddenly indecisive.

"Well, don't just stand there. Get going!" Mr. Whitman commanded.

"Yes, sir!" Joe said as he absent-mindedly handed his Thermos to Mr. Whitman. "Thank you, sir."

Mr. Whitman looked at the container and wondered what he would do with it.

"Wait, I'll need that," Joe said as he took the Thermos back from Mr. Whitman and then shook his hand profusely. He then worked his way through the gathered crowd, shaking their hands while receiving slaps on the back and attaboys. As he broke through the crowd, he quick-stepped to the elevator and up to his room.

After packing, he hurried downstairs with suitcase in hand and stopped to say goodbye to Lil. "Guess I won't see you for a few days. Merry Christmas, Lil."

Lillian was emotional. "You work things out with that General of yours, and if you see Evie, don't you be shy. A woman needs to know you're interested, or she'll think you're not."

Joe smiled and kissed Lil on the cheek. "Thanks, Lil."

Out the door and down the steps, Joe hailed a taxi. One passed him by, but it did not stop. Frustrated, he quick-stepped down the street, looking for the next taxi to hail. Another was just ahead, but two women jumped into the vehicle before he could reach it. Walking further, he spied a taxi with the off-duty sign lit. He took a chance. He knocked on the window and then pulled the door open to address the driver. It was Huck.

"Say, pal. I'm in a real pickle. Is there any way you can drive me to the bus station?"

"Can't you read? I'm off duty," Huck protested.

"I realize that, and I sure do apologize for bothering you. But if I don't get to the bus station by 9 a.m., I'll miss my bus to Vermont."

Huck was irritated, but he stopped and processed Joe's request. His aggravation turned inquisitive. "You with the 151?"

Huck had seen Bob's announcement on the Ed Harrison show. Joe's spirit jumped. "I am. I mean, I was. Listen... Huck. I can't miss that bus. Is there any way you can get me to that station?"

Huck flipped off the off-duty sign. "I was with the 1st Armored Division under Harmon. Seems like we trailed you boys in the 151st for half the war. Get in."

Joe was ecstatic. He whipped open the cab door, threw his suitcase in the back seat, and then jumped into the car. "I owe you one, pal."

It was twenty blocks to the Greyhound station. Huck, an experienced cabbie, weaved his way through side streets, back alleys, and main roads and arrived at the station in under fifteen minutes.

"I'm grateful, Huck," Joe said as the taxi whipped to a stop in front of the station. "What do I owe you?"

"This one's courtesy of the 1st Armored. You boys in the 151st did some good work for us. It's the least I can do."

Chapter 38

Joe tipped his hat to thank Huck and then entered the bus station to purchase his ticket. Outside once again, he found the correct bus, boarded it, and then scanned for open seats. He found one next to a pretty blonde. He had no choice but to approach her. "Most of the seats are taken. You mind if I sit next to you?"

"Be my guest," the woman said.

"Thanks." Joe sat down and then laid his overcoat across his knees.

The woman took note of him. She suspected him to be among several other men on the bus that were part of the 151st Division. "I take it you're headed up north for Christmas?"

He made eye contact with her and then looked down into his hat. "Yes— to Vermont. And you?"

"I'm headed up north, too. Christmas in Vermont. That sounds nice."

Joe thought for a moment. "I guess it does. Christmas in Vermont. It has a nice ring to it."

He looked into his hat once more and then returned his gaze to the woman. "You have family up there?"

"My sister."

The brakes of the bus loosened, and the bus lurched forward. A voice was heard outside the bus door. "Last call for Waterbury, Hartford, Springfield, and Pine Tree."

A hurried couple entered the bus after making a frantic dash from the ticket counter. As they made their way down the aisle, the man recognized Joe. "Well, I'll be. Joe Ross! It's good to see you."

Joe looked at the man. "Well, what do you know. Sergeant Baxa! It's been a long time."

"You headed to Pine Tree to see the old man?"

"And to be with the unit," he replied.

"Swell! This is my wife, Amy Lou."

"How do you do, ma'am."

"How do you do, Joe."

Sergeant Baxa noticed the woman sitting next to Joe and waited for him to introduce her until it became uncomfortable. "Aren't you gonna introduce me to your wife?"

"I'm Betty Haynes," she said quickly. "We came separately."

"Take a seat," the bus driver called out. "We're ready to depart."

"Say, we'll catch up after the bus gets going. It's nice to see you, Joe. Ma'am."

The couple walked to the back of the bus and took the last two seats. The bus embarked. Betty had recognized the name— Joe Ross. It was the same name that her brother Benny had written about during the war and the same name that Evie had told her about in Florida. "Joe Ross. Did you serve with the 151st Division under General Waverly?"

Joe was surprised. "I did. With A Company. I was a Captain."

"How remarkable. I believe my brother Benny was a Private in your Company."

Joe put the names together. "Betty Haynes? You're Benny Haynes's sister!"

"I am. And my sister Judy is already in Vermont waiting for me."

"Sure. Benny was a good man. Some soldiers turned out to be worthless bums, but I could always count on him. It's been a while, but I remember him telling me that you and your sister did a little singing for some local USO shows. I remember him being awfully proud of you for that."

"We did. Not too bad for a couple of farm girls from New Jersey, huh? We have our own floor show now."

"I guess I don't remember Benny mentioning you being a farm girl, but it's been a while. So, how did you end up in show business?"

"You might say it was in our blood. Our farm was located just outside Westfield— about fifty minutes west of New York City. Our mother, Lorna, was a chorus girl— in Ziegfeld's Follies, no less. She met my dad at the end of WWI as he was on his way back to the family farm. She was tired of dancing by then, so she gave it up to be with him. We learned to dance and sing from her."

"You have quite the talented family. What a change for your mom, though. Going from Broadway to a family farm, I mean."

"It was, but she couldn't have been happier. She raised four healthy kids, and we had a wonderful time of it growing up in the country."

"Four?" Joe said.

"Oh, yes. My youngest brother, Kenny, he runs the farm now. We used to call him *Squirt* when he was little. Benny was supposed to take over the operation when he got back from the war, but... Well, that never really happened."

Joe sensed sorrow in Betty's voice. "So, Benny's not on the farm?"

Betty looked into her lap. She was being unusually forward. It was not her style. She quickly appraised the man sitting next to her and decided to extend to him a measure of trust. "Benny's in Alaska now, but who knows where he'll be tomorrow or the next day. He was never the same after the war. He came back to the farm for a while, but he's been a drifter ever since, and we've never stopped worrying about him. He needs help, but he never quite stays around long enough to get it."

"I've seen that with a few soldiers I've come in contact with. I've seen it a little in myself, too. Lucky for me, I landed in a spot where I could be of some use. It helped to heal the wounds."

"You landed at the YMCA?" Betty said.

"Wow. How would you know that?"

She pointed to the overcoat draped across his knees. "You're YMCA pin. On your overcoat."

He felt chagrined. "Oh, yeah. I left so fast this morning I forgot to take that off. Yeah, I landed at the Y. I found the more I focused on others, the less time there was to wallow in my own miseries."

The bus rattled across a bad stretch of road, interrupting the conversation. As the road smoothed out, so did the conversation. "You wouldn't happen to know a young lady named Evie Sanders, would you?" Betty asked.

Joe was astonished. "Ms. Haynes, I'm beginning to think you're a bit of a mind reader. Do you know Evie?"

"I met her briefly in Florida. And then I spent more time with her in Vermont. I'm with the show you're on your way to see tonight. Or at least I was."

"You were? But not anymore?"

"Well, Joe, friend of Benny and Evie, it's like this. I believed something about a man that I shouldn't have believed, and rather than dealing with it head-on, I ran away like a little schoolgirl. I left the show and went to New York City. Since then, I've come to see just how wrong I was. So, now I'm on my way to Vermont to see if that man will take me back. Nothing like baring your soul to a complete stranger," Betty said mirthlessly.

"Well, Betty, friend of Evie and brother of Benny, the important thing is you've realized your mistake, and you're on your way to make amends," Joe offered softly. "That's a good road to be on."

"I appreciate that, Joe."

As they traveled, they spoke intermittently with one another in between conversations with Sergeant Baxa, Amy Lou, and several other soldiers who had recognized Joe and who were surprised to see that he was still alive and kicking.

New York turned into Connecticut. The nearer the bus came to Vermont, the more Joe thought about seeing Evie again. He was still unsure of what he had done to alienate her, and he was increasingly anxious about meeting the General. He needed to talk with someone, and Betty was the nearest someone.

"Betty, would you mind if I share something with you?"

"Go right ahead."

"I believed something about a man once that wasn't true either. But I took it one step farther, and I called him a coward."

Joe leaned in close so that those around him would not hear. "But you see, I was the coward. I wasn't man enough to accept my circumstances, so I blamed him for what happened to me and for letting the Division down— even though that wasn't true. He's never forgiven me for that."

"Would you mind if I ask who that man is?"

Joe put his head down. "General... Tom... Waverly."

"Oh, dear. I see your predicament. You're on your way to honor a man who may not want to see you. That's a hard spot to be in."

He exhaled deeply and leaned back into his chair. "It sure is."

Betty sat quietly for a moment before questioning her traveling companion further. "Joe, why come? Why

come all this way to see a man who may not have forgiven you, and in fact, may hate you?"

"I didn't want to at first. But for better or for worse,
I'm a soldier. And it's my duty to stand with my Division.
When we're called, we respond, no matter the cost.
That's just how it is."

"But you're not a soldier anymore. The war is
over, Joe."

"Yes, it is. But there's still a war going on *inside of
me*. For ten awful years, I've carried this burden that I've
wronged the General. Until I can tell him how wrong
I was, that war will continue."

Betty came to admire Joe in that moment. Evie was
right; Joe was a good man. "And what about, Evie?"

"Evie?"

"Yes, Evie. I hope you don't mind, but she told me
about you while we were in Florida. If I understand
her story correctly, you and I aren't the only ones who
believed something about a man that wasn't true."

Joe took the hint. "I don't know what I did wrong,
Betty. I've examined every word, every look, trying to
see how I hurt her. But I can't figure it out."

"You really like her then?"

"More than anything— and Bobby, too. He's such
a great kid."

"It seems like we both have a challenge ahead of us
then," Betty stated.

Chapter 39

The train pulled into Pine Tree Station. Soldiers joyful and exuberant exited the train laughing, joking, and anxious to commence with the invasion. The town of Pine Tree awaited them. Archie stood inside the bed of his Ford half-ton truck and called the men to attention. "Men and ladies. My name is Archie Andrews, Captain of the 76th Infantry Division. I'm a friend of General Waverly's, and I live right here in Pine Tree. The people of Pine Tree welcome you!"

Hurrahs lifted from the soldiers.

"We are grateful that you've sacrificed your Christmas plans to honor our friend and beloved commander, Tom Waverly."

More hurrahs.

"Captains. Please step forward."

Captain "Buck" Beckley, Captain "Bunny" Bunnell, Captain "Rog" Teeling, and Captain "Al" Mallie stepped to the front and exchanged salutes and handshakes with Archie, who had stepped down from the truck. "Thank you so much for being here, Captains."

"Wouldn't miss it for the world," Captain Beckley said.

"Captain Wallace will have special instructions for you during the performance tonight. Don't worry, nothing too dramatic," Archie said. "For now, I'll need your help in organizing the men. We'll need to be efficient at quartering and directing the Division in order to make the show on time."

"You can count on us, sir," Captain Bunnell said.

Archie climbed back into the truck bed and addressed the crowd. "We have an exciting night ahead of us. But to pull this off, we'll need your help to take the General by complete surprise."

A voice called out from the crowd. "What do you want us to do, Captain?"

"For those of you who are lodging at the Columbia Inn, I'll need you to make two lines behind Captain's Beckley and Bunnell. For those of you staying at the Sunshine Motel, make one line behind Captain Teeling. For those of you lodging in town, make a line behind Captain Mallie. Please remain in your street clothes until you reach the Columbia Inn. You can change into your uniforms in the backstage dressing area. If you have any military hats or insignias, please remove them at this time."

An old grunt named Birch swiped the hat from his friend Collier's head and handed it to him. The crowd laughed.

Archie pointed to the town folk standing behind him. "Ladies and gentlemen. The good people of Pine Tree will escort you up the mountain in their vehicles. Please remain silent as you enter the inn. If all goes as planned, General Waverly will be detained in a rear area. If he happens to see you, please do not make eye contact or acknowledge him in any way but proceed directly to the lodge. Any questions?"

A murmur arose from the crowd, but no questions were asked.

"All right," Archie said. "It's time to commence with Operation Waverly."

A roar lifted from the soldiers while the roar of engines arose from the townspeople. Bel Aire's, De Soto's, Hornets, Town and Country's, Roadmaster's, Packard's, and an assortment of pickup trucks roared to life after Walt, Clancy, Curtis, and all the townspeople had entered their cars and started their engines.

One by one, the vehicles pulled up to the line of soldiers who awaited transport to their lodging destinations and then the two miles up the mountain to the door of the Columbia Inn. Within minutes a steady stream of vehicles made their way up the darkened mountainside forming a parade of lights. As they rounded the last bend and entered the inn's parking area, the drivers turned off their lights, slowed to a stop, and then released their passengers to the front porch, then turned to go down the mountain to pick up more passengers.

Mayor Allison and his wife Alice were responsible for the last maneuver. They led each carload of soldiers quietly through the inn and into the lodge. Alice seated the spouses at the dinner tables while Mayor Allison escorted the soldiers to the dressing area to change into their uniforms. The entire operation ran like clockwork.

Back in Pine Tree, the bus from New York pulled into the station. Six cars, led by Thurl and his Pontiac Torpedo Woodie, awaited the soldiers. As the passengers exited the bus, Thurl lifted the ear flaps of his Kromer hat and called out to those who had come to see the General. "If yer lookin' for a ride to the Columbia Inn you can line up right here. My name is Thurl."

Joe, Betty, Sergeant Baxa, Amy Lou, and a dozen soldiers and their wives lined up next to Thurl.

"Now, don't you worry none. We got plenty of cars to get you up this here mountain. We have to get moving if we're to be on time, though."

Joe impulsively grabbed Betty's hand and called out to Thurl. "Thurl, this young lady is in the show tonight. Is there any way she can go in the first car?"

"Not a problem. Clarke, we got a special delivery."

"Hop in, lady. I'll take you first," Clarke said.

Betty turned to Joe. "Thank you, Joe. I'll see you on the mountain!"

One by one, the cars pulled up to the line of soldiers and loaded as many as would fit into their vehicles. Joe, Sergeant Baxa, and Amy Lou were the last to procure transport.

"You're the last ones," Thurl said. "Hop on in. I had a couple old carbs in the back seat that I was rebuilding, but I cleaned off the seats the best I could."

Sergeant Baxa was uneasy. "Ah, Amy Lou. Why don't you sit in the front with Thurl? I'll sit in back with Joe."

Amy Lou was appreciative that she would not have to sit in back and soil her dress. The trio entered Thurl's car and then sat back as he raced up the winding and weaving mountainside to catch the other vehicles.

With every turn, Joe's heart pumped rapidly from the realization that he was one step closer to seeing General Waverly for the first time in ten years. A sense of embarrassment and shame overshadowed him as he remembered his last word to the General— *coward.* His mind struggled for a meaningful word that he might speak upon seeing him. But what word was available in the human vocabulary that could soften such a blow? '*I'm sorry*' seemed so trite and overused.

There was no time to overthink it. Within minutes Thurl pulled to a stop in front of the Columbia Inn and released his passengers. Joe paused before exiting the vehicle and weighed the benefit and disadvantages of meeting the General face to face or playing the coward and returning to town with Thurl.

Sergeant Baxa was concerned. "You coming, Joe?"

Joe bowed his head, composed himself, and then cast an easy look toward the man. "I'll just be a minute, Sergeant. You go on."

"Well, okay, then. We'll see you inside."

Joe took another moment to collect his thoughts. Uncertain if he was engaging the enemy or on a peace mission, there was one thing that he *was* sure of—he was not a coward. He looked at Thurl. "Well, I should get in there. Thanks for the ride, Thurl. I'm sure the men appreciate what the town is doing for the General."

"Every town needs a good General. And he's about the best. Enjoy the show, Captain."

Chapter 40

Joe exited the vehicle and then fixed his eyes upon the inn. It was beautifully crafted— the arched windows, the large front porch, the inviting entry, the ski lodge so artfully positioned next to the inn. The General had built himself a first-rate establishment. It was a darn shame he could not enjoy it. For, from the moment he stepped into the bus in New York City to the moment he stepped out of Thurl's car and onto Columbia Inn ground, he had mentally prepared himself for court-martial, or at least a very cold if not frozen shoulder from the General.

He gathered his courage and forced himself up the stairs and into the inn. Mayor Allison questioned him on his rank— a Captain. He would be seated at the same table with General Waverly. Mayor Allison then escorted him through the inn and into the expansive lodge where he would join up with the rest of the Division.

Backstage, it was a merry time for Bob and Phil. Their plan was working. As the soldiers changed into their uniforms, they bantered ardently with one another while Bob relayed instructions to the men on the evening's performance and their part in it.

As Bob completed his instructions, he noted that the men began to look past him and that he was no longer the center of their attention. And then, one by one, they solemnly stood at attention and saluted.

Phil grabbed Bob by the arm. "Bob," he said and then gave the nod to look behind him.

Bob turned to see Joe, who had just entered the dressing room. Surprised and instantly overjoyed, he stood straight and tall and offered a salute with the rest of the men. Overwhelmed by the response, Joe returned the salute.

"Joe! You came!" Bob said as he rushed forward to greet him. The band of soldiers followed his lead and rushed forward to shake Joe's hand and slap him on the back. They had not seen him since the day he left Montepolina as a bloody hero lying on a stretcher. Most had thought the ground would see him before they would. Bob then refocused the group. "All right, men. It's showtime! Captains come front and center and wait for the signal to march out."

Joe changed quickly and took his place at the front of the line. He was nervous and unsure. He peered out into the packed crowd of happy women awaiting their significant others and smiled a melancholy smile. Feeling instantly forlorn and quite alone amidst the happy crowd, he turned his gaze back to the stage and unexpectedly caught sight of Bobby standing on the opposite side of the stage. He was looking at him, just as he had in New York City during their first performance together at *Playing Around*. Bobby smiled and waved at Joe, who joyously returned the wave.

From the shadows, Evie stepped forward and put her arms around Bobby. She did not take her eyes off of Joe, communicating with her body language how she longed for him. She quivered from the hope that Joe hadn't given up on her and that he would love her back.

He did.

His eyes communicated everything he could not speak aloud as he stood on the opposite side of the stage. She interpreted his look and nearly jumped out of her shoes.

Upstairs at the inn, Emma and Susan were hard at work to awaken the General. Emma's plan of subterfuge had worked too well. A double dose of sleeping powder in the General's afternoon brandy had sent him to la-la land. After washing, he stood in his bathrobe, looking indignantly into his empty closet after Emma had artfully sent his small array of dress suits to the cleaners. His military uniform was now the only appropriate attire to wear for the evening.

After dressing, Susan escorted the General downstairs. Emma went before them to signal Bob that the General was on his way. Bob dispatched the Captains down the aisle to wait for him. Joe's heart palpitated as he marched toward the lodge door. His palms were sweaty, and a sense of dread overwhelmed him. It was an unbearable moment.

Finally, Emma opened the lodge door to allow the General through. The packed audience rose to their feet and welcomed him with wild applause. He stood in disbelief, being wildly snookered by their scheme. The sight of the lodge packed with people and of his unit commanders standing before him was an extraordinary sight. It had been so long since he had seen them.

And then he saw Joe. He nearly wept. The man that haunted his dreams was now standing in uniform before him. He cast a warm expression toward Joe, who perceived the expression, but was unsure how to read it. The General quickly composed himself and walked down the steps to face his unit commanders. Joe took his traditional place at his side. General Waverly did not protest.

Suddenly, the stage became alive with activity as Bob and Phil led the men of the 151st Division across the stage and down the aisle while singing, *We'll follow the Old Man.* The General watched the proceedings while Joe took time to observe his disposition, which he discerned to be a mixture of surprise and bewilderment. The soldiers then lined up in two single-file rows as the song came to its completion.

"The men are ready for inspection, sir," Bob said.

"It's just routine, sir," Joe added.

Resuming a role that he had played out in the Army for nearly thirty years, the General walked between the lines of soldiers, correcting them on their shoddy appearance and reminding them of their duty and the need for discipline. As he reached the stage, he turned to the men of *his* Division, and with extreme gratitude, he relayed to them that he had never seen such a wonderful sight in all his life. Those simple words resonated deeply among the men and made the sacrifice of leaving home and family for Pine Tree worth the effort. The General then retraced his steps through the line while shaking the soldiers hands. Upon reaching Bob and Phil, he thanked them for orchestrating such a wonderful event.

The first routine was to begin. Joe helped to seat the General while Bob and Phil met Judy and a recently returned Betty on stage to begin their performance of *Gee, I Wish I Was Back in the Army*.

Joe sat at the same table with the General and attempted to watch the performance— but he could not. With no time to confront the General and make restitution for his transgressions before the show, he found that he was trapped in a DMZ— a no man's land— and his nerves had become raw. He could not move forward, and he could not sit still while the issue remained unresolved. He did the only thing he knew to do— retreat. He quietly stood from his chair and hurried away, to the General's dismay.

Emma and Susan were stationed at the top of the stair. Joe walked past them and made his way into the inn and then out the front door. A cold chill bit at his neck as he came to an abrupt stop on the front porch. Unsure what he would do next, he ran his hand through his hair with intensity and looked up into the sky, wanting nothing more than to scream. He peered down the darkened road and thought how easy it would be to lose himself in the wilderness that surrounded the lodge. He advanced aimlessly down the stairs. A voice called out from the doorway. It was Emma, along with Susan. "Leaving so soon?"

Joe turned toward the two women. The sober reality of his situation brought forth an unencumbered confession. "I don't belong here."

"Your name is Joe, isn't it?" Susan asked.

"It is. How would you know that?"

"We would know you anywhere. The General has a very special photograph of you. He's so longed to see you," Emma said.

"Me? He's longed to see me?"

"He's had dreams— nightmares, really. He says they won't go away until he sees you again," Susan explained.

Suddenly, from the dimly lit sky, it began to snow and snow steadily. Emma and Susan jumped for joy as they spotted the flakes falling from the heavens. It was an ethereal sight. They stepped onto the porch with Joe.

"Oh, Grandpa will be so happy!" Susan exclaimed.

"You tell him, Joe," Emma said.

"Me?"

"Yes. You! The General's been waiting for snow, and he's been waiting for you. I'd say that makes you the right person to deliver that information."

"He won't want to see me."

"Why not? You're a Captain, aren't you?"

"Yes."

"And you're one of his men, aren't you?"

Joe could not avoid the question. It was time for him to decide if he was with the General or against him. He straightened his back. "I am."

"Well, those are his men in there, and you're one of his men. It's only right that one of his men brings him urgent news. Now get in there, soldier. That's an order!"

The logic was sound. Joe's duty was clear. As Emma and Susan waited, Joe re-entered the lodge and approached the General. Bob and Phil were on stage singing their new Christmas song *Waiting for Christmas to Call.*

Joe leaned into his ear. "General, there's an urgent matter. Come quickly."

The message was unexpected and bewildering, and yet it had come from Joe. The General knew it must be important. Without hesitation, he rose from his chair and followed Joe out of the lodge and into the inn where Emma and Susan were waiting. They smiled profusely and pointed at the front door. The General stepped through the doorway and onto the porch. He looked up into the glorious sky and then lifted his hand to catch the flakes. It was beautiful, wonderful, snow! Emma and Susan beamed with delight as they stood in the doorway and rejoiced with him.

Emma identified a fortuitous opportunity. She turned toward Joe, placed her hands on her hips, and looked at him sternly. "Get out there, soldier."

Joe did not resist. "Yes, ma'am."

He stepped onto the porch, faced the General, and saluted. "General Waverly."

The General saluted him in return. "Captain Ross. It's been a long time."

"Yes, sir. It has." He did not delay in confessing his insubordination. "General, ten years ago, I was out of line when I called you a coward. I'll never be able to take those words back, but I would like to apologize profusely for disrespecting you, sir. You are the bravest man I have ever met. If you say the word, I will re-enlist tomorrow so that you can begin court-martial proceedings against me. I will not protest."

Any demurral the General may have harbored was softened by the confession. "Tomorrow is Christmas Day, Captain. The recruitment centers are closed. I think you may find it hard to re-enlist."

Joe had not considered that fact. "Yes, General. Sorry, sir. The day after then."

"At ease, Captain," the General said as his heart softened further. "I looked for you everywhere, Joe. I couldn't find you. I wanted to tell you that you were right, son. I should have never left the Division to General Carlton. I knew he was out to get a medal and that he was putting my boys in harm's way."

"You were just following orders, sir."

"Yes, I was. And that was my dilemma. You know that as well as anyone, Joe. The absence of discipline leads to chaos, and chaos is the puppet master of death and destruction. That was my choice, son. Don't you see? If I rejected my orders, I would break the chain of command, and that would break discipline, and then chaos would have its way. So, I chose discipline over chaos and prayed like hell that General Carlton had an ounce of salt in him to lead this Division. And that's where I was wrong. I hope you can forgive me for that."

Joe was relieved. "If there's anything to forgive, I forgive you, sir."

General Waverly smiled. "It appears we've both been in need of a pardon, son. I'd say we've made a healthy step in that direction."

"Yes, sir. I believe we have, sir."

Inside the door, Emma and Susan were teary-eyed at the sight. The General then relaxed and placed both hands upon Joe's shoulders as a father would a son. "I can't tell you how happy I am to see you. I'd like to hear all about your life these past ten years."

"You'll have to tell him later," Emma barged in. "Bob and Phil's song is finishing up. You better get back in there before your Division thinks you've deserted them."

"We wouldn't want that. Would we, Joe."

"No, sir. We wouldn't."

"Hurry up, you two. I don't want to miss the next number," Emma huffed.

The group re-entered the lodge and watched the remainder of the show in joyous peace. For the finale, Bob, Betty, Phil, and Judy met behind the Christmas tree and shared a romantic kiss. Then, seeing the snow falling for themselves, they opened wide the lodge doors behind the stage to the wonder and amazement of the audience and then sang the finale *White Christmas*.

With the song and show complete, the foursome was as giddy as elves the day after a successful Christmas. They exited the stage to join the General at his table. Evie and Bobby raced from the stage to find Joe. Bobby nearly jumped into Joe's arms as they met. Joe embraced him and then Evie. Finally, they were together. Trudi and Doreen, overjoyed at the sight of Joe and Evie together, joined them at their table. Emma and Susan took their place next to the General.

With the exuberance of an eighteen-year-old who had his whole life ahead of him and who had just enlisted in the United States Army, the General stood upon his chair and offered a toast to the men and women in the crowded lodge.

"In all my life, I could have never imagined this night. Tonight, on this Christmas Eve, I am reminded of friendship, faith, charity, and forgiveness." He then pointed to the crowd and to all the men and women who had gathered about him. "Your presence tonight is the greatest gift I could have ever received. Thank you, one and all. Merry Christmas!"

Mark Streuber

Christmas Day 1954

Dear Joe,

It is late. Many of the men and their wives are still here enjoying Christmas Day with us. It was such a fine day. I was sorry to see you leave so soon for New York City, but I understand you have commitments you must keep. It was a pleasure to learn about your life over the past ten years and how you've been such an influence on those young men you work with at the YMCA. You are a natural leader. I am not surprised that you've continued to be a leader of men, even of men in the making.

The snow continues to fall. It must be a full-on six inches that's fallen to this point. A good thing, too, as I needed a diversion to keep the men occupied with more than what a handful of old stories and few bottles of wine could provide. The snow is not deep enough for proper skiing, but it's been enough to put skis on those old boys and send 'em up the ski tow and let 'em get a feel for what it's like.

Bob and Phil, Betty and Judy are still here. We've had a great opportunity to catch up and talk a little about show business. I'm glad they put their show on hold in New York until New Year's Eve. I think they're embracing their time together as well as the rest they're enjoying. They're convinced they need to take the new show on the road, and I think they will. But I get the feeling Bob and Betty are already thinking about settling down somewhere. I'm not so sure about Phil and Judy, but time will tell.

Your friend Evie sure is a lovely gal. I wish I had the time to get to know her better the few days she was here, but we were so busy with the show there wasn't enough time. Of course, you know that Susan did spend a fair bit of time with little Bobby and she even showed him how to ski before you left.

I'm happy that you and I had an opportunity to make amends. You're like a second son to me, and I'm happy that I no longer have to carry the burden that I let you down, which brings me to a question.

I'd like to offer you free room and board anytime you and any of those boys of yours want to visit Vermont. It would give those boys a chance to get out of the city and experience cows, and mountains, and fresh air, and for them to see a little more of the world than just what the city has to offer.

And God willing, I'll still be here, and the Columbia Inn will be thriving. It turns out a few boys in the Division had gone on to become Wall Street investment bankers. They so loved the Columbia Inn and the people of Pine Tree that they're begging me to let them invest in the ski resort, which I think I might.

But mostly, I've decided to take the advice of my friend Archie and use some of my land for apples, which will bring visitors up here year-round and will be another reason for you to bring those boys up here. It sure is beautiful in Vermont in the fall.

Consider my offer, Joe, and please keep in touch. I was sorry to lose track of you the first time. I would hate to do that a second.

Sincerely,

Tom Waverly

December 29, 1954

Dear General Waverly,

Thank you so much for your letter. I was honored to be in your presence again and experience even for a day the life that you have built in Vermont and at the Columbia Inn.

In all my life, I never thought I would get the chance to apologize for my grievous mistakes. I am thankful I was so well received by you and that you allowed me the opportunity to make amends.

I'm glad that you approve of Evie. She and I and Bobby have had dinner together each night since we arrived home. She is everything a man could hope for. In fact, it's my hope that she and I will become more than just friends.

We've only known each other a few months, but I have every intention of asking her to marry me (please do not mention that if she corresponds with you.)

I thought it right to wait a few months before making my declaration so that she has time to see that I am stable and constant. If our relationship proceeds as planned, I will ask her to marry me on Valentine's Day.

If she approves of me, General, I have a favor to ask of you. I can think of no better place for her and I to marry than at the Columbia Inn. It has already created such wonderful memories for us, and I've heard a certain General say Vermont is beautiful in the fall and winter. I'm sure it is just as beautiful in summer! I would like to ask Bob and Phil, and Betty and Judy to be there. I hope their schedule will allow it.

And yes, what a wonderful gesture to invite me and the boys from the YMCA to come to the inn. It would be an experience of a lifetime as many of these boys have never been outside the city.

I appreciate the offer of free room and board, but one thing I have learned, General, is that hard work can be its own education.

Perhaps you'll allow us to develop a work-share arrangement where the boys and I can work for our room and board? If you have a new orchard to plant and trails to groom, and a lodge that needs repair, then many hands can make the work light.

I'm sure the boys will get a kick out of working with Susan and Emma and all the wonderful townspeople of Pine Tree. It will be an experience they'll never forget. I know I'll never forget.

I'll write soon, General. Until then, I wish you good health, a prosperous New Year, and that you enjoy the many Christmas's that are sure to be ahead for you!

Sincerely,

Joe Ross

Made in the USA
Monee, IL
28 August 2022

12697087R00201